THE BUTCH

Mahendra Jakhar is an ex-journalist currently working as a scriptwriter for feature films and television shows. He did his BA (English Literature) from Kirori Mal College, Delhi University, and started working as a freelance photo-journalist for an English daily. Soon, he was working full-time as a crime reporter.

He shifted to Mumbai in 2006 to pursue a career as a freelance scriptwriter. His first film project was a Mahesh Bhatt film, *The Killer*, starring Irfaan Khan and Emran Hashmi. He has done scripts for shows like *CID, Mano Ya Na Mano, Seeta aur Geeta*, and others. He also did research and writing for the documentary on the hijack of IC-814 from Kathmandu to Kandahar for Discovery Channel.

His latest film project is the soon-to-be-released *Mountain Man* directed by Ketan Mehta. Currently, he is working on a script for a film to be directed by Ashwini Chaudhary. He has also worked with Tigmannshu Dhulia on the film script of *Shaagird*, starring Nana Patekar.

A voracious reader, his all-time favourites are crime thrillers and murder mysteries. Jakhar says he hopes to come up with more such interesting and universal stories.

His film script, *Bhiwani*, was selected for the Co-Production Market at the India International Film Festival, 2013, held in Goa.

Interestingly, he shares his birthdate, 15 September, with the likes of Agatha Christie, Marco Polo and Oliver Stone.

THE BUTCHER OF BENARES

Mahendra Jakhar

Westland Ltd

westland ltd

61, Silverline Building, Alapakkam Main Road, Maduravoyal, Chennai 600 095
No. 38/10 (New No.5), Raghava Nagar, New Timber Yard Layout, Bangalore 560026
93, 1st Floor, Sham Lal Road, Daryaganj, New Delhi 110 002

First published by westland ltd 2014

10 9 8 7 6 5 4 3 2 1

ISBN: 978-93-83260-77-5
Typeset: PrePSol Enterprise Pvt. Ltd.
Printed at Thomson Press (India) Ltd.

To Hawa Singh Jakhar,
my father, my hero!

ACKNOWLEDGEMENTS

First and foremost, I would like to thank all my teachers, who moulded me into the person I'm today. Especially Mr Allan Lewis, who hooked me onto reading and writing, Mr K.B. Kain, my history teacher who turned history into an exciting mystery, and Mr D.N. Saxena who taught me the art of discipline. Also, my mother, who has been a teacher throughout her life and packed me off from a small town infested with criminals to a boarding school near Delhi. It changed my life.

Heartfelt gratitude to the exceptional team at Westland, for their superb guidance. Extra special thanks to Gautam Padmanabhan, CEO, Westland, who believed in this book from the start, and to Prita Maitra, my editor, who slogged with me to craft this book at every stage. My sincere thanks to Gunjan Ahlawat, art director, and the entire art team for coming up with an exceptional cover design. I also express my thanks to publisher Paul Vinay Kumar, Vipin Vijay, general manager production, and Shatrughan Pandey, manager production.

I wish to express my sincere appreciation to Anuj Bahri and Shravani Pandit of Red Ink Literary Agency, who motivated me to complete this book. They led me by the hand into the amazing world of publishing, of which I had no idea.

I thank my entire family, especially my wife, Priya Raman, for her patience while I researched and redrafted (thanks for letting me off those shopping trips for vegetables and milk!), my son, Hridai, whose enthusiastic questions helped me spot any holes in the story, and my father, Hawa Singh, whose name I have borrowed for my hero. My father was a simple army man who always found the money to buy me books (although I sometimes squandered it on movies and fast food), and who didn't once object when I resigned from three jobs in less than a year, assuring me that he would always be there for me. Well, he passed away, and that has left a deep void—one that I can fill only by my writing. It's his spirit that lives in the character of Hawa Singh in this book.

PROLOGUE

Eventually everyone dies, but death, in various forms and ways, still comes as a shock. Then they throw dirt in your face. Then the worms eat you. Or they consign you to the flames. The flesh sizzles and the bones crackle. Be grateful it happens in that order.

There are very few who have tasted death and come out of it alive. It could be the cold barrel of a gun pointed at one's head, a mountaineer hanging from a slender rope, or lying on a hospital bed surrounded by one's family all waiting for the last breath, or simply a car stopping an inch away from you that could have struck you dead. Everyone will tell you that the taste of death is not of this earth.

Death is all around us and it takes a fraction of a second to blow out the flame of life. A simple toaster or a gas stove in your kitchen could fry you. That fine vegetable knife could chop you to pieces. And the car you drive could crush you to pulp.

Full of such thoughts, Hawa Singh, a thirty-one-year-old sub-inspector with the Delhi Crime Branch, inched ahead through the dust-laden air. He led a team of eight policemen armed with self-loading rifles and police-issue pistols towards a brick kiln on the Delhi-Ghaziabad border.

Hawa Singh had received information that the dreaded dacoit of Chambal valley, Nirbhay Singh Gujjar, was hiding there. He had kidnapped Kavita Venkateshwaran, star reporter on a prominent English news channel.

In the afternoon heat of June, the police team hiding in the fields of sugarcane fought a combination of sweat, dust and fear. They could see dense black smoke spewing from a chimney, the clay bricks stacked around a huge furnace and the baked red bricks that labourers carried to nearby trucks.

The policemen waited with bated breath for some sign of Gujjar's gang. There was none.

This was the kind of time when they smelled and tasted death. To some it was the smell of rusted iron but for Hawa Singh it was like pure steel between his teeth. Any moment a bullet could come ripping through the sugarcane and make a hole large enough to let out life.

It takes nerves of steel to hold on waiting for the first bullet to be fired. Then it would be a free-for-all. Only the lucky would survive. Only the very lucky.

Hawa Singh towered over the others. He was six foot, two inches tall and of athletic build, with a shaved head from which the sweat now trickled down to his brow. No way could he botch this operation. Nirbhay Singh Gujjar was on the most wanted list of seven states for cases of murder, kidnapping for ransom, robbery and abduction of women.

More important was Kavita. She was precious. It was only for her that he braved death.

Kavita and Hawa Singh had met some two years earlier when they started seeing each other. A fortnight ago they had got engaged after much bickering between their families. Hawa Singh was a Jat from Haryana and Kavita, a south Indian, Tamil Brahmin.

'You couldn't find a girl in our own community?' his family asked him. 'She is dark. Short. She talks too much on TV. Does she know Hindi? Can she make chapattis? Those people eat only rice and dosa!'

'Jats!' countered Kavita's family. 'They are uncouth. Rowdy. All they know is to eat, drink and *sleep*. Uncultured!'

Finally, both families came to terms and the couple were engaged. They had planned to get married both south-Indian and north-Indian-style. They couldn't help laughing whenever they thought about what their wedding would be like—Jats from the villages of Haryana mingling with the Brahmins of Chennai.

Just a week earlier, Kavita got a call that promised her an exclusive interview with Nirbhay Singh Gujjar. She took the risk and ventured out all alone to meet him.

But Gujjar held her captive and demanded a ransom of five crore rupees from the government, along with the dismissal of all cases against him. Kavita was a prize catch.

The government didn't want to give in to a dacoit. They sent in the right man to get Kavita back—Hawa Singh.

Hiding in the field, he could hear the faint voices of labourers and the rustle of sugarcane leaves all around them. They had been waiting at the same spot for four hours. The men were nervous. They had heard stories about Gujjar beheading policemen. They wanted revenge.

Hawa Singh focused on the brick kiln, waiting for the right moment to charge in, grab the captive woman and lead his team out safely.

Around sunset, as red, orange and crimson streaks spread in the sky, intersected by the dense black smoke from the brick kiln, he got the sign. Through the foliage he saw two jeeps coming towards the kiln. Spotting them, he hurried ahead, signalling to the team to be prepared to strike.

The jeeps came to a halt, one of the drivers stepped out and walked ahead calling out, 'Everything is ready.'

At this point, Hawa Singh made a sign to his men to surround the area. Four men then charged from the left and another four from the right.

Hawa Singh looked at his men as fear gave way to a new high, 'We are not here to make arrests. Shoot to kill. I'm going to get Kavita.'

The guns were cocked and ready, in sweaty palms. There was a rattling sound and Hawa Singh saw a large circular sheet of iron being lifted off the dusty ground. Out from there appeared the members of Gujjar's gang. They were armed with AK-47s, police rifles and pistols. They stood guard, looking around the veil of darkness slowly enveloping the place.

Hawa Singh was sitting on his haunches to hide his tall frame. The crouching position he adopted also allowed him to emerge, at a chosen moment, to attack with the ferocious speed of a wild animal. The motto he lived by was that of the Delhi Police: 'With you, for you, always.' And he would go to any length to save the city and its citizens.

As he looked ahead, he saw Nirbhay Singh Gujjar coming out of his underground bunker. He was dressed in a kurta and dhoti with an AK-47 casually slung around his shoulder. He wiped off the sweat lingering around his heavy handlebar moustache.

He shouted at his men to hurry, and two of them pulled Kavita out of the bunker. She looked in bad shape but her spirit was pretty much intact.

'You better kill me because I won't let you get away with the ransom money,' she shouted at Gujjar.

Nirbhay Singh Gujjar smiled at her, and turned to nod to his men to climb into the waiting jeeps.

They had let down their guard and that was the moment Hawa Singh was looking for. He leapt from his hiding place towards the Gujjar gang. He didn't need to signal the team or call out to them. They knew the drill and ran right behind him, fanning out around the dacoits.

Hawa Singh moved determinedly, with the sure footing that came from years of experience in battle. One wrong foot, and you could be food for the worms. He was aiming for the head of the notorious dacoit who had massacred twenty policemen and had beheaded two senior superintendents of police.

Suddenly, a small group of reporters hiding in the nearby fields came out with their cameras, wanting to catch the action live. One of the police officers looking for a big jump in his career seemed to have leaked out the information to them.

As the reporters approached, the members of the gang shouted in warning, 'Press!'

Hawa Singh had already aimed and fired. A dacoit's head exploded in crimson as grey matter and shards of skull flew out.

Hawa Singh had given out the battle cry and a bloody encounter ensued. The police team took cover behind the stacks of bricks and fired at the Gujjar gang. Nirbhay, hiding behind one of the jeeps, opened up his AK-47, tearing through a wall of bricks and ripping apart two policemen behind it.

By this time, the camera-toting reporters had run back to cover in the fields. They were seeing more action than they'd catered for.

Hawa Singh kept shooting, cracking open three more skulls. The sound of gunfire, the screams of dying men and the smell of blood brought vultures out into the grey sky. They silently circled the sky overhead, waiting for the living to turn dead. Flesh. Blood. Death. The birds had only to wait.

Three other policemen were knocked out by the heavy onslaught from the Kalashnikovs that the Gujjar gang had commandeered from soldiers of the Central Reserve Police Force. Hawa Singh saw his men falling one by one as he took cover behind the long chimney of the brick kiln.

The sun had disappeared and the sky was turning black. Flames. Fumes. Fury. Fear.

Kavita was being held by two men while three more stood around her, barring any attempt from her to run. Nirbhay was in a hurry to escape and take Kavita with him. As he pushed her into the jeep, the remaining three policemen charged towards him. Before Hawa Singh could even shout to them, all three were shot through their eyes. It was said that the dacoits of Chambal were the greatest snipers and the most accurate marksmen. They lived up to their reputation.

Kavita finally managed to free herself and run. She ran towards the fields crying, 'Singh! Singh!'

Hawa Singh shot at the gang member trying to run after her. He saw Nirbhay turning towards Kavita. Nirbhay raised his AK-47 and fired at her. The bullets found their mark. Suddenly, the battlefield became quiet; the shrieks of the vultures grew louder and louder.

A deep fury washed over Hawa Singh and he came out of his cover shooting wildly, shouting in grief, 'Kavita! Kavita!'

He could smell death and steel right close to him. Inside him. Blood was oozing from his head. He held it and ran through the darkness with shots ringing all around him.

He ran towards the Gujjar gang speeding away in their jeeps. He raced across the field of sugarcane, over the dusty roads, through the narrow lanes, and hit the tarred road.

He felt the gravel under his chin, the smell of tar coiling up his nose, and then saw a line of blood trickling down from his head onto the road. Then, darkness engulfed him.

***

As Hawa Singh opened his eyes, he felt the hard, cold ground under him. He felt a severe pain in his head and his legs refused to move. He looked around to see dense fog. The visibility was almost down to zero; he couldn't see even his own hands.

Then he heard the sound of temple bells and the chanting of mantras. He could hear the sound of waves rippling in water. The fog brought with it the sweet smell of incense. The loud clang from the clock tower shattered his dream state. Hawa Singh realized that the ground under him was a cemented floor and he was lying on the Dashashwamedh Ghat in Benares, on the river Ganges.

It had been more than seven years since the encounter with Nirbhay Singh Gujjar, in which a bullet had lodged close to his brain.

Kavita had died on the spot.

He was bedridden for more than ten months and underwent multiple surgeries. The doctors were unable, however, to remove the bullet from such a sensitive part of his skull. Finally, it was decided to let the body itself take care of the bullet. With time, a layer of fat covered it, preventing it from moving in further.

Luckily, it was a bullet from a small-calibre pistol and didn't find its way right up to the brain. But it gave him a constant headache, and at times he would lose consciousness for hours. Hawa Singh had tasted death and had learnt to live with it.

The shoot-out with Nirbhay Singh Gujjar, in which he lost Kavita and his entire team, was a nightmare that wouldn't go away. It was almost two years later that Hawa Singh, in a joint operation with the Madhya Pradesh police, managed to kill the dreaded Gujjar. He had emptied twelve bullets into the hated body.

But the revenge could never sooth his soul. The nightmares remained. The smell of death was his constant companion. He was already half-dead, and people called him 'the Ghost'.

With great effort he curled up his legs and sat up on the steps of the Dashashwamedh Ghat. He tried to remember how he had got there in the first place, and then his father's voice echoed in his ears.

'I'm not going to die lying on a hospital bed or in that cramped room of yours. Just take me to Benares. Finally, with my death on holy soil, I will acquire salvation,' said Fauja Singh, his seventy-nine-year-old terminally ill father.

Now thirty-eight years old, with a seven-year-old near-mortal wound, Hawa Singh was a senior inspector with Delhi Police, crime branch. He had brought his ailing father to die peacefully in Benares.

He still carried the six-inch-long zigzagging scar from the cut that opened his cranium from the left ear up to the crown of his head. There was a time when he tried to hide it by growing his hair long, but he soon gave up. He preferred to keep a crew-cut that clearly showed the mark—his medallion from the battle.

It was 4 am as he came out of his nightmare, lying on the ghat in Benares. The darkness was still hanging over him, along with fog that was waiting for the sun to melt it away. There were a few naked tungsten bulbs hanging above him, emitting the golden glow of haloes around them.

As his brain started registering more sounds, he heard a tremendous uproar, as if hundreds of feet were pounding along the ground. Then the wind carried the chanting to him—*'Om namo Narayana!'* The air vibrated with the sounds and the fog parted to give way to the godmen.

He saw hundreds and hundreds of naked men, their bodies covered in ash, carrying trishuls as they fiercely rushed with impressive speed and strength towards the holy waters of the river. These were Naga sadhus, who had come to bathe in the Ganges on the holy day of Makar Sankranti, which fell on 14 January that year, one of the coldest days in the coldest winter month in northern India.

Naga sadhus cover their bodies with nothing more than ashes, supposedly as a mark that they consider their bodies dead and already cremated. For this they use the ashes of open fires, where they burn tree-trunks, the roots facing the sky. The trident is the only real physical thing they possess. And the only things they wear are the beads of Rudraksha. They believe that wearing eleven thousand Rudrakhsa beads will help them attain the form of Lord Shiva.

To Hawa Singh, they looked like ghosts. He noticed that they were led by a man much fairer than the rest, with long dreadlocks and a heavy beard.

As they reached the Ganges, they all gave way to their leader to first step into the waters. He took the dip and chanted, '*Om namo Narayana!*' At that, the entire crowd of sadhus jumped into the icy waters.

The leader of the Naga sadhus raised his hand in the air and the chanting stopped. He folded his hands and took a dip inside the waters. He was followed by the hundreds of sadhus who all momentarily disappeared under the waters. Suddenly, the water went still. There was no sound. The ghostly sadhus seemed to have vanished.

On top of the water, something came floating by, something that looked like a white shroud. Then it came closer and closer. Hawa Singh could smell it. The taste of death intensified on his tongue.

The mass of bearded, long-haired sadhus reappeared above water, throwing out air from their lungs. It took a moment for them to register the floating body and they parted to surround the dead body of a beautiful woman.

Hawa Singh saw that the young woman had long blonde hair, which fanned in the water around her head. She was wearing a flowing white dress, and there were bloodstains on the breast. Her lips were painted bloody red and her eyes were closed. She looked serene as if she had slept while her heart pumped out blood from inside her body. There was no sign of pain on her face.

The body came closer and the Naga sadhus scrambled out of the water. Hawa Singh could see that the body was fair-skinned and looked like it had belonged to a European or American.

Then he saw a wooden stake stabbed into her heart.

mocked his [illegible] her lips were pursed but [illegible] and [illegible] were [illegible] she [illegible] and kept walking [illegible] jumped out [illegible] her body. There was [illegible] on [illegible] face.

[illegible] by [illegible] the [illegible] [illegible] and looked like [illegible] belonged to [illegible] or [illegible]

Then [illegible]

> 'Benares is older than history, older than tradition, older even than legend, and looks twice as old as all of them put together.'
>
> — **Mark Twain**

CHAPTER 1

The prospect of a bullet that could quickly put an end to the miseries of life holds allure to some. But those who wish to die in Benares have to wait. Death in the City of Moksha does not come that simply.

Thousands come to Benares every year, looking for mukti, or release from the cycle of rebirth and death. Seventy-nine-year-old Fauja Singh had a similar pursuit in mind, when he asked his only son to accompany him to the holy city.

They had taken a room at Mukti Bhawan, just a short walk from the river. This place is the preferred last destination—a final stopover—for elderly Hindus. Their hope is to end up on one of the hundreds of funeral pyres on the sacred Harishchandra Ghat, lit for cremation each day.

Mukti Bhawan, or Salvation House, offers twelve bare rooms arranged around a courtyard in a hundred-year-old red-brick building with green shutters. While those who can afford to pay their electricity and food bills do so, the poorest families pay nothing.

After checking in at the hostel, a guest has two weeks to die or else they are gently asked to leave. Between thirty and seventy people die here every month.

It had already been five days since Hawa Singh brought in his father to the Bhawan. They had been given two blankets and bedsheets to sleep on the hard cement floor. The yellow paint on the walls was peeling and bore the marks of dampness and seepage. The cold was terrible.

Fauja Singh munched on a hot oily kachori, saying, 'I'm not going to eat their dead food. I'm not dead yet. I want to taste all the delicacies of Benares before I attain moksha. Do you hear me?'

Hawa Singh, lost in his thoughts and waiting for a phone call, just nodded. He had made the call to the local police about discovering the body in the Ganges at Dashashwamedh Ghat. He knew the police procedure and that he could be called in any time to record his statement.

'Tell me one thing. Once I achieve salvation, what will happen to my soul? Will it merge with God? Will I become part of God?' asked Fauja Singh, popping a large gulaab jamun into his mouth.

But Hawa Singh had never given thought to the concept of rebirth. For him the human body was like a non-rechargeable battery, one with a limited life. The battery finally loses its charge and dies. The End.

'What the hell has happened to you? Here I'm talking about my death and you are fiddling with your cell phone. You policemen will never understand spirituality. I'm telling you, you are never going to attain moksha.'

Hawa Singh looked up at his father and shouted with gritted teeth, 'I don't want moksha and I don't want to see God! I have seen enough deaths to understand there is no God.'

'Oh, so you think you can defy death with your guns?' the old man shot back. 'It was God who saved you with that bullet still stuck in your head. There will come a time when you will want to die, but death will not come. Dying a good death is as important as living a good life. Death is the ultimate bliss.'

'Enough!' warned his son. 'I don't want to hear another of your lectures on death and salvation. I have enough problems on my mind.'

'You have nothing but a bullet in your head. Fool! Come, I'll make you a big one.'

Fauja Singh took a bottle of rum out from his rucksack with a naughty smile, 'This is going to perk you up big time.'

He poured rum into two steel tumblers with his big hands. There was a time when these very hands had punched the wind out of top international boxers. Fauja Singh had won two consecutive gold medals in the heavyweight category at the Asian Games during the '60s. On his third outing, he was disqualified on technical points.

The infuriated Fauja Singh proceeded to punch one of the judges of the tournament. That one punch threw Fauja Singh's life out of gear. He was barred from the Indian Boxing Association and was banned from competing in any sporting event. Those were times when, in India, people didn't even respect the sport of boxing. One of the greatest champs of Indian sparring was plucked out and thrown into anonymity.

From then on, Fauja Singh did odd jobs to take care of his family. Finally, he settled in his village, near the Delhi border, in Haryana, to work on the fields. His wife died early due to tuberculosis and he single-handedly raised their only child, Hawa Singh.

Hawa Singh had inherited all the qualities of his father—a short temper, the tall and wide frame, the big hands and the strength of a boxer. Only a strong man would survive a bullet in his head. Fauja wanted him to take up a secure government job and Hawa Singh ended up in Delhi Police.

He was the most ferocious of his force, the most daring, and had the most number of problems with his seniors, although that did not prevent him from acquiring a long list of commendations. They had not been able to throw him out. They needed him to face the bullets. The war never stopped for Hawa Singh.

Fauja Singh had developed a serious heart problem and the doctors gave up on him. The champion who once weighed ninety kilograms was reduced to a body weight of fifty-five. The bones protruded under his skin, giving him the look of a skeleton covered with a thin layer of tissue.

In Benares, Fauja decided that he wouldn't complain or cry. He would instead make the most of his last days. So he indulged in all the delicious food and drink he could avail of.

'Soon, I'm going to be with God so I don't need these priests—or any doctors—to teach me anything. I am going to be on a one-to-one with the Almighty Himself.'

Little did the sellers of moksha know that soon this father-son duo would make Benares cry for salvation.

Fauja handed the steel tumbler of rum to Hawa Singh. Father and son looked at each other and brought the glasses together, saying, 'Cheers!'

'Cheers to your life and cheers to my death,' said Fauja Singh smilingly.

With that, they did a bottoms-up. The dark rum caused a pleasant burn, bringing warmth and a heady determination to go on with whatever life they had lived as they pleased.

Finally, the cell phone rang.

*

Hawa Singh walked through the narrow lanes of the old city. These galis, or lanes, are a maze. He walked hurriedly, cutting through a group of students dressed in saffron, going to their Sanskrit lessons, and vendors selling artefacts and sweetmeats on the sides of the lanes. There were kids flying kites on the tops of their houses, girls learning Kathak in a courtyard. The sounds of the shehnai and flute emanated from some corners, along with the fragrance of incense and flowers that mixed with the stink rising from the open drains and garbage strewn around.

The sound of temple bells never seemed to stop in Benares. They were a constant reminder that you were in a holy city. Hawa Singh saw many people who had come from all parts of the globe in search of peace, spirituality or to gain wisdom. He could never understand it. For him Benares was just a city that stank.

The only source of comfort was the marijuana freely available in various forms. One could smoke it, eat it or drink it mixed with milk, tea or lassi. Hawa Singh preferred to eat the small laddus, the form in which they were sold from government-owned stalls. They were not perceived as a drug but as the prasad of Lord Shiva who was said to have founded this ancient city, once called Kashi.

The little balls of bhang, along with country-made liquor, had become his constant companions on the dark highway called life.

Hawa Singh came out onto the main road and took a rickshaw to the office of the city's senior superintendent of police. To prepare himself for such official meetings, he preferred marijuana over alcohol, as it didn't smell and eased the pain in his head.

Sitting on the rickshaw, he looked around at the riot of colours in the market. The tourists, along with daily-wage workers, crowded around the shops selling hot samosas, kachoris dipped in potato-and-peas curry, golden jalebis filled with sugar syrup and hot milk laden with dry fruits.

A sharp, stinging pain took over his head as the images of the floating body returned to him. Then he saw the Naga sadhus gasping for air as they came out from their dip in the waters. The naked, ash-smeared Shiva worshippers, the self-claimed authorities on the Hindu way of life, were known for their austere living and quickly aroused temper. They were possessive of their lot, and would go to any lengths to protect and guard what they considered sacred.

Hawa Singh spotted the old dilapidated building which housed the SSP's office. Some fresh paint had been applied in a vain attempt to hide the many cracks and peeling plaster. A few saffron-clad sadhus were on the road outside, with a group of young and restless foreigners tailing them—in search of God.

The crime rate in Benares had never made it to the headlines, in spite of the attacks by fanatic Hindu organizations on film crews and young romancing couples, cases of thefts, missing persons—most of whom were elderly people abandoned by their families on the many ghats, some sporadic murders—but nothing that commanded the attention of the world outside Benares.

The long corridors of the SSP's office were guarded by lazy policemen. The warm sun on a cold day had made them drowsy. Hawa Singh walked past them with a stride that spoke of confidence gained by diving headlong into many battles. This office had nothing to do with those, stinking as they did of inactive bureaucratic stench. He hated the air here.

The SSP's office was at the end of the corridor. Hawa Singh saw the big nameplate stuck on the door: 'Neeraj Thakur, SSP, Benares district'. He was the man who controlled the entire police force there—a veritable army.

A thought crossed Hawa Singh's mind. 'What would happen if the entire police force went on strike? Will the animal instinct tempt people to prowl the streets looking for prey, or have we become civilized enough to take charge of our affairs? Maybe the fear created by the police keeps us grounded and civilized. You can domesticate animals, keep them as pets, but you need to keep them on leash so they do not to cross the line.'

He shrugged off his thoughts and, before the guard at the door could stop him, Hawa Singh entered the office. Right ahead on the wall was the huge emblem of the Uttar Pradesh Police and underneath it sat the top boss of Benares Police.

Neeraj Thakur, forty-seven years old, looked like the foodie he was—round. He was dressed in finery, his immaculate uniform adorned with the Ashoka emblem and several stars and medallions. The wall on each side of the office was covered with the statistics of solved cases. In front of Neeraj Thakur sat his coterie of junior officers, munching on hot samosas and slurping sugary tea.

Hawa Singh walked up to desk and said, 'I was asked to come and meet you here. I'm Hawa Singh, senior inspector, Delhi crime branch.'

The SSP and others looked up at him, astonished.

'Well, if you want to finish your breakfast, please carry on. I'll come back later.'

The SSP laughed. 'Hawa Singh, this is Benares. Wherever we meet to talk, first we eat. I have heard a lot about you, and finally, we get to meet.'

The SSP and Hawa Singh shook hands. The SSP looked at the officers. 'This man looks like a boxer or a wrestler,' he said. 'Look at his massive hands.' Turning to his visitor, he added, 'Just don't break mine!'

'No, sir, I'm just a policeman. It's my father who was a boxer.'

'See, didn't I tell you? Tell me, is it really true that the size of one's palm is equal to the size of one's dick?' laughed the SSP.

The gang of police officers cackled. Hawa Singh hated such jokes at times of crisis. He could clearly see that none of them was capable of handling a sensitive case, nor had they ever stepped out of the confines of these walls.

'Well, sir, can we get down to work?' he asked the senior officer. 'It seems you wish to take down my statement, as it was I who had discovered the body and made the call to the police.'

The SSP got up and walked around Hawa Singh. He placed his hand on his shoulder, in an attempt at propitiating him. 'It *is* a very serious case,' he conceded.

'A foreigner has been found murdered. The report has gone to Delhi as we had to inform to the embassy.'

'Have you been able to identify her?' asked Hawa Singh.

The SSP's tone suddenly changed to one of anger. 'What do you think we have been doing here? She is a US citizen and was murdered with that wooden stake. The body has been sent for autopsy and we should get the report by this evening.'

'So, sir, what do you want from me?'

'Well, the Home Minister knows about your presence in Benares and he has specifically asked you to help us in this case. Maybe they want to hang you soon.'

'It's your territory, and I came here only to accompany my father, who wished to die here.'

'Now, it's your neck in the noose. I don't want you to step out of line, get in our way, or hamper our investigation in any way. Everyone comes here for mukti and I hope you get yours. Understood?'

Hawa Singh nodded in affirmation.

Neeraj Thakur sat back in his chair and looked at Hawa Singh. 'So how do you wish to start?'

A faint smile crossed his lips, as Hawa Singh thought, 'So, they have not even started yet.'

'Well, sir,' he put the question to the SSP, 'How did you figure out that she was a US citizen?'

One of the junior police officers spoke up, 'We found the receipt of her hotel bill in her pocket. We searched the room and found the passport. It's that straight and simple.'

Hawa Singh knew that these idiots had ransacked the entire room. It would be difficult to find any more clues there.

'Did you find anything else on the body?' asked Hawa Singh.

The SSP pushed a large brown paper envelope across the high wooden desk towards Hawa Singh, saying, 'Everything that we found on the body is here. You can check it for yourself.'

Hawa Singh was aghast that these guys hadn't taken any precaution to avoid tampering with the evidence. He looked at the SSP and nodded. Then, very carefully, he removed and laid down the items from inside the envelope.

First to come out was a long chain with the Holy Cross dangling from it. It looked like it was made of steel but could have been platinum or white gold. The next object Hawa Singh placed on the table was an ID card with a clip to wear it around a belt or on a jacket pocket. It was clear that the woman preferred to wear Western clothes.

Hawa Singh looked at the ID card and read out, 'Eva Marie Cassidy, age 31 years, research scientist working with the Vatican Observatory Research Group.'

Then he saw the seal of His Holiness, the Pope.

Hawa Singh failed to find the connection between the Vatican and one of the oldest Hindu cities in the world, Benares. He fumbled and asked, 'Where is that wooden stake?'

The SSP took out a sealed plastic bag from a drawer and placed it on his desk. At least they had taken care not to smudge the fingerprints.

In the early hours of dawn, when Hawa Singh first saw the body, he had not been able to fully see the shape and contours of the wooden stake. To him, it looked like another dagger. Now, he saw it up close.

He saw that it had a pointed end and that the wood was polished, probably teak. It was approximately an inch-and-a-half thick and twelve inches long. Deadly. Dangerous. It had achieved its purpose.

He tried to figure out why anyone would use a wooden stake to kill. Why not simply use a knife or a dagger?

It was then that he saw the hilt. It was in the form of a cross.

The Holy Cross.

CHAPTER 2

It was 3 am, and a thick layer of fog shrouded off this part of the Earth from its satellites. Below it, the inhabitants of Benares could hardly make out the numerous stars in the vast sky. Their very breath condensed into vapour and mixed with the fog. The Ganges looked like it was boiling, as the foggy smoke rose from its waters.

This was the time when ghosts or vampires ventured out. This was also Hawa Singh's favourite time for conducting investigations. This was the time when most people were deep in sleep, but for Hawa Singh it was just the start of day. It was not surprising that they called him the Ghost.

He had repeatedly requested Neeraj Thakur that he be allowed to go through Eva's hotel room. But the SSP had denied him permission, saying, 'We have already searched the place and collected all the evidence. Now the room is sealed, and only with the permission of the court can it be re-opened for further examination.'

Finally, the Ghost had decided to knock on the door himself.

According to the police reports, Eva Marie Cassidy had been staying at Yogi Palace in Karthik Gali, close to Dashashwamedh Ghat. Hawa Singh waded through the thick fog as the street dogs barked and howled at him. He was smoking a bidi for warmth. He disliked cigarettes because of the filters, and the chemicals they put in the tobacco. This was perfect. Nothing came between the tobacco, the drag and the smoke.

He felt the icy-cold body of his constant companion, a Colt .45 that he kept tucked in at his back. He preferred this to the service pistol policemen were issued. He had snatched it from a Russian arms dealer in Paharganj. Since then it had become his weapon of choice and had stood right by him in many encounters.

It was called the peacemaker, a fire-arm forbidden even in America. Hawa Singh preferred to use cross-filed bullets that could singly kill an elephant. If you shoot it at a man from a distance of five metres, the bullet makes a wound as big as a dinner plate. Hawa Singh kept the trigger filed to make it quick and more sensitive. He could have taken down six Clint Eastwoods in a matter of five seconds with his Colt. It made him dirtier than Dirty Harry.

Through the fog he could see a bulb shining above a signboard. As he stepped closer he saw it was a board painted in yellow, with hand-written black letters: 'Yogi Palace, The Best And The Cheapest. All Are Invited.'

Hawa Singh took his hands out from the pockets of his leather jacket and felt the chill running into his veins. His heavy stubble worked as a light cover for his face but his crew-cut left his scalp cold. The bullet inside was slowly absorbing the cold and, soon, his vision could turn foggy.

The main door was a glass one and there was no one outside. The Ghost sneaked in and saw a man snoring at the reception desk. He looked at the rate card: 'Dormitory—Rs 150', 'Double Bedroom—Rs 500', 'Single Room—Rs 650', 'Private Room—Rs 800' and 'Ganges View Room—Rs 1000.

'Not bad at all. This is the true haven for all backpackers in Benares,' thought Hawa Singh.

The Yogi Palace was more of a cheap lodge and nothing of a palace. Still, the clean rooms and cheap accommodation, and the proximity to the Ganges attracted a lot of foreigners.

Totally uncaring of disturbing anyone, he climbed up the creaky stairs, his heavy boots clomping. He knew that Eva had taken up a single room on the first floor. There had to be something there that the local police had missed.

As he walked up to the room, he saw that the room was sealed with a big lock on the door, wrapped in a white cloth and bearing the insignia of the Uttar Pradesh Police. Any attempt to break in would destroy the seal. Hawa Singh knew that the window inside the room, which overlooked the street, would be sealed too.

Hawa Singh had entered many such sealed rooms. He took out his Swiss knife and unscrewed the entire bolt. It was a fake Swiss knife that he had bought for a Rs 100 or so from Karol Bagh Market in Delhi. He was fascinated by the multi-tool device and always kept it by him.

There was another wire that was wound around the two handles of the door, also sealed. He unscrewed the two handles—and the Ghost 'walked' in through 'sealed' doors.

Hawa Singh had been a policeman for fifteen years. During that time several of his colleagues had been killed in the line of fire. It had hit him hard every time it happened and he was painfully aware of how dangerous his work was. But the risk itself, the fear and the nervousness involved in it, had kept him alive. The fear bestowed on him the spirit to stay alive, to win against all odds. If there was no fear, heroes wouldn't be heroes.

He stepped inside the room. It was neat and tidy. There was a single bed carefully made up, with a bedsheet tucked in and a blue bedcover over it. A wooden table with a reading lamp on it stood by the bed, along with a foldable, rusted aluminium chair. A simple wardrobe stood opposite the bed, close to the attached bathroom. The walls were painted a light blue, adorned by framed pictures of Lord Shiva and the ghats of Benares.

The floor was of cheap imitation marble, and Hawa Singh could make out hundreds of footprints left there, courtesy the local police. They must have swarmed in like a herd of hippos to take charge and had ruined all possible prints.

Hawa Singh stepped closer to the study table and saw there were a few books piled on top—a travel guide on India, a book telling the history of Benares, another about many Hindu gods and goddesses, and underneath them all, a book on Vedic astrology.

He could make out another pile of oily prints on the books. The policemen must have flipped through the books in the hope of finding a love letter or some nude pictures of the white girl. However, they had left the books lying there, deeming them the useless things that foreigners seem to find fascinating.

Politicians say the police profession calls for the highest intelligence and exceptional mental, physical and moral qualities. Hawa Singh knew differently.

Many high-profile and sensitive cases had been botched by untrained policemen who merely trampled over the scene of a crime. They brought in another pack of apes, the journos, to show them around the place for photo opportunities. By the time the forensics arrived, everything was a mess. Then, when the local police failed, the Central Bureau of Investigation—the CBI—was called in. By that time, they had nothing to go on.

He looked under the bed, under the mattress, but found nothing. He opened the cupboard and met with a strong waft of some feminine fragrance. The local police seemed to have taken away all the young woman's possessions. He opened one of the drawers and saw a few beads of Rudraksha—another pet purchase of foreign tourists in Benares.

He looked at the bathroom door. It was made of plastic, to cut the cost of a more expensive wooden one. Inside the bathroom were a few leftover bottles of shampoo, bath gel, sunscreen lotion, a tube of toothpaste and a few twigs of neem, something used by locals to clean their teeth.

The dustbin contained old newspapers that had once wrapped oily samosas or kachoris. The policemen must have brought these with them.

On the plastic door, there was a picture of Hanuman ripping his chest apart to show Lord Ram and Sita residing in his heart. The celibate Hanuman clearly had to watch nude guests during their ablutions in the bathroom day after day.

There was nothing that yielded a clue. Hawa Singh looked for signs of blood but there were none.

The question that rose to mind, was, 'Was she killed inside the room and then dumped in the Ganges? Or was she killed somewhere else?'

He found some traces of ash in a corner of the bathroom. It looked like cigarette ash. He touched it with a finger and smelled it. A familiar smell. Then he tasted it. It was weed.

In all, it seemed Eva had been quite adventurous. She had wanted to soak in the local flavour, grew interested in the myriad colours of Hinduism and tried all the stuff associated with its mystic side.

Hawa Singh turned and stood at the bathroom door looking inside the room thinking, 'There has to be something here.'

He was not a married man, but from his limited experience of the opposite sex, he knew that all women loved to collect things. They have their own memorabilia. It could be gifts received from their first boyfriend, the wrappers of chocolate bars, birthday cards, pictures, a diary or a scrapbook.

He had already gone through the pictures in Eva's digital camera that lay with the local police. It contained all the usual touristy pictures of temples, ghats, boats in the river, burning pyres, the narrow lanes, shops and dishevelled sadhus. However, they had not yet found her cell phone.

The police had informed the Vatican Observatory on the mail id they found on her ID badge. Her body would be sent to her family in the US. The Vatican had made a special request to the Indian government to look into the murder and had also requested the

American investigative agency, the FBI, to help with the Indian investigation.

The FBI had chosen one of their young and highly trained agents, Ruby Malik, to be sent to Benares to work with the police and apprehend the killer.

Hawa Singh had no idea about all this. For him, it was more about fighting the darker forces and keeping himself alive. The more he worked, analyzed and investigated, the more his brain kept up with him. The moment he slackened, the bullet started to pinch.

He looked at the bed and thought, 'Women are not the ones to keep things under or inside their mattresses. But they do keep stuff close to or under their pillows.'

There was nothing. Maybe it had been cleared by the local police.

The cupboard.

Hawa Singh thought, 'The cupboard is usually the place where everything is piled by women. They prefer to have diaries with locks, notepads and stick-on notes, along with an army of markers and stickers. This is their temple. They keep it covered and won't allow their husbands, boyfriends and even mothers to look inside. It is their world.'

Hawa Singh maintained that one look at the contents of a cupboard told you about the kind of person using it—organized, structured or just plain messy.

He went to the wardrobe again. He opened it but there was still nothing. There were sheets of newspapers lining the shelves. He removed the paper but there was nothing underneath it.

He moved his fingers along the line of shelves, hoping against hope to find something stuck there. Nothing.

He opened the drawers. Empty.

The shoe box. Dust.

Hawa Singh bent closer to look at the dust. It was red sand. There was hardly any sand of this colour in and around the Ganges.

'Where did this come from?' he mused.

As he bent to look into the shoe box, he raised his eyes to one of the open drawers. Inside it, he could see another box. One feature you would find in most Indian almirahs. They're used to keep jewellery and other precious items.

Hawa Singh put in his hand and felt something. It was a small pocket diary. He flipped through it and saw some telephone numbers written on a page. There was a name underneath them. He tore out the page and pocketed it.

There was something else. Bigger.

It was a framed picture of Baba Ramtirath, the leader of the Naga sadhus. He wore a soft smile, his deep blue eyes twinkling behind his rimless glasses.

At the bottom of the photograph, he had signed: *'For Eva, with lots of love, Baba Ramtirath'.*

CHAPTER 3

'The idea of the existence of some religion called Hinduism was created by Western imperialists out of a desire to describe the world according to the system of their own values. It is impossible to estimate the ancient world from the point of view of the modern one. Hinduism is a way of life, not a religion. It was there even before Judaism, Christianity and Islam came into being. It is the true way to the supreme goal—realizing God. And we Naga babas are an ancient and wild order of naked yogis whom I call the "Hell's Angels" of Indian spirituality,' intoned Baba Ramtirath, the head of the Naga sadhus, while talking to a group of media persons.

Baba Ramtirath was unlike other Naga sadhus. He had deep-set blue eyes and fair skin. A flowing peppered beard completed the resemblance to Tolstoy. He was actually an American, born and brought up in California. It was during the '70s when, as an eighteen-year-old young man, he wandered to India and met with the Naga sadhus.

He was struck by their way of life, and became a disciple of a Naga baba, a master shaman sadhu from Rajasthan. As foretold by an astrological prophecy, he soon found himself the first foreigner to become an initiate of the Juna Akhara, the oldest and largest grouping of Naga babas, with more than 200,000 members.

At the Kumbh Mela in Haridwar, in 2010, Baba was honoured with a permanent seat in the Juna Akhara Council and given the title *Antahrashtriya Mandal ka Shri Mahant* (World Circle Guide).

But the spiritual path wasn't quite what the young Ramtirath had expected. He was accused of using his tantric powers to murder his own guru. That accusation remained a riddle to be solved. His life was full of accounts of magic, miracles, ghosts, and austerities. He was a mystic who bore the true heart of India.

He had led more than five thousand Naga sadhus for a bath in the Ganges on the sacred day of Makar Sankranti. The entire ritual was disrupted by the body of a murdered woman that floated in between them. Taking it as a sign from the universe that the dark forces were gathering together their powers, Baba Ramtirath had organized a huge Shiva puja to protect the holy city of Benares.

Hundreds of naked Naga sadhus covered in ash, squatted, smoking chillums filled with marijuana. The media people had left and Baba Ramtirath was giving directions to prepare for the big puja.

Hawa Singh, dressed in his usual leather jacket, leather boots and an old pair of faded jeans, walked up to meet Shri Mahant Baba Ramtirath.

As he moved ahead, he was stopped by Naga sadhus holding tridents. He could see that there was an organized structure to the mass of sadhus. They sat in circles, one within the other, making a kind of a barrier around their leader. It was not easy to break through this as these Nagas were jealously loyal, ruthless, and could kill with their bare hands.

Hawa Singh cleared his throat and shouted, 'Police! I need to talk to your leader.'

The sadhus looked at him and one of them went to inform the Mahant. Through the mass of sadhus, Hawa Singh could only see two blue eyes peering from behind the thick, round rimless spectacles. Then the eyes settled on him.

For the past two days, Hawa Singh had been running from the SSP office to the government hospital to get the autopsy report. However, they didn't have an expert to conduct the post-mortem and they had to wait for one to come from Allahabad.

The local police and the SSP office had been of no help to Hawa Singh. On the other hand, his father, Fauja Singh, was constantly on his case as the old man wanted Hawa's constant company in his last days.

Hawa Singh himself had gone to the government hospital to study Eva's body. She was lying on the steel platform, almost melding with the cold white metal. He saw that she was of medium height, five feet, six inches. She had brown hair with streaks of blonde. She must have dyed it.

Her face was not exactly beautiful but she had good features, with a shapely nose and thin lips. The eyes were grey, below very thin eyebrows. There was something about death that changed the face of a living person into cold marble. With her body having been in water, the skin had become paler. Yet, she had not bloated a lot.

It was clear that she had not been in water for long before her body was discovered.

One question haunted him. Did the killer walk past him carrying her when he lay passed out on the ghat? Was it possible that the killer threw her in the water right before Hawa Singh's sleeping eyes?

The killer may have stepped over his prostrate form, a thought that would add to his nightmares.

He had gone back to the ghat to look for clues. There were no signs. It came as a consolation that the killer may have been on the opposite bank of the river, and that he never came up to the ghat itself.

Hawa Singh had checked the young woman's hands for any signs of struggle or wounds. The fingers were long and artistic. She definitely was not used to any manual work.

The thing that shocked him was the gaping hole in her chest. The medic conducting the autopsy confirmed that Eva's heart was wrenched out while she was still alive. The wooden stake had been stabbed in later, after her death, into the very place where her heart had been.

However, there were no signs of sexual violence or even struggle on her body. Hawa Singh specifically checked her wrists, her feet and the neck area to ascertain whether she had been tied up before the entire ritual of killing began.

Apart from that, a few pieces of paper had been found in her stomach. They contained blurred drawings with some chants pertaining to Hindu astrology. Nothing could be made of that.

This connection of an astronomer with astrology confounded Hawa Singh.

He tried to gather as much information about the Vatican Observatory from the Net. He found that the Vatican Observatory is one of the oldest astronomical research institutions in the world. Originally based in the Roman College of Rome, it now has headquarters and a laboratory at the summer residence of the Pope in Castel Gandolfo, Italy.

The Vatican Observatory Research Group operates the 1.8m Alice P. Lennon Telescope with its Thomas J. Bannan Astrophysics Facility, known together as the Vatican Advanced Technology Telescope (VATT) funded by the Vatican and directly under the Pope.

However, nothing seemed to fit for Hawa Singh. A research scientist working with the Vatican studying the vast galaxies, the presence of Hindu astrological drawings, Baba Ramtirath's signed picture, the removal of Eva's heart, and then her being dumped into the Ganges impaled by a Holy Cross. Hawa Singh decided to meet directly with Baba Ramtirath.

He was trying to break through the ring surrounding him when, suddenly, two massive hands started to frisk him. A strongly built sadhu pulled out his Colt and looked at it with a smile. Then he threw it down to the others sitting in a circle. They passed it around, examining it with amazement. The Naga sadhu who had frisked Hawa Singh pushed him ahead.

Hawa Singh could feel the raw power in that gentle push. The Naga sadhus were a tough lot. Even when they went high up into the snow-covered mountains of the Himalayas, they stayed there for months on end in the same condition—unclothed, and persevering with the same austerities.

Their lifestyle had confounded the greatest of spiritual gurus. The Nagas tried to emulate the life of Lord Shiva—a mystic figure most often misunderstood.

They moved through the fumes of marijuana, and Hawa Singh found himself standing in front of Baba Ramtirath.

Baba took a long drag from his chillum and threw out a dense cloud of smoke. 'So, what are you looking for, officer?' asked Baba Ramtirath in what was clearly an American accent.

Hawa Singh felt awkward in the mass of naked men and mumbled, 'I wanted to talk to you regarding the murder of an American woman.'

Baba gave him a look and then nodded, saying, 'Why don't you sit down and be comfortable?'

The local papers had covered the murder of the white girl and everyone knew about it. However, the findings of the autopsy were not yet made public. Many a time, the herd of inquisitive journalists had tried to charge on Hawa Singh, but he had so far escaped unscathed.

Hawa Singh sat on the ground facing the blue-eyed American, introduced himself and then updated him on events surrounding the murder. They both stared at each other as the smoke-filled air hung between them.

Finally, Baba Ramtirath spoke. 'Do you know why we smoke so much?' he asked rhetorically. 'We want to keep a curtain of smoke between ourselves and the world. There are times when people desperately try to break our order.' He smiled to himself.

'Did Eva meet you personally to get that autograph on the picture?'

'Oh yes, she did come around ten days back, when we had just come into Benares. Everyone wanted to come for my darshan and she took an appointment to meet me personally. She was interested in Hindu astrology, especially the *Bhrigu-Samhita*, and wanted me to explain it all to her.'

Hawa Singh looked dumbfounded. '*Bhrigu-Samhita*?'

Baba Ramtirath took off his spectacles and carefully polished them with a soft cloth. He then looked at Hawa Singh and explained, 'The *Bhrigu-Samhita* is an astrological classic attributed to Maharishi Bhrigu. It was written in pre-Vedic times. It is said to contain predictions on current and future lives, as well as information on past ones. Maharishi Bhrigu had given a system of calculation, alongside planetary positions, with which one could make accurate predictions.'

'So this Eva, an astronomy researcher, wanted to learn astrology?'

Baba Ramtirath laughed out loud. 'That's what India is all about. Everyone gets attracted to this land because of its mysteries. I took Eva to be just another of those foreigners who are here on a trip. Most of them enjoy all this and then get back to their lives in the West.'

'She didn't go back to her life,' said Hawa Singh.

Baba Ramtirath nodded, looking around at the throng of sadhus. He turned to Hawa Singh and said, 'I knew that she wouldn't live long.'

'What?'

'While I was explaining astrology to her, I drew out her horoscope and could see clearly that soon she would be dead. Her time was up.'

Hawa Singh was quiet for a moment. Then he spoke. 'A few pieces of paper were found inside Eva's stomach with some drawings and chants on them.'

'Ah, it must be the *mrityunjay-yantra* that I had given her. I had asked her to keep it close to her. It was meant to protect her.'

'She seemed to have taken things so literally that she ate it. It was close to her all right, but it didn't protect her,' said Hawa Singh.

'When one's time is up, nothing can stop it. Death finds its way.'

Baba Ramtirath took a long drag on his chillum and exhaled heavily. He then offered the chillum to Hawa Singh.

The chillum was filled with the best marijuana from the fields in Himachal. As he took a long drag, Hawa Singh could feel weightlessness taking him over—he was floating in the air sitting cross-legged.

The trance was broken by Baba Ramtirath. 'So what are you looking for?'

Hawa Singh looked at him under eyelids that felt paradoxically heavy. 'I suspect that some Hindu fanatic was involved in the murder.'

'To me it looks like the work of some orthodox Christian who planted the Holy Cross in her heart.'

Hawa Singh looked around and realized that most of the Naga sadhus didn't understand a word of English, so he continued, 'Just to tell you she worked with the Vatican directly under the Pope.'

'Then you should ask the Pope. He seems to have all the answers.'

Hawa Singh chuckled. 'You, along with these sadhus, were the only ones present in the Ganges when her body was found.'

'Are you saying that I'm a suspect?' asked Baba Ramtirath.

'I'm trying to make a list.'

Baba Ramtirath smiled, 'You're an interesting man. Do you know these Nagas can cut you into pieces at the slightest flick of my finger?'

'I just love to jump into the lion's den,' smiled Hawa Singh.

Baba looked at him with his crystal-blue eyes, 'Finally, I have met a true man. You seem to have already tasted death.'

'I'm half-dead. They call me the Ghost,' laughed Hawa Singh.

'So tell me, dear Ghost, what makes you think I could have killed her?' asked Baba Ramtirath.

Hawa Singh was quiet for a moment before speaking. 'It looks like your sadhus may have carried the body in that dark hour to leave it in the Ganges. It looked like a sacrificial killing, a ritual in which her heart was removed.'

Baba spoke softly, 'Your simple mind came up with a simple calculation—strange men perform strange rituals. Let me tell you, the Naga sadhus might portray themselves to be fiery but they are the most peace-loving men. The Nagas were organized into a sect by Adi Shankara in the fifth century BC. We are the ultimate protectors of the Sanatan Dharma, or what some call the Hindu religion. The killing of a fellow human being is totally against Hinduism and we would never commit such an act.'

Hawa Singh nodded, but added, 'I have seen many loving fathers, brothers and relatives commit the most heinous crimes. There are times when the human mind goes out of control when it is filled with rage, and there are times when the human mind coolly calculates and plans. Then there are those individuals whose minds are shadowed by the veil of religion, traditions and rituals. They prove to be the most dangerous.'

'There is a whole world of difference between what is and what seems,' countered Baba. 'It's all an illusion. You are trying to use your logic and reasoning, but it won't work. Don't forget, that day was also one of the most auspicious days in the Hindu calendar.'

Hawa Singh looked puzzled.

Baba spoke with a smile and twinkling eyes, 'The fourteenth day of January, or Makar Sankranti, apart from being a harvest festival, is also regarded as the beginning of an auspicious phase. It marks the end of an inauspicious period which, according to the Hindu calendar, begins around mid-December. It is believed that any auspicious and sacred ritual can be sanctified this day onwards.'

'Sankranti is the Sanskrit word in Hindu astrology which refers to the transmigration of the Sun from one Rashi—or sign of the zodiac—to another. Hence, there are twelve such Sankrantis in all. However, the Sankranti festival usually refers to Makar Sankranti or the transition of the Sun from Dhanu Rashi, or Sagittarius, to Makar Rashi, or Capricorn.'

'The winter solstice marks the beginning of the gradual increase in the length of days. Scientifically, the shortest day of the year is around the twenty-first or twenty-second day of December, after which the days begin to get longer and the winter solstice begins. Hence, the Uttarayana, northern movement of the Sun, is actually 21 December, which was originally the day of Makar Sankranti too. But because of the Earth's tilt of 23.45 degrees and sliding of equinoxes, Ayanamsa, longitudinal change, occurs. This has caused Makar Sankranti to slide further down the ages. A thousand years ago, Makar Sankranti was on 31 December and is now on 14 January. Five thousand years later, it shall be by the end of February, while in 9,000 years it shall come in June. The dates may change but its importance will not. A Hindu would not kill on such an auspicious day.'

'A fanatic Hindu might kill just to mark the auspicious day and to show its might to the Holy Cross,' argued Hawa Singh.

Baba nodded thoughtfully, saying, 'You will have to move beyond the borders of knowledge and science and step into the world of faith and God, to get this one. Religion and reasoning don't go together.'

'Whatever might be, I want to request that you and your followers don't leave Benares till the case is solved.'

'Well, that might take an eternity—and I don't have the luxury of all that time.'

Hawa Singh got up saying, 'I won't keep you waiting.'

He turned to leave and saw long, sharp swords in the hands of the assembled sadhus. It would take one strike to separate the head from the rest of the body with one of those. Hawa Singh would disappear forever. The Nagas were waiting for a word from their leader.

'There will be time to kill. Time to fight and time to sacrifice,' declared Baba Ramtirath.

CHAPTER 4

Hawa Singh walked towards the SSP's office, adjusting his retrieved Colt at his back with some relief, and covering it with his jacket. He could hear a cacophony of laughter, clapping, people shouting at the top of their voices in Hindi and English. He had heard this kind of commotion too often and knew it was going to be a scene typical of any press conference. The herd had arrived.

He opened the door to see an army of mouths munching on sweets and slurping colas. In between, they threw questions at the police team sitting in front. Hawa Singh saw Neeraj Thakur, the SSP, sitting alongside the Deputy Superintendent of Police, and another five junior officers. Between them sat a young girl, dressed sharply in a grey suit and white shirt.

She wore fiery red lipstick and her hair was finely cut. She was pretty, with big dark eyes, a shapely nose and high cheekbones. It was clear that she worked out regularly—unlike Hawa Singh, who sought nothing more for his body than survival.

It was an impromptu press conference called by the SSP to introduce this FBI agent to the press. Ruby Malik was half-Pakistani and half-American, the closest the FBI could find to an Indian. Back in the US, they didn't differentiate between Indians and 'Pakis', anyway.

Her very introduction had caused a furore among the herd. They were trying their best to shake up and stir the unknown fear and mania that they were so good at creating. Many frivolous questions were being flung at the woman from across the room.

Q. *Do you think, being as you are a Pakistani, you will be able to do justice to the investigation?*
A. *Yes, I do.*
Q. *Have you ever been to India before?*
A. *No.*
Q. *Do you understand India and its culture?*
A. *No.*
Q. *Where do your loyalties lie, with Pakistan or with the US?*
A. *With my work.*
Q. *Do you think the Indian police are not capable of handling the investigation?*
A. *I'm here only to assist.*
Q. *What do you know about Benares?*
A. *Nothing.*
Q. *Do you like Indian food or American food?*
A. *I eat to live!*
Q. *What did you learn at the FBI?*
A. *A lot!*
Q. *Would you prefer to shoot the killer or arrest him?*
A. *I abide by the laws.*

Q. *You are so beautiful... were you a fashion model before joining the FBI?*

A. *No.*

Q. *Are you interested in modelling, or in Bollywood?*

A. *No.*

Q. *How do you keep yourself so fit? Would you like to give us any tips on dieting and exercise?*

A. *Run.*

Q. *Have you seen any Hindi films?*

A. *No.*

Q. *Who are your favourite actors and actresses?*

A. *We better get working.*

Hawa Singh loved her simple, straightforward answers. It showed that she was not here on a tourist visa or to while away the time. She meant business.

The SSP felt the cold vibes between the journos and Ruby. The moment he saw Hawa Singh, he got up and called out, 'Look, we have Hawa Singh here. Come, Hawa Singh.'

Hawa Singh felt awkward, hating to stand in front of the pen-pushers, and more so to answer their inappropriate questions. He looked at Ruby and she smiled at him. He was too taken aback to smile back.

'Let me introduce you both. Ruby, this is Hawa Singh, and this is Ruby,' said the SSP with a big smile.

Ruby got up to shake hands with Hawa Singh. He saw that she looked about five feet and eleven inches tall. She had a firm grip. After a very long time, he felt a sense of security and comfort as she held his hand.

The SSP was declaring to the media persons, 'Hawa Singh from the Delhi Crime Branch and Ruby Malik from the FBI will be assisting us in the full investigation.

However, let me make it very clear that it is our team that will lead, as this is our territory.'

Hawa Singh knew the SSP was playing his cards smartly. He was putting Ruby and him right in the dock, while ensuring his chair was safe. If the investigation failed, it would be Hawa Singh and Ruby who would be questioned.

'We will keep updating you all, from time to time, as the investigation proceeds. I'm sure that we'll be able to catch the killer very soon,' the SSP smoothly assured the press.

The herd munched on the free chips and nuts, and downed their cokes. Crunch. Slurp. Breaking news.

Ruby looked at Hawa Singh and said with her American accent, 'So let's get working.'

Hawa Singh nodded.

For Hawa Singh the press conference was the most idiotic move by the SSP. He had displayed the faces of the investigating team to the killer. Either he'd escape before they laid their hands on him or he'd go out of his way to get them out of the way.

CHAPTER 5

It was around five in the evening. The cold wind coming in from the Ganges had chilled everyone to the bone. Women scurried on their errands covered in layers of sweaters and shawls, bargaining for fresh vegetables. The men sat around bonfires on roadsides, smoking bidis and drinking hot tea laced with ginger, cardamom, tulsi and black pepper.

The water was bitingly cold. It took some courage to wash even your hands in it. In Benares you could nevertheless see the devout take a full dip in the near-freezing Ganges. Religion was their opium, allowing them to do things they wouldn't dream of without it. God worked in various ways.

The children had disappeared from the streets, and were now huddling inside their quilts. The light outside grew diffuse as the sun prepared to bow down to the night. The cows, the street dogs, the cats and the rats were all busy scampering for their last meal before settling in groups to sleep. Only ghosts came out on such nights.

Hawa Singh walked through the narrow street with long strides. Right behind was Ruby Malik, trying to catch up with him.

'It would be better if you went back to your hotel. I need to check on my father,' said Hawa Singh, without turning around.

'And I need to look around the city. I need to understand it.'

'There is nothing to understand. There is a killer out there and we have to catch him,' retorted Hawa Singh.

A few passers-by stopped to look at Ruby, so smartly dressed—not a common sight in the streets of Benares. The men stood gaping as she strode past with Hawa Singh.

'I have been assigned by the SSP to be with you. We are a team,' said Ruby.

Hawa Singh stopped and turned to look at her. 'I don't take orders from that SSP—or from anyone else. I prefer to work alone. If you want to be with me, work with me, you'll have to listen to me and do as I say.'

'I should tell you I don't like taking orders from anyone either,' Ruby shot back curtly.

He looked into her deep dark eyes. He could sense in her the same spirit that ran in his veins. They were people with independent minds, who had their own style of functioning. They were not clerks at desks given to writing reams of reports to prove their worth. They preferred to act. Accomplish something. They were rushing to reach an end.

Such people need to be left alone. They are used to the darkness, the silence, the waiting. They belong to the same family. That of leopards.

'Look, I'm going to meet my father. He is a slightly deranged man. It sometimes gets difficult to control him,' warned Hawa Singh.

Ruby's scarlet lips parted in a big smile as she said, with some excitement, 'I would definitely like to meet him. And you also need to apprise me on the details of the case.'

He sensed the same headstrong, stubborn bull's attitude in her. It was useless to argue with his double.

They moved ahead silently as Ruby got the view of the narrow *galis* of Benares. She saw open flowing drains, garbage strewn around with pigs having a party on the leftovers, vendors rushing up to her with their incense sticks and flowers, while the pandits clamoured around her, vying to get a puja done for her at the cheapest rates.

Hawa Singh kept walking ahead, leaving her to deal with them all. Ruby was not at all used to this kind of attention and she fought her way through the growing crowd around her. It all came to a standstill, when a man, his skin painted black, in a flowing black robe, and holding a long sword, blocked her path.

Such men dressed themselves as various Hindu gods and goddesses and went around collecting alms from the superstitious. The man in black, with a red tongue lolling out, was emulating Kali Mata. He kept leaping about around her, demanding a thousand rupees to let her move ahead.

If it had been the streets of Washington, she would only have to flash her FBI badge, to bring the matter to an end. Or if the situation demanded it, kicked the man in the groin and laid him out flat on the ground.

Here, it was a different world. She was not allowed to carry her pistol. She was, like any other tourist, stuck in a jam. There seemed no way out except to pay this toll to walk in the streets of Benares.

The man moved his sword over her head. A fine strand of hair got sliced off her head and floated up in the air.

'Give me the money or I'll curse you,' shouted the man, who now seemed to be totally possessed by Kali Mata.

In this jamboree, a hand caught 'Kali Mata' by his throat and banged his head against the nearby wall. The hand caught hold of Ruby and pulled her away from the crowd. No one uttered a word. Ruby, too, was stunned by this act of Hawa Singh.

The man possessed by Kali Mata lay sprawled in the drain. He somehow got to his feet, picked up his sword and ran away.

Holding her hand, Hawa Singh led Ruby to Mukti Bhawan. Ruby looked at the dilapidated red-brick building. The bricks were jutting out of the walls. The cement looked like dust as it crumbled and kept falling on the ground. She was apprehensive that the building itself might just fall on them.

Hawa Singh looked at her and said, 'Don't worry, you won't get moksha that easily. Come on in.'

He walked inside and she followed him into a room. The first thing she saw was an old man who looked like he'd recently pooped in his pyjamas because he wasn't wearing any. Fauja Singh was shadow-boxing, standing on the cold cemented floor, dressed only in a kurta, his legs bare and shrivelled. A long line of saliva trickled down from his mouth as he gasped and panted. Hawa Singh picked up a towel and cleaned his father's mouth.

'Look at me. I can still beat the hell out of many boxers,' Fauja boasted in an old man's quavering voice.

He turned to look at Ruby standing near the door. She was shocked to see the conditions they lived in. There was not even a bed in the room. There was a tattered mattress on the cement floor covered with two blankets, and a dirty pillow with oil marks on it that had turned black. There was no place to sit. It was worse than a prison cell. But then, everyone came here to die. What was the need for luxury, when you were leaving it all behind?

Fauja Singh laughed suddenly. 'Finally, you got yourself a girl.'

He turned towards Ruby and extended a large hand. 'Myself Fauja Singh, international champion. Boxer.'

Ruby, smiling, took his hand. 'Ruby Malik, FBI.'

Fauja looked amazed. 'FBI! Isn't that the American CID? What the hell are you doing with this Hawa Singh?'

'I'm here to assist him on a murder case.'

Fauja could only understand the word 'murder' and he latched onto it. 'Murder. Are you talking about the murder of that American girl? This Hawa Singh never tells me these interesting things but I read them in the newspaper.'

Hawa Singh held his father, urging him to rest. Fauja flung off his hand and said, 'We are talking murder and crime—and you want me to rest! Let me tell you, Ruby, it's the fortunate ones who get to die in Benares. From here you directly achieve moksha.'

'Enough, you better stop with your shadow-boxing or your heart will give out,' said Hawa Singh.

'Don't give me all this love and care. I'm going for my final rest. The gods are waiting for me, but I'm going to keep them waiting. Tell me, Ruby, do you believe in rebirth?'

She was taken aback by the abrupt question and said, 'I've never really thought about it.'

Fauja spoke like an excited child, 'I know for sure that there is rebirth. We all are caught in this process of reincarnation till we expend all our karmas and mingle with the One Source, God.'

Hawa Singh handed him a few pills with a glass of water. Fauja was about to take the pills but threw them away suddenly, shouting, 'What are these medicines for? I have come to Benares to achieve moksha and give away this body. You are trying to take away my Godliness.'

Ruby was quiet, looking uncomfortable at being caught in an argument between father and son.

Fauja realized it and said, 'Ruby, there is no need to feel awkward. This boy is like this only. I'm the one worried about him, more than he about me. He is like a kid. When I'm gone, please take care of him. Or take him with you to your American CID.'

'Enough, champion, it's getting late. It's time for you to eat something,' said Hawa Singh.

'I have ordered some hot chhole-bhature. I am not going to eat the food of these dead people. Remember, I'm not here to die like them. I'm here to achieve moksha. Now go and call your mother to prepare some tea for the guest.'

These were the moments that brought tears to Hawa Singh's eyes. In his ramblings, Fauja would often call upon his dead wife, believing her to have gone out to buy vegetables, or in the kitchen, cooking, or knitting on the terrace.

It was the shrill tone of his cell phone that distracted Hawa Singh from an emotional moment.

It was Neeraj Thakur, the SSP. 'The Naga sadhus and the Aghoris are about to battle each other,' he shouted. 'I want you here right now.'

Hawa Singh couldn't hear anything further as the voice crackled over his old and broken handset. He had held it together with cellotape. He had never been tech-friendly.

But there was one word he heard clearly.

Murder.

CHAPTER 6

It was eight at night. Dark water. Black sky. Temperature 1 degree celsius. Windy.

The hundreds of Naga sadhus led by Baba Ramtirath, and armed with tridents and swords, stood chanting, 'Om Namo Narayana! Har Har Mahadev!' In front of them on the same bank of the Ganges stood another group of sadhus, the Aghoris, also armed with tridents, axes, hatchets and clubs. They carried torches of wood picked up from the burning pyres.

In between them lay the body of Tailanga Swami, Mahaguru, or the leader of the Aghoris. His head had been struck off and lay a few feet from the body on the blood-stained sand. There was an axe with blood on the blade next to the body. It had probably been the weapon that killed him.

The Aghoris blamed the Naga sadhus for the murder of their guru. The Nagas refused to hear them out. The two groups of mystics stood on the bank of the river sacred to them both, ready to kill each other.

A few paunchy policemen tried to diffuse the tension. They had flood-lit the area.

The SSP was trying to get reinforcements in case the situation spiralled out of control.

He was already under the pressure of the American woman's presence in his team, and now they had another murder to look into. Neeraj Thakur, the upholder of law and order in the city, was tremendously worried. There would be a lot of questions from the political circles and he'd have to produce results or be ready to be axed.

A group of media persons with cameras stood at a distance from the war zone, illuminating the entire battlefield with their flashbulbs. They waited for the moment when they would be allowed to take pictures of the dead Aghori Baba. It would make for an exciting front-page display. The smell of blood had brought the hounds out.

Baba Ramtirath stood at the head of his followers, calling out, 'We would never even touch these Aghoris who call themselves the descendents of Lord Shiva. They are nothing more than roadside tantriks.'

The rage among the Aghoris was growing. No one dared insult them. They were the custodians of Benares, of life and death. They are known for their extreme and outlandish violations of typical Indian and other social mores. Their unorthodox, taboo rituals have caused many mainstream Hindus to condemn them as non-Hindu.

They are known to engage in post-mortem ritual cannibalism, residing in cremation grounds, and taking part in tantric sexual rituals. They smear cremation ashes on their bodies, and have been known to use skulls from human corpses for crafting bowls. They either go naked or wear the shroud of a corpse.

Though both Naga sadhus and Aghoris are devotees of Lord Shiva, the Nagas hold the latter in contempt due to the rituals they engage in.

The SSP spoke to them all, trying to keep his nervousness and stress in check, 'We understand your emotions but this is a murder case. Please let the police do their work. We assure you we'll soon catch the killer.'

The Aghoris refused to budge an inch from their ground. 'Blood will be spilt right now. Our guru has been killed and these Nagas are responsible for it. Since the time they have arrived in Kashi, things have gone wrong. They are an evil breed and need to be cast out from our holy land.'

The Nagas shouted back, 'Let us see who can move us out of Benares. This is the land of Shiva and we are the true devotees, not these Aghoris who live in cremation grounds and eat half-burnt corpses.'

Tailanga Swami commanded great reverence from the local population. He was known for his tantric strength and was supposed to possess miraculous healing powers gained through intense eremitic rites and practices of renunciation and tapasya.

He was the only one in the entire history of Benares who performed worship of Shiva at the Kashi Vishwanath temple using his own filth.

He said, 'Dirt is as much part of the Universal Soul as roses, holy water, incense and flowers.'

The priest who saw Tailanga Swami indulging in such an act had slapped him. Later, the priest was mysteriously found dead outside the temple. After the cremation, Tailanga Swami and his group of Aghori sadhus feasted on the priest's half-burnt body.

'The dead and the living are all one. By eating him we become one with him,' Tailanga Swami had stated.

Aghoris believe that up to seven human murders are forgivable. There have been instances of human sacrifice, but human sacrifices did not count as murders.

The greatest of all Aghoris, the most powerful tantric, the man supposed to cure diseases and bring life to the dead, had been killed. No powerful mantras or tantras—just one powerful stroke of an axe.

Hawa Singh and Ruby hurried to the spot, to see the warring clans standing in all preparedness to battle it out. Ruby had never seen something so extraordinary—an army of men with phalluses dangling for all to see. She turned her face away.

'These Aghoris have no right to even take Lord Shiva's name. They are the ones who need to be thrown out of Kashi,' announced an angry Baba Ramtirath.

'This Kashi has been our home for hundreds of years. Why don't you go back to your mountains and hide in those caves? Don't forget Kashi was founded by Lord Shiva and we are His only true followers,' cried out Neelambar Nath, the second-in-command of the Aghoris.

The Nagas gave a war cry that shook all of Benares—'Har Har Mahadev!'

Hawa Singh knew that the situation needed to be diffused. He snatched a rifle from one of the constables and rushed right in amidst the two groups. He pointed the rifle up in the air and fired two shots.

A deathly silence filled the air.

Hawa Singh shouted at the top of his voice, 'This Benares doesn't belong to you, it belongs to the people. You have no right to disrupt the harmony of this holy land that you all are so proud of. I want all of you to lay down your weapons now.'

The SSP was shaking with nervousness. What was Hawa Singh up to?

Hawa Singh saw no one had put down their tridents, axes or clubs. For them they were not weapons. They were an extension of their bodies.

Hawa Singh almost stepped on the patch of bloody sand surrounding the body, and quickly withdrew. A shiver ran through his body as he looked upon what he feared to see—a headless body.

Ruby couldn't bear to look at the ghastly spectacle. Hawa Singh took a few deep breaths and turned to the SSP. 'Yes, we have another murder here. It's Tailanga Swami, the Aghori guru,' said Neeraj.

The very thought of murder filled Hawa Singh with deep sorrow, because the implication was that such heinous acts of crimes would never stop. More and more violent crimes dominated public life. Society was moving towards an ugly darkness that had changed the face of the friendly neighbour, the friend, the kinsman.

Newspapers and television channels were full of stories of violence. Crime today was selling like sex. People seemed to derive a secret satisfaction from the thought: 'At least, I'm safe.' Being safe was being alive.

Hawa Singh looked at the Aghoris crowding close to the headless corpse and shouted, 'Get back! No one will come close to the body.'

Neelambar Nath of the Aghoris stepped forward, calling out, 'We want to claim the body of our guru, and would like the police to keep out of our affairs.' He called his men to pick up the corpse of Tailanga Swami.

Hawa Singh raised the rifle, pointed at the group of Aghoris armed with tridents and axes, and shouted at full volume, 'Listen to me very carefully! The body needs to be taken for post-mortem. We are here to help you out and catch the killer.'

'Our guru's body will not be cut open for any reason!' roared back Neelambar Nath. 'We have our own means of tantra-mantra and we'll make sure the killer dies a painful death!'

The SSP was shaking with the knowledge that it was almost impossible to argue and to make the Aghoris comply with the law of the land.

Hawa Singh stepped up close to Neelambar Nath, looked him in the eye and said, 'Do not interfere with police work. If I have to shoot you all, I will. The police will take away the body. You do your work and let us do ours.'

He then turned towards the Naga sadhus and looked at Baba Ramtirath questioningly.

'Just to tell you, officer, a Naga sadhu doesn't use an axe,' said Ramtirath. 'The only thing we carry is this trishul. Just look back at those Aghoris, they are the ones who are carrying axes. It could be anyone of them who killed their own guru. It could even be Neelambar Nath himself.'

'Don't you dare say that again or we'll cut you to pieces. Our guru was our God!' cried Neelambar.

'Enough! Now I want you both to step back from here and let the police do their work. I said now!' commanded Hawa Singh.

The Nagas and the Aghoris slowly stepped back.

A forensic team rushed up with a few armed policemen. The SSP was continually giving an update on the situation on the phone to the District Magistrate. For the first time since the danger had escalated, he felt a bit relieved. He didn't know if anyone else on his force could have handled the sadhus. Only a man who is not afraid of dying would jump into a war zone.

Ruby and Hawa Singh scrutinized the crime scene with their torches. 'Most of the blood has been soaked into the sand,' Ruby observed.

Hawa Singh was more interested in the axe. He saw it had a heavy wooden handle and hoped to find some fingerprints on it. The blade, too, was heavy. It looked as if it had been sharpened for the kill.

Ruby pointed to a set of footprints in the sand, calling attention to them. 'Singh, we have these prints here. They could be of the victim or of the killer.'

Hawa Singh nodded and indicated them to the forensic team. It was difficult for them to work in the near darkness.

Ruby sat close to the body. It was lying stomach down in the sand.

Hawa Singh stepped closer and called out to a medic to turn the body upward. The medic carefully, with gloved hands, did so.

The Aghoris were chanting mantras and slowly drifting back towards their cremation ground. They had decided to leave the police alone and call on the spirits to guide them to the killer. Only Neelambar Nath remained, keeping an eye on the police and on his dead guru.

Baba Ramtirath chanted a prayer for the dead and called out to his men to come away.

Finally, they left the dead alone.

The hounds were still circling the grounds, in their perpetual thirst for blood.

'These Aghoris live in the cremation ground. It seems that Tailanga Swami came here all alone,' said Hawa Singh.

'You mean to say that the killer was prepared and waiting for him here?' asked Ruby.

Hawa Singh looked at Neelambar. 'Swamiji was sitting with us in the cremation ground till around 7.30 pm. After that he suddenly got up, saying that he had to meet someone and left,' said Neelambar Nath.

'The killer himself had called him,' said Ruby.

'It had to be someone close to him. Someone whom he knew well, trusted and went out alone to meet,' said Hawa Singh.

Neelambar was quiet. Hawa Singh asked him, 'Where were you at that time?'

'You think I killed my own guru? I would have given up my own life any time to keep him alive,' protested Neelambar.

'Then you will have to answer my question.'

Neelambar took control of the anger boiling in him. 'I followed Swamiji for a while, just to be with him. But then he disappeared in the darkness. He used to do that to us. He must have sensed me.'

'That means you were also not with your group in the cremation ground.'

'You can say that, but it doesn't mean I killed him.'

'We'll find out.'

Ruby pointed her torch at the severed head. 'There is a distance of more than ten feet between the body and the head. The cut shows that the killer used only one stroke to decapitate him. Only a really powerful blow could fling the head that distance.'

Hawa Singh saw that Neelambar was a lanky, scrawny man—but then, these Aghoris were capable of amazing feats of strength.

'A lot of blood has flowed. Since the killer was standing close to the victim, he must have been drenched. That means his clothes would be heavily stained. Someone must have seen him,' said Ruby.

Hawa Singh looked at the sand, the blood, the Ganges, and finally spoke. 'The killer could have washed himself clean in the river. No one would suspect a man coming out wet from the Ganges. The other possibility is that he crossed the river to the other side.'

They looked towards the opposite bank. All they saw was darkness.

Hawa Singh summoned a young local police officer, Gaya Prasad Sharma, and instructed him to talk to people around the nearby ghat, the shops, vendors, beggars, lepers and all, to find out if anyone saw a man carrying an axe coming towards the area. He hoped someone would have seen the killer coming armed to the secluded spot to kill.

The head of Tailanga Swami was wrapped in opaque plastic by the forensic team. That was a big relief for Ruby. She wouldn't have to see it again.

The body was picked up to look for signs underneath it. There was nothing. Only blood.

Hawa Singh wanted to make sure that this was an, unconnected incident and told the forensics team, 'Just check if his heart is in place.'

The medic looked and said, 'Yes, it's right there.'

Hawa Singh was relieved. Going by the modus operandi, at least it was not the same killer.

'You might not believe us but this is the work of Naga sadhus. They are no less tantriks than we are. They can disappear into thin air and dissolve into darkness. They are here to capture the city,' persisted Neelambar Nath.

Hawa Singh was looking far into the darkness. He turned to Neelambar and asked, 'Did your guru often come out for such secret meetings?'

'No, this is the only time that I saw him doing so.'

'That means he could have been meeting this person on a regular basis, or at least knew him well enough to venture out in the dark to meet him.'

'If it was so regular, we would have known about it. And Guruji was not scared of darkness. For us Aghoris, the good and bad, light and dark, are all part of the same sacred source.'

Hawa Singh nodded thoughtfully, adjusting his Colt. 'Did Swamiji have any enemies? I mean, did anyone ever threaten him or did he ever have a rift with someone?' asked Hawa Singh.

'Here, in Benares, people worshipped him. Even the Kashi Naresh doesn't cross his path.'

Ruby came up to Hawa Singh and said, 'I don't know whether I should be involved in this or not. This is an isolated case and has nothing to do with the murder of Eva. The FBI didn't send me for this.'

The SSP was sweating helplessly, surrounded by reporters. He was trying to answer their questions as best as he could. The best remark he could come up with was, 'I assure you and the people of Benares that the killer will be caught.'

Hawa Singh knew that it was not all about power, the uniform and grabbing headlines. The police all over the country were understaffed, underpaid and overworked.

Still, they have to act. They have to forget everything once they are out on streets.

It was not only about intelligence, it was about who would endure longer and stick around to the end. One needed to act, be patient and have the strength to bear pain.

Sleepless. Loveless. Ruthless.

The crux of the matter was that, within a short span of time, they had had to contend with more than one murder in Benares.

Hawa Singh was forced deeper and deeper into an endless fog. He already had too much on his mind—his dying father, the memories of Kavita, the bullet that constantly worried at his brain, the murder of Eva, the many riddles of astrology, and the mysterious *Bhrigu-Samhita*. And now this.

'It would be better that the local police handle this. We both are out of jurisdiction here,' said Hawa Singh to Ruby.

Ruby had a sudden idea. 'Could it be that the swami was killed to take away the focus from Eva's murder?'

Hawa Singh looked at her and said, 'It would have been better,' replied Hawa Singh, 'for the killer to have left Benares and disappeared till we tired of the hunt and gave up.'

Ruby nodded in agreement.

'Also, Eva's killer left his signature in the form of the Cross, and her heart was wrenched out. The Holy Cross and the axe don't fit together,' said Hawa Singh.

They did not know it at the time, but there was one factor that tied them together.

CHAPTER 7

The water was warm enough for comfort, and not hot enough to burn. It was dark and the fog was at ground level. The outdoor pool was lit and its bottom shone with polished tiles as Ruby Malik did her customary daily fifty laps.

She wanted to unclog her brain, clear it of all the blood and gore. She wanted to tire herself out physically, to give her mind some rest.

She loved the water cascading down her body as she glided ahead, knifing smoothly through the warm water of the heated swimming pool at Nadesar Palace. It was built in the nineteenth century to accommodate illustrious guests of the East India Company. The white stucco, colonnaded mansion became the residence of a maharaja before its transition into a luxury, ten-suite guesthouse, combining the traditional elegance of a colonial country-house hotel with the joys of modern gadgetry and plumbing.

The FBI had earlier booked her in a guesthouse. The Vatican made sure that the investigative officer had all the comforts, so she could focus at ease on her work. The Vatican too was interested in finding the killer of their trusted and loyal employee at the observatory.

It was already 11.30 pm and the fog had covered everything. Ruby was on her last few laps, almost sweating inside the warm water. Hawa Singh walked towards the pool, cutting through the curtain of fog. His hands were chilled. He couldn't believe that Ruby was swimming in this temperature.

He stood close to the pool, watching her move gracefully, like a smooth dolphin. He could see the contours of her body as her long legs kicked the water and her slender hands stretched ahead to touch the wall.

Hawa Singh realized that she was fair-skinned, but still no one would call her a foreigner. She had the typical features of an Indian or a Pakistani girl. Dark black hair. Black eyes. An oval-shaped face. Overall, she had a perfect body. He could see the workouts behind it all. While he was getting bulkier, drank a lot and had a bullet lodged in his head.

Ruby finished her fifty laps, saw Hawa Singh standing on the rim of the pool, and smiled up at him, breathing a little fast after the exertion.

'Why don't you join me?'

Hawa Singh dipped his hand in the pool to check the temperature and said, 'I prefer the Ganges. Are you ready for an early morning dip?'

She climbed out saying, 'I don't want to freeze in the river.'

She was wearing a sleek, backless swimsuit. She removed the cap from her head and flicked her hair. It had been a long time since he had seen a beautiful woman.

He picked up a towel and handed it to her. 'I wanted to discuss certain things with you.'

Ruby wrapped the towel around herself saying, 'Well then, let's go to my room.'

Hawa Singh followed her, trying not to stare. He couldn't help but notice her beautifully shaped legs, still shining wet from the pool, and the gleam in her hair.

Kavita had always kept her hair open, letting it dance in the wind. He had loved to play with it. All that love now gone.

They stepped into her room. Hawa Singh was not used to seeing such luxury. He had stayed in cheap guest-houses or lodges most of his life. He had never been able to afford something like this, nor could the rest of the Delhi Police.

Swathes of pink raw silk draped the four-poster bed. Works of art from the Maharaja's collection were displayed on the walls. The room had original pieces of furniture to recreate the atmosphere of a bygone era. The décor of the room was intended to evoke the colours of marigold, jasmine, and the pale pink lotuses that are offered to the Ganges. Hawa Singh sat hesitatingly on one of the prized chairs, lest he break it.

Ruby went into the bathroom, leaving the door slightly open, enough for Hawa Singh to see that this room was equally a feast for the eyes—retro fittings, shining white marble and Venetian mirrors. In one of the larger mirrors, he watched, transfixed, Ruby removing her swimsuit. She dried herself and slipped on a t-shirt and shorts. As she emerged back into the bedroom, he looked away.

'I'm ordering some hot coffee,' said Ruby from near the phone. 'Why don't you update me on some details while we wait for it? The police did provide me with the file but I need to know more directly from you.'

Hawa Singh nodded, realizing that, suddenly, he felt very warm. He was not used to these heated rooms. He removed his leather jacket and his Colt, placed the jacket on a side table, and quietly slipped the gun under it.

Ruby jumped onto the bed and sat on it cross-legged, tying back her hair. 'Okay, I'm ready, so let's start.'

To Hawa Singh she looked like a girl out of some television commercial. Bubbly. Chirpy. Smiley. She looked different from the confident suit-clad FBI official at the press conference. Her armour had gone.

He controlled his thoughts and focused on narrating to her the series of events that occurred right from the time he saw the body of Eva in the water. In between, Ruby was constantly taking notes. He told her that the forensics team were not able to come up with any prints. Obviously, there had been a stampede of flatfoots in Eva's room.

By the time he finished she had a list of pointers. 'I don't understand the connection between astronomy and astrology,' she began musingly. 'Secondly, the motive of the murder is not clear. Is it a ritual killing, part of a human sacrifice? Thirdly, where was she killed? It is clear that she was brought to the Ganges and left there.'

To Hawa Singh she spoke like any trainee detective trying to show off her intelligence. Still, she had explored the basic question. Motive.

'Well, the way I remember it, it was pretty clear that the crime scene was artificial and arranged,' admitted Hawa Singh. 'I mean, the way the body was left in the Ganges with the wooden stake. It was meant to call for attention.'

Ruby looked thoughtful and said, 'We need to find out whether it is a beginning, or an end.'

Hawa Singh was peeling away the layers of the mystery one by one. He believed that there are marks left at the scene of every crime. It's left to you to find them.

'The Naga sadhus and the Aghoris are right now our prime suspects,' he continued, still lost in his train of thoughts. 'They are the ones who go in for tantric rituals and sacrifices, and consider themselves to be the controllers of life and death.'

The coffee arrived and Ruby got up to serve it in what looked like, to Hawa Singh, expensive cups. He was afraid that if he broke one, he'd have to pay for it.

'What do you think about the murder of Aghori Baba?' asked Ruby.

'It could be a case of gaining power in their circle. I mean, one of them could have killed him to take his position.'

'In that case, Neelambar is the person to gain. He was the second-in-command,' reasoned Ruby.

'Forensics have found thumbprints on the handle of the axe. They will lead us to the killer.'

Ruby spoke her thoughts out aloud. 'You think Eva ever met this Tailanga Swami?'

Hawa Singh looked stunned at this new perspective. 'We could look into that! In fact, we need to find all the places that Eva visited here, all the people she met in Benares.'

He suddenly remembered, took out the small piece of paper from his pocket, and handed it to Ruby. 'This was what I found in Eva's hotel room. I have checked the telephone numbers. One of them is the private number of the king of Benares.'

Ruby looked surprised. 'The king of Benares! They still have a king here?'

'He is a figurehead, actually. Monarchy was dissolved post-Independence. The current "king", or "Kashi Naresh" as he is called, is Maharaj Abhay Narayan Singh. He is a descendant of a highly orthodox Brahmin family. Even today, the Kashi Naresh is deeply revered by the people of Benares. The people here consider him an incarnation of Lord Shiva. He is also the chief cultural patron and an essential part of all religious celebrations,' explained Hawa Singh.

'Here, everyone seems more mysterious than the last person,' exclaimed Ruby.

Hawa Singh gingerly replaced his porcelain cup on the table. He rubbed his scalp uncomfortably as the indoor heating went to his head.

Ruby looked at him curiously. 'Is it really true that you have a bullet lodged near the brain?'

He nodded silently.

'Man, that's crazy. Does it hurt?'

Another nod, followed by a dry 'Can we get on with our work?'

Ruby sat down on a cushion resembling a marigold. She looked like a goddess, sitting amidst its velvet petals.

'Right, then,' Hawa Singh continued, 'the second number I checked is the mobile number of Suryadev Singh, minister of state for social development. He happens to be notorious.'

At Ruby's questioning look, Hawa Singh elaborated, 'Suryadev Singh, approximately fifty-five years old, is the son of B.P. Singh, the most powerful coal mafioso during the late '70s and '80s, just after the nationalization of mines in Bihar and the Jharkhand region. When all mines were taken over by the government, B.P. Singh began to run parallel mines illegally. Many other small coal mafia gangs followed suit.'

Ruby was all ears. 'So now, the mafia thickens the plot. Go on.'

'Due to intense rivalry with other gangs, the rising violence, killings, and political turmoil, B.P. Singh sent his son, Suryadev Singh, to London to study. Suryadev studied in London and throughout was well aware of his father's activities.

'Suryadev acquired a fine taste in wine, women and photography. It is said that he still loves to develop black-and-white pictures in his personal darkroom. After he graduated, he came back to Bihar to work for his father. Suryadev had high ambitions and wanted to transform the illegal activities into a legal business empire. He went from one minister to the other for a permit to take over the mines. They simply refused. Suryadev grew utterly bitter with the government, beginning to believe his father had been right all along. It was power that ruled.

'There were other rival gangs that targeted B.P. Singh's business and their fleet of trucks. To neutralize them, Suryadev went underground to live with the workers. There he posed as a poverty-stricken labourer and learnt everything about how men could be sold as slaves, about illegal mines, and about those working against his father. He successfully put an end to all the rival gangs. Except for one gangster, Hassan Ansari, who succeeded in killing Suryadev's father in a shootout between their gangs.

'Suryadev tracked down Hassan Ansari and killed him. He then resolved to carry on with his father's work, taking over the entire illegal coal business. Many top engineers, officers of the government-owned Coal India Ltd, worked for him. He was generous and was prompt with his payments. All the ministers and bureaucrats were very happy with him.

'In fact, Suryadev turned out to be more lethal and cold-blooded than his father. He was not interested in the workers or their lives. He was interested in coal and the money that coal brought him. A well-read, intelligent man turned to the world of crime.'

Ruby looked impressed. 'You seem to have done a whole lot of work on this coal guy.'

'Two years back,' Hawa Singh resumed, 'I was assigned to look into the death of a mining inspector whose body was found in a goods train carrying coal from the mines of Jharkhand to Delhi. Everyone knew that it was Suryadev who had got him killed. We got the hit-men. They were nothing but hired hands that would kill anyone for a few thousand rupees. There was nothing that connected them to Suryadev Singh. He doesn't leave any traces or tracks that can lead anyone to him.'

'So now he is a respectable politician in your country and he can't be touched?' asked Ruby.

'As he gained more and more power and wealth, Suryadev looked for higher things to gain respect in society. So he decided to contest the elections instead of funding the morons that he used to do. He even married a local girl to gain the loyalty of the people.'

'Why would such a big shot murder a girl like Eva?' asked Ruby.

Hawa Singh returned to his coffee, although it had turned cold. 'Suryadev loves to throw lavish parties. He gets girls, scotch and wine from different parts of the world. He has a son, Prashant Singh, who is known to abduct young girls, rape them and throw them on the road. Yet, no charges have ever been filed against him.'

'But the autopsy confirmed that there was no sign of sexual violence on Eva's body,' put in Ruby. 'In fact, there were no signs of even a struggle.'

'Her killer could be Suryadev Singh himself. He is a big sympathizer of many Hindu fundamentalist groups and funds many of their activities. Also, Eva had access to his personal number.'

Ruby held her face in her hands. 'What the hell was she doing with all these men?'

'There is another one,' Hawa Singh went on. 'I checked on the third number that was struck off with the same pen. Maybe Eva herself cut it out. For what reason, we don't know yet.'

Ruby looked at Hawa Singh attentively, her eyes suddenly shining bright.

Hawa Singh looked at her, 'What?'

'I am listening to you, carry on.'

'So this third number connected me to Pandit Vishnu Shashtri, a professor of Sanskrit at Benares Hindu University. He is also one of the prominent astrologers of Benares.'

Ruby got up excitedly, 'He must be Eva's connect with astrology. We need to meet up with him.'

'We'll be meeting all three of them. They are high on our list. There is something more.'

'What, more numbers?' she asked.

'No, it's a bird.'

'Bird?'

'Underneath these numbers she wrote a word, "SPARROW".'

CHAPTER 8

The nightmare slipped in under cover of fog and found its way to him. It clutched him with its strong arms and dragged him into black fear.

Hawa Singh saw himself running, in a direction he couldn't tell, with blood from his head filling his nostrils. He was gasping for air. He couldn't see anything. But the sounds came loud and clear.

'Singh, Singh!' he heard Kavita cry out to him.

He was running, tearing through the darkness with his head pounding. He heard the gunshots.

Silence.

Darkness.

A sudden shiver woke him up. There was a sharp pain in his head. Images of Kavita floated in front of his eyes. He had to force himself to shut them and cut her off. She would never die for him. She was still there, smiling and laughing, narrating her experiences to him with girlish enthusiasm—and then stealing a quick kiss.

Love. You couldn't find it these days. It's extinct.

He looked around and found himself on a couch in Ruby's room. He checked his watch: it was 5.30 am. He saw Ruby curled up between the silken sheets, fast asleep. He picked up his jacket, tucked in his Colt and was ready to leave.

Something pulled him back to Ruby. He went to her and moved a few strands of hair away from her face. She smiled in her sleep. He bent closer, and as if in sudden reflex, Ruby opened her eyes. She clutched the hand he had placed on her cheek, and fell contentedly back to sleep.

It had been a long time since he felt something in him that had lain dormant. He wanted to reach out to her, to hold on to something normal, real, maybe just a smile.

He kept gazing at her. She had eyes much like Kavita's and the same childlike zest for life, the same infectious smile and spring in her stride. He couldn't resist a smile himself, that moment. He gently withdrew his hand from her tender grip, and walked out into the fog.

Hawa Singh had to take care of a man whom he considered to be in a more precarious position than himself. Fauja Singh.

The temperature had dropped by a few more degrees. The papers had said it could be the coldest winter in a hundred years.

Inside Mukti Bhawan, Fauja Singh sat bare-bodied, with a thin towel wrapped around his waist. A pandit was performing puja, chanting mantras.

'What the hell is all this?' yelled Hawa Singh as he walked in on the scene. 'You want to die now, champion, sitting as you are?'

'What else have we come here for? Death. Moksha. Did you get my jalebis?'

Hawa Singh picked up a blanket and threw it over his father. 'I'm not going to get you anything till you start taking care of yourself. You are not a child.'

Fauja laughed. 'I like it when you behave this way. But I'm not this body. I'm a divine being. I'm a spirit. I'm God.'

'Don't start all over again. I have enough on my mind.'

'If Kavita had been here, she would have solved your case in minutes. She was a star reporter,' cried Fauja.

They regarded each other. Both their eyes were moist. Then Fauja broke down altogether. 'It is I, who should have died,' he mourned. 'She had so much life in her, so much to live for, for you, to make *you* live.'

Hawa Singh wrapped his arms around his father and let the tears flow.

'Let's forget the jalebis,' said Fauja Singh through his own tears. 'I want to have idli-sambar. You remember how often Kavita would get dosas, idlis and sambar for me? She filled my life with love and care. Maybe I'll meet her up there.'

That morning father and son had a hot, scrumptious south Indian breakfast. They talked about Kavita. On her first visit to their village in Haryana, she had sat with the village elders and smoked a hookah. It had scandalized the entire village. She had driven a tractor through the fields. She had gone around taking pictures of village women, the buffaloes, the camels. Everything was an awesome sight to her.

All the time Fauja stood beside her proudly. 'My daughter-in-law comes on TV,' he had boasted.

Now, she was gone, creating a vacuum in their lives. Suddenly, they had been left with little to talk about, nothing to laugh about. A fog had engulfed them. Fauja finally decided to break through it and free himself. Death is equal to freedom.

It was already 11 am. Hawa Singh had to go and pick up Ruby Malik.

'This CID girl is not bad,' said Fauja smilingly.

'She is from the FBI,' corrected Hawa Singh.

'It's all the same. I like her. I'm telling you, God has sent her to you. Take your chance, boy, before she flies away.'

Hawa Singh shook his head and walked out.

Ruby and he were going to meet Kashi Naresh, the king of Benares.

*

They took a rowboat to cross the Ganges, as Ramnagar Fort was situated on the opposite bank. As they drifted away from the ghats, Ruby gazed with delight on the many sights of Benares. 'I have never seen so many colours in a city. This is beautiful!' she said.

Hawa Singh was lost in his own thoughts, but nodded in acknowledgement.

Why, he asked himself, had he chosen to be a policeman?

There was no answer. It had not been, then, about right and wrong. Maybe it was because, when he was a kid, he had been bullied in school. Maybe it was then he'd resolved to become the tough guy.

Now, he knew right from wrong, but not everyone else appeared to. Today every kid on the street believed in the adage: 'Behind every great fortune there is a crime.'

The world was filled with attractions that distracted minds. Everyone was greedy, wanting to possess and hoard. Everyone wanted it all, fast and easy. But there was only one way to get there: the criminal way.

His thoughts were broken by Ruby. 'Is it possible,' she asked, 'that the killer of Aghori Baba crossed the river like this on a boat? It could be any of the hundreds of boatmen.'

'The possibilities are numerous,' Hawa Singh responded. 'But yes, he could have crossed the river and disappeared. There would be no trace of blood. They say the river Ganges purifies everything.'

They looked ahead to see Ramnagar Fort situated majestically on a hill. There were hardly any houses or temples on this side of the river.

It had taken them twenty minutes to cross the river and another fifteen minutes on a tonga to reach Ramnagar Fort. It was like being transported to an altogether new world.

The fort was built in a typical Mughal style of architecture with carved balconies, open courtyards, and picturesque pavilions. It was built by Kashi Naresh Raja Balwant Singh in the eighteenth century. Today, one part of the fort was used as a residence for the royal family while another was converted into a museum.

Hawa Singh strode resolutely to the residence. There were armed guards all around, who escorted Ruby and Hawa Singh to the private quarters of the king.

Inside, the walls on either side of the long corridor were covered with oil portraits of the many kings of Benares, from the very first maharaja, Balwant Singh, who presided over Kashi in 1740, to the last, Maharaja Vibhuti Narayan Singh.

Hawa Singh and Ruby were left in a room stacked with books and artefacts. They sat there on large ornate chairs waiting for Maharaj Abhay Narayan Singh to show up.

They sat in silence for almost half an hour, and finally, Kashi Naresh walked in. They stood up like automatons in the presence of royalty, shook hands and introduced themselves.

Hawa Singh noticed that Abhay Narayan Singh wore gloves that covered his hands. He also wore a high-collared sweater that covered his entire neck. It was only his face that was visible. He was a well-groomed man, with carefully plucked eyebrows, hair dyed black and a clipped, thin moustache. He looked close to fifty-five years in age.

Ruby could see the guards with guns poised at all doors and windows.

Hawa Singh softly cleared his throat and spoke, 'You know that a foreigner, Eva Marie Cassidy, was murdered in Benares under mysterious circumstances.'

'I heard that Tailanga Swami was also killed mercilessly. Why does a murder of a foreigner become so important?' asked Kashi Naresh.

'It's like this: in Eva's hotel room I found a slip of paper with three telephone numbers on it. I have checked that they were written by her. One of them was your personal telephone number.'

'Are you treating me as a suspect?' Abhay Narayan asked curtly.

'We don't want to leave any question unanswered,' chipped in Ruby.

Abhay Narayan looked at her and smiled. 'Okay, I'll clear everything for you. She wanted to meet me, to discuss the *Bhrigu-Samhita,* and to go through the manuscripts in our small museum, Saraswati Bhawan.'

Ruby and Hawa Singh exchanged a look.

'I have been told that you don't meet anyone just like that. How come you agreed to meet with her at such short notice?' asked Hawa Singh.

'Just the way I agreed to meet you,' laughed Abhay.

Hawa Singh was quiet. Ruby checked out the guards and saw that their guns were cocked and ready.

Abhay regained his composure and said, 'Let me tell you, very few get to meet Kashi Naresh. According to orthodox Brahmin traditions, no one has seen Kashi Naresh eat, and none of the kings has travelled abroad and thereby defiled himself. During the religious occasion of Shivratri, Kashi Naresh is the chief officiating priest and no other person or priest is allowed to enter the sanctum sanctorum. It is only after he performs his religious functions that others are allowed to partake of the ceremony. And I think you should know, there is much mystery surrounding this fort.'

'You didn't answer my question,' said Hawa Singh.

Abhay Narayan looked stern. 'Well, I got to know that Eva worked with the Vatican, which is the centre of Catholicism, just like Benares is nodal to Hindus. I have to respect that.'

'So did you take her around your museum?' asked Ruby.

'Yes, I did and I'm sure that you both would also like to retrace her footsteps. Maybe the same track will lead you somewhere.'

Before they could say anything, Abhay was up and out of the room. The guard at the door signalled them to follow.

They moved through many corridors and narrow stairways that led them to a secret passage used by the kings and the royal families to enter Saraswati Bhawan.

It was a large room with an interesting collection of royal carriages, weapons, coins and exquisite artefacts.

Abhay Narayan explained, 'Here we have a rare collection of manuscripts, especially religious writings. There is a handwritten manuscript of the *Ramayana* by Goswami Tulsidas, and books illustrated in the Mughal miniature style, such as the *Balwant Naama, Vansa Vivaran,* and many others.'

Ruby looked at a collection of coins with holes in them and asked, 'What are these?'

Abhay guffawed out aloud and said, 'Maharaja Prabhu Narayan Singh had a penchant for target practice. He used to have coins tossed high in the air, and shot at them with a rifle. The holes in the damaged coins show his perfect aim.'

Hawa Singh looked around and saw pistols, unique swords and the legendary Ramnagar Clock.

Abhay pointed to the clock saying, 'Eva was particularly interested in that. It was made in 1872 by the state's official clockmaker, B. Mulchand. It still gives accurate chronological and astrological readings.'

'Astro readings!' exclaimed Ruby.

'It shows the placement of the sun, moon and stars at any particular time. Astronomy and astrology go hand-in-hand.'

Hawa Singh looked puzzled. 'What else was she interested in?'

'She wanted to check the original manuscript of the *Bhrigu-Samhita*. Sadly, we don't have that. It could be 5,000 years old, or even 10,000. The original manuscript got lost in time as Brahmins took it to various parts of the country. It doesn't exist.'

Hawa Singh was quiet as he tried to fit the new revelations with the motive for Eva's murder.

He looked at Kashi Naresh and asked, 'One more thing. What does "sparrow" mean to you?'

Abhay looked shaken, but for only a moment. He regained his composure and laughed, 'You must be joking.'

Ruby and Hawa Singh looked at each other, puzzled by his reaction.

'The guards will escort you out,' said Abhay, signalling an end to their interview. 'I hope your visit was fruitful. By the way, Suryadev Singh is throwing a lavish party at his guesthouse. You should talk to him. Eva told me all about her meeting with him.'

Hawa Singh and Ruby looked stunned.

Maharaj Abhay Narayan Singh walked out.

*

They stood on the bank of the river, with Ramnagar Fort in the background, staring down at them. A vast stretch of sand separated them.

'Astrology and astronomy are the keys to all this. The planetary positions of the sun, moon and stars are used in Hindu astrology. There was something that Eva knew, and something else that she was looking for,' observed Ruby Malik in a thoughtful voice.

'It could be that we are reading too much into it,' interjected Hawa Singh. 'It's complex. The killer seems to have tried to build a mystery where, perhaps, there is none. It could be a simple case of jealousy, revenge, lust, a simple crime of passion. This entire circle of astrology and astronomy has been created to keep the focus away from the main motive.'

'You mean she could be like any other foreign tourist with an interest in astrology?' asked Ruby.

'Yes, it could be as simple as that.'

Ruby looked around at the rippling waters and asked, 'Do you think she may have had a boyfriend here?'

'I have checked with the hotel and they said she didn't have any visitors there. Outside, in the city, too, she was mostly engaged in the mysteries of astrology and the colours of Hinduism. However, the local police have yet to get back to us about all the people she met with in Benares.'

Ruby looked puzzled, 'So what are we looking for?'

'We have to hit the nerve centre. The killing machine. The mafia boss. Suryadev Singh.'

CHAPTER 9

Despite the increase in vigilance, and the enforcement of stricter laws and punishment, the crime rate is ever on the rise. The number of murders, robberies, kidnappings for ransom, rapes, trafficking of girls, illegal drug and liquor sales, and lynchings just keep going up, year after year.

There have been cases of eve-teasing in which people who took exception were stabbed to death. And with the Net broadening its bandwidth, the rate of cyber crimes, too, has increased. The moment the regulatory authorities ban a noxious product, an entire army of black marketeers rises.

It is as if society as a whole has no fear of the law. The rich know the ways to get around restriction, while for the downtrodden; crime is the only sure way to success.

Even the judiciary seems to have collapsed, with judges reduced to court clerks, with cases piling up and hearings adjourned day after day. The police look helpless. And the politicians don't seem to care. It seems as if even godliness has disappeared from what was once the land of gods and goddesses.

Hawa Singh reflected on the miasma surrounding most people today. India was not shining, it was rotting. Frustration, rage, anxiety and depression were its hallmarks.

But he was a lone soldier. What could he do?

Standing with Ruby Malik outside the palatial bungalow of Suryadev Singh, he thought bitterly that crime really did pay. It was built of white marble, a high structure to rival even the fort of Kashi Naresh.

It was unusual for politicians to make Benares their base, but Suryadev had opted to, turning the holiest of holy Hindu sites into a centre for arms-dealing. Suryadev Singh controlled the vast trade in illegal arms, supplying guns and explosives to underground rebels in Bihar, Chhattisgarh, Jharkhand, Orissa and Andhra Pradesh. And when the Indian government began selling out coal blocks to private companies, it looked like his every dream was coming true. The wealthy corporates couldn't take a step without his blessings in the dense forests and mines of these states.

Soon Suryadev Singh would hold sway over hundreds of crores worth of coal. None of the big mafia guys, not even those in Mumbai, Hong Kong or Dubai, would have thought one could earn as much as ten crore rupees a day, from illegal mining and trade in coal. And none of them dared to step into Suryadev's territory.

Outside the massive marble edifice, Hawa Singh and Ruby saw imported cars—BMWs, Mercedes, Jaguars, Ferrari, Lamborghini, along with some vintage cars that commanded prices double that of the Jaguars—snaking down the drive.

The driveway had turned into a ramp for the guests to show off their luxury cars. Hawa Singh and Ruby had arrived in a pedal-rickshaw. It's good that they got down a little distance before the bungalow and preferred to walk in.

Ruby was dressed in a short black dress, showing off her long legs. There was a deep vertical slit at the back, showing her beautiful skin right down to the waist. She wore high heels and deep red lipstick, and had her hair tied back. Hawa Singh was dressed in his usual leather jacket and jeans.

He couldn't help but let the forbidden thoughts cloud his mind. It'd been a long time since he had had a woman.

He moved in hesitatingly, nervous about gatecrashing the party. He felt a bit nervous doing all this. He never felt comfortable with these sophisticated wine-drinkers and makers of polite conversation. He kept his head down—from no angle did he look a part of this crowd. Ruby flashed a smile at the guests as she walked past them.

Inside, they walked into the hall where a huge chandelier—probably Italian crystal—hung from the ceiling. Expensively attired guests crowded the place, as wine, cheese, scotch and a variety of exotic snacks floated past on salvers carried by liveried servants. On the walls were large black-and-white photographs, obviously taken by Suryadev, of poverty-stricken miners. It was said that Suryadev hated to touch coal himself, even though the precious black mineral had taken him to where he was.

The guests in the party included top police brass, powerful politicians, industrialists, senior MNC executives and bureaucrats that included the SSP, Neeraj Thakur. It was for males only. Many looked glad to have left their wives and daughters behind. Different pleasures were awaiting them.

There were many semi-nude white foreign girls dressed up in shiny costumes, who helped to serve the guests. The girls had been hired for the entire night, giving the men complete freedom to vent their lust in the private bedrooms upstairs. There were various guns and antique swords displayed along the stairway going up.

After the last such party, some of the girls were found to be badly beaten, cut and abused. There were two who disappeared altogether, consigned to lime or the river. No reports were ever filed.

Who said crime didn't pay?

Ruby felt lost in the crowd and grabbed Hawa Singh's hand for a sense of some security. He himself found all the extravagance around him claustrophobic. He had no problems with people being wealthy, but despised ostentation. And hypocritical small talk infuriated him.

His line of thought was broken by the sound of thunderous clapping. He looked up to see Suryadev Singh walking down the staircase into the hall. He was dressed in an immaculate white kurta-pyjama and had a glass of what looked like scotch in his hand. He had the look of a suave man—clean-shaven face, soft voice, an Oxbridge accent and always chivalrous to ladies. He also looked pretty young for his age.

The SSP was the first one to go and greet him. Suryadev put his hand on his shoulder, a sort of blessing to the police chief. Soon, the others clustered around to shake hands with the coal king.

Suryadev loved to be treated like royalty. It boosted his already inflated ego. From the top politicians to the seniormost cops, no one dared to oppose him.

Neeraj Thakur, the SSP, turned around and seeing him, Hawa Singh pulled Ruby away from his line of vision. They stood with their backs to the SSP, pretending to gaze intently at a black-and-white photograph of coal-mine-workers stuck inside a flooded mine. The weeping helpless workers were a ghastly sight as they appeared to plead for help. It was said that Suryadev Singh dumped a truck full of coal inside that mine. The workers were never found. The mine was illegal and so were the workers, paperless refugees from Bangladesh.

Suddenly, the lights went off. The guests cried and hooted with fear and excitement. One didn't know what Suryadev might have in mind for them. For the first few seconds the guests felt anxious, but as music filled the air, they realized this was just another of Suryadev's party games.

Hawa Singh saw a few well-respected politicians and bureaucrats grabbing at the breasts and buttocks of the young girls serving them. In the darkness they all turned into animals. Hawa Singh held Ruby close to him, her head resting on his broad chest. Frightened as she was, she felt strangely secure in his arms.

The entire hall was suddenly illuminated by colourful lights and the music grew even louder. Then, smoke started filling the hall. Was Suryadev planning to gas them?

Slowly, out from the dense fog, a group of girls came out dancing, dressed only in g-strings. The guests went crazy. Then, like a Bollywood hero who appears from nowhere, Prashant Singh swaggered out of the smoke. He was dressed in a designer suit and expensive handmade shoes. Hawa Singh would have never known those labels. They had never mattered to him.

Prashant, the only son of Suryadev Singh, and the more vicious of the two, had turned thirty and this was his birthday party. He had been involved in the abduction of girls, violent fights and was known to kill people with the knife that he carried with him.

Some said that he loved to cut open the stomachs of his victims and then closely inspect their guts. With him, too, no cases were ever filed. No witnesses. They called him the 'Madman'.

He should have tried his tricks on Hawa Singh's turf.

Prashant went up to his father and touched his feet. Suryadev blessed him. The guests cheered loudly, 'Happy birthday!' Most of them were already drunk, and ogling the semi-nude dancers.

A large cake in the shape of a cricket stadium was brought in. The boundary was marked with mounds of cream in the shape of tits, and red cherries served as nipples. The guests went ecstatic. Prashant cut the cake and licked one of the red cherries with his tongue. 'Now it's your turn,' he called the guests.

The men rushed to the cake to have their share of the red cherries. The cream filled their mouths and like kindergarten kids they smeared it on each other's faces.

Suryadev Singh smiled, looking at these so-called arms and legs of the government machinery. He was the power source and could switch off the supply any time he wanted.

Prashant opened a champagne bottle and poured it over the girls. They were Russian and East European girls. Hawa Singh could never understand the fascination of Indian men for white girls. They just couldn't handle their testosterone levels seeing one of them. To him it was the slave mentality persisting in a country once dominated by a white race. Witness the demand in the market for cosmetics that promised to turn skin fair!

There lay the sickness. Everyone wanted to be white—in their lifestyle, in their looks, in their eating habits, almost everything.

With music and drinks flowing, the men started to dance with the girls, fondling them all the while. They were waiting eagerly for the lights to be switched off.

This was an opportune moment for Hawa Singh and Ruby. They could slip inside to look for signs or clues in the inner rooms. They went into what looked like a study. The walls were stacked with book shelves; only God knew who studied those books. Once, Suryadev had been a voracious reader. Now, things were different.

There was a large mahogany desk faced by a revolving chair. They tried the drawers of the desk, but they appeared to be locked. Hawa Singh took a hairpin from Ruby and picked them open one by one. Inside the drawers were various knives and daggers—it was likely to be Prashant's private collection, because he was known to love knives. There were some antique knives from China and Korea, an African blade, one that seemed to date back to the Mughal era, and another of the US Army issue during the Vietnam War.

The knives were of stunning beauty, but Hawa Singh didn't want to touch them. They closed the drawers and looked around the room. There were a few large portraits on the wall, more of Suryadev's black-and-white photographs and a silver cross. The Holy Cross.

'What is this doing here? They are not Christians. Suryadev is, if anything, a practising Hindu who funds many fanatic Hindu organizations,' whispered Hawa Singh.

Ruby hurriedly clicked a picture of the Cross on her mobile phone. There was nothing else that caught their attention, so they slipped out of the room.

They moved through a narrow corridor that led towards a wider passage with rooms on both sides. They checked to see if there was anyone around—there wasn't—so they pushed open a heavy wooden door and entered one of the rooms.

The door was padded thickly on the inside, like those in recording studios. The walls, too, were padded; the room seemed to be completely soundproof.

Ruby pressed a switch and a pale blue light filled the room. There was one large bed in the centre, and a tall glass-fronted cupboard containing some transparent jars.

The very sight of the stuff that floated in those jars made Ruby gasp in horror. Hawa Singh, too, for all the terrible scenes he had witnessed as a policeman, had not seen anything like it. Inside the glass jars were heads and other human body parts floating in liquid. Numbed, Hawa Singh and Ruby took a while to recover from the dreadful spectacle.

When they did, Ruby began to take photographs on her cell phone. Hawa Singh busied himself searching the room for more clues. Ruby stopped near one of the jars and pointed. It held a human heart.

'So we have gate-crashers in my house,' said Suryadev Singh, from behind them in his customary silken voice. They hadn't heard the door opening or his padding right up to them. Hawa Singh's hand directly went to his Colt in reflex.

'You won't need that Hawa Singh saab,' purred Suryadev. *So he knew who they were.*

Suryadev came close to Ruby and said, 'I know all about Hawa Singh. He has been after me for the last many years. Well, so many of them have been… you must be Ruby Malik, the FBI girl.

'Let me introduce you to these pieces of art,' he continued, pointing to the body parts in the jars. 'These are pieces of the men who were killed by my father, Baldev Pratap Singh. The only way to kill the competition was to kill the competitors. So he did so—and left these preserved souvenirs to me.'

Hawa Singh went straight to the matter. 'I wanted to talk to you about Eva, the girl who was found murdered,' he said to Suryadev.

'So you came here to talk, but then you took a detour,' smiled Suryadev.

'Did she meet you or not?'

Suryadev took a sip from the glass of scotch he held in his hand. 'Yes, she did come. She was a beautiful girl. I showed her my art collection.'

'Why did she come to you?' asked Ruby.

'Ah, the FBI interrogation. All right, I'll try to be of help—although I'm not accustomed to being questioned, ever. She came here to party. She was fun. She smoked weed, drank and was pretty high. This is why foreigners come to Benares, to smoke weed.'

'What does the word "Sparrow" mean to you?' asked Hawa Singh abruptly.

'Those are beautiful birds. I love their chirping. Now, it seems, their music has faded. I don't see them any longer. Many of them have died—but who cares? And the few that are left have forgotten how to sing; the noise of traffic confuses them. And then, the cities are spanned right across by high-tension wires. One touch can burn a sparrow to ashes.'

Now, Prashant barged into the room. 'What happened?' he demanded to know, and directed his glance to Ruby, looking her long legs up and down.

Suryadev spoke, again softly. 'These are the ones who crashed our party. I caught them checking out our art collection.'

Prashant's maniacal smile turned to a quiet laugh. 'Sounds like fun. Let's go down and celebrate. It's my birthday, after all.'

Hawa Singh and Ruby hesitantly walked out of the room, Prashant following right behind, escorting them down the staircase and into the hall.

The orgy in the hall was still on. The guests, totally drunk, were mauling the girls. 'This shouldn't happen in Kashi,' thought Hawa Singh.

A little alcohol, a little licence, brought out the worst in everyone. Maybe people seized such opportunities to exorcize their demons. It was in such circumstances that crimes spiralled out of control.

Prashant pulled Ruby to the centre of the hall and called to everyone, 'Look, we have a special guest here.'

Hawa Singh stood quietly close by. The first among the guests to recognize the two was the SSP, Neeraj Thakur. Mercifully, he was too drunk to do much about the situation except shout to Hawa Singh, 'What the hell are you doing here?'

Hawa Singh didn't answer.

'Please, they are our guests,' said Prashant. Then, with a swift stroke, he took out a sleek gold dagger and sliced Ruby's dress from the neck to the bottom. The dress parted like two lengths of curtain. Fortunately, she was wearing a bra and panties. The drunken men stared and cheered and whistled.

'Now who wants to ride her?' said Prashant loudly.

'Don't you dare touch her,' shouted Hawa Singh.

'Oh, so you are going to stop me? Let me see,' said Prashant, calling out to his guards, 'Throw him out.'

About a dozen heavily armed men surrounded Hawa Singh. He had to act now. His head was buzzing. The bullet was like a needle in his head.

He pounced on Prashant and grabbed him by the neck, holding the Colt to his temple. 'You filthy bastard, you touched her. You dared to put your hands on her. I can put this bullet right through your head, and spray all in the room with the rest.'

'Hawa Singh, put it down,' said the SSP.

Hawa Singh ignored him and looked in Suryadev Singh's direction. 'This is your son,' he said. 'You better teach him some manners.' He then kicked Prashant, who fell to the floor, his face hitting the marble hard. Nevertheless, even as he lay prone, his maniacal laugh continued.

Hawa Singh took off his jacket and put it around Ruby, saying, 'Come, Kavita, we need to get out of here.'

Ruby was looking at him, shell-shocked. She was not Kavita. And no one had ever stood up for her like this before.

CHAPTER 10

Hawa Singh walked out with Ruby, boiling with rage. Outside the bungalow, there was a police jeep, and inside it, Sub-Inspector Gaya Prasad Sharma and a team of four constables on duty.

The SI leaped out of the jeep on seeing Hawa Singh and saluted, 'Sir, I didn't know you had also come to the party.'

The condensed breath coming out of Hawa Singh's mouth looked like smoke from a fire. 'We need to drop Ruby madam at her hotel,' he said curtly.

'Please, sir, I'll drive myself. We had a heater fixed in our jeep last year. Now, we can all stay warm in here.'

Gaya Prasad hurriedly opened the door of the jeep and asked the constables to step out. The sleepy policemen grumbled and reluctantly did so.

Hawa Singh didn't realize that he was still holding Ruby's hand as they climbed into the jeep.

Gaya Prasad told his men, 'Listen, I don't want any of chaps going to sleep in some corner. Be alert, I'll be back soon.'

He started the jeep, smiling at Hawa Singh conspiratorially, 'You know everything about Suryadev Singh, but we are totally clueless. All we know is that he is a powerful politician and we have to guard him, salute him. We have to keep our jobs.'

Hawa Singh strongly believed that police should never feel helpless—or what use was there for a police force? Political arrogance was what had decreased their morale, used as they were as personal guards and servants by more powerful people.

The jeep moved slowly, the yellow fog lights attempting to pierce the mist. As they sat together on the backseat, Hawa Singh and Ruby were still holding hands.

Gaya Prasad looked back and said, 'Sir, I checked out on all the people at the ghats, like you told me to. I questioned every single boatman, pandit, beggar, leper, vendor and flower-seller, but none of had seen a man carrying an axe.'

Hawa Singh didn't seem to hear anything. He was quiet. Ruby looked at him and pressed his hand. There was no reaction.

'There is one possibility, sir. There are these doms who conduct cremations on the ghats. They use axes to cut the wood for pyres.'

Hawa Singh didn't respond.

The jeep crept through the winding road. The fog was so dense, making Ruby feel that they were sailing over clouds. Gaya Prasad continued with his conjectures. 'Did you know, sir, that Neelambar Nath has become the leader of the Aghoris? I'm telling you, he is the one who killed Tailanga Swami, to take his position. He has been given the title of Swami Neelambar Nath.'

Ruby looked enquiringly at Hawa Singh. 'What do you think?'

Hawa Singh was still staring wordlessly into the fog.

They were quiet till they reached Nadesar Palace. Gaya Prasad got out and opened the door for them. Hawa Singh stepped out, holding Ruby's hand.

Gaya saluted. 'It'll be an honour working with you, sir.'

'Kill them before they kill you,' mumbled Hawa Singh.

Gaya Prasad was stunned, looking to Ruby for explanation. She gestured for him to leave.

Hawa Singh was wearing a thin cotton t-shirt. The freezing cold didn't seem to bother him. They walked into Ruby's warm room.

She led him to a chair and made him sit. 'Let me get you a drink. You need one.'

'No, I'd better leave,' said Hawa Singh, getting up.

Ruby, still wearing the bulky leather jacket, stepped up close to him and examined his face. 'Back there you called me "Kavita". Who is she? You seem to be carrying a lot in your head.'

She made him sit on the bed. She removed the jacket and her torn dress revealed much of her body. Hawa Singh seemed to be staring right past it, a splitting pain in his head taking over. The bullet was nudging at his brain.

'There seems to be lot of rage hidden inside you, you need to spill it out or it will kill you.' She knelt on the bed, held his hand again and said gently, understandingly, 'You loved her a lot.'

This brought tears to his eyes. He fought hard to hold them in, but they spilled over quietly.

'Why don't you tell me about her?' persisted Ruby, softly.

Hawa Singh finally looked directly at her. 'I lived for her and now I'm just this body. I failed to save her and my team. I killed her.'

Ruby drew closer to him. 'She still lives in your heart.'

Hawa Singh shook his head, struggling to escape from the fragmented images and voices that crowded it. Then he nodded. 'Yes, she will always live inside me.'

Then Hawa Singh poured his heart out to Ruby, telling her everything about Kavita, about their love and planned life together, her abduction, the encounter and her killing.

Ruby couldn't speak for a long time, leaning her head against his shoulder. 'I wish someone loved me as much,' she finally whispered.

Then, briskly telling him 'You need some sleep', she helped him remove his boots and urged him down on the bed. They lay there, wrapped in each other's arms. Hawa Singh held her tightly, seeming to want to dissolve into her.

'I don't know why, but I have this strange feeling. It's like an unknown fear that is creeping towards me. Something bad is about to happen,' he told Ruby.

'Forget everything,' said Ruby comfortingly. Hawa Singh managed to close his eyes. And they slept like babies.

It was just after 2 am that he woke up with a start. Was it fear, anxiety, stress, or something he didn't know? There was only one thing he knew—he had to act.

He dressed, left the room and walked out into the fog. The killing fields were calling him.

CHAPTER 11

SSP Neeraj Thakur was facing his own nightmare. Thousands had crowded around the Kashi Vishwanath temple, one of the most famous dedicated to Lord Shiva in Benares. The doors to the main shrine, where the Shiv-linga is located, had not yet opened.

It is believed that a simple glimpse of the linga inside the temple cleanses the soul completely, leading the believer to the path of knowledge and bhakti. It was Monday, the day of Lord Shiva. Devotees had come from nearby cities and from as far away as Kolkata, Delhi, towns in Punjab and Maharashtra, and abroad.

The temple opens daily at 2.30 am for mangala aarti, and by 3 am, devotees are allowed to join in the prayers. From 4 to 11 am darshan is allowed to all visitors. It was already 6 am. Why were the doors to the main shrine not yet open? They seemed to have been locked from the inside. The crowd was getting more and more restless. This had never happened in the history of Benares.

Baba Ramtirath, along with hundreds of Naga sadhus, was at the front of the crowd, as the Nagas were given the first preference for darshan. The SSP, along with a large contingent of the police force, was trying to calm down the crowd.

'This seems to be the work of those Aghoris. They have done some tantra-mantra and closed the doors,' Baba Ramtirath told the SSP.

The police they didn't want to force open the sacred gates—it would have triggered a major riot.

The SSP called the Ghost.

***

Hawa Singh ran through Vishwanath Gali and tore his way through the humongous crowd of devotees. Above him soared the three domes of the temple— two of them golden—shrouded by fog.

It was in 1839 that two domes of the temple were covered in gold donated by Maharaja Ranjeet Singh of Punjab. The state government was taking a keen interest in gold-plating the third. There would probably now be a dome scam.

Baba Ramtirath spotted Hawa Singh and came up to him. 'You planning to open the doors yourself?' he asked him sarcastically.

Hawa Singh looked back at the mass of men, women, children and the elderly, all of whom were carrying vessels filled with milk and sweets to be offered to the linga. The SSP looked furious. Helpless.

Hawa Singh knew there was a deep-seated hatred and mistrust of the police in all classes of society. It didn't need much to trigger it off. This could be that trigger-moment.

Yes, prevention was better than curing a situation. But then society itself didn't own up to its crimes. Policing would never solve the problem. The media would be quick to label the area a 'police state'.

Hawa Singh realized what he had to do. He would have to play the devil.

Hawa Singh pushed at the door in front of him. It felt like something was stuck on the other side to prevent it from opening. Another, stronger, push and he glimpsed a horizontal wooden bar between the two handles on either side of the door inside. There was no way out. They would have to break in.

Baba Ramtirath urged his people on. 'It seems Lord Shiva wishes the Naga sadhus to push open the door. We are the closest to the lord. We'll have to do it.'

There was pin-drop silence.

***

Maharaj Abhay Narayan Singh, the king of Benares, had been woken from sleep. He stood on the rampart of his fort, watching the commotion through a telescope, one he used at night to observe the stars and their constellations. The kings of Benares have always been lovers of astronomy and astrology. In the day time he would observe his citizens

Baba Ramtirath, along with the heaviest-built of the Naga sadhus, came forward. Hawa Singh winked at the SSP and they started to push at the doors.

The heavy door creaked and groaned in protest. There was a cracking sound.

Silence.

The crowd bit its tongue to ward off bad luck. The breaking down of the door could spell doom for all humankind. It could anger Lord Shiva, the destroyer of the universe. They waited.

The naked sadhus pushed with all their strength. The wooden obstruction inside tensed. There was a growling sound, and then it started to crack under the joint force. The wooden bar inside broke, and the door to the jyotirlinga was flung open. The crowd erupted in cheers—'Har! Har! Mahadev!

They didn't see what Hawa Singh and the other Naga sadhus saw. The body of a naked man, smeared with ash, was bent over the linga. Blood flowed onto the silver altar.

A wooden cross protruded from his back.

***

Kashi Vishwanath temple, through the ages, had been visited by great saints like Adi Shankaracharya, Ramkrishna Paramhansa, Swami Vivekanand, Goswami Tulsidas, Maharshi Dayanand Saraswati, Guru Nanak and several other such spiritual personalities. This time, it was visited by death.

A bloody murder.

The SSP made a public announcement that the temple would be closed to all visitors till further notice. It was something that had never happened over the last several centuries. Slowly, the crowd parted and vacated the temple premises.

'I don't want the police inside. Let only the forensics team come. Till they do, no one else is allowed inside.' Hawa Singh's orders were clear.

But an exception was made for FBI agent Ruby Malik. When she arrived, Hawa Singh said grimly, 'It has happened again.'

The body was that of a foreigner, white. He was lean but not in an athletic way.

Ruby looked at the body and spoke out, 'Again, the Holy Cross. It seems we have a serial-killer in our hands. He seems to be targeting only the whites.'

Hawa Singh examined the inner sanctum. Right ahead of the jyotirlinga was a solid wall. There was no other door or window through which the killer could have escaped after killing him.

He looked up at the domes but there were no windows, no openings. 'He locked the door from the inside. Then where did he go?' Hawa Singh puzzled over the matter.

It looked like a magic trick. The way a magician disappears from inside a locked trunk in front of the audience and appears somewhere else. 'Is it possible that the killer is a magician?' wondered Hawa Singh.

He knew that behind every magic trick there is a setup. You just had to look for it.

It was then that he saw a round hole in the floor. It was around four-and-half feet in diameter.

He called in the priest and asked, 'What is this?'

'That's a well and it has been here for many centuries. It is called the Gyana Vapi, or the "wisdom well",' he said. 'It is believed that the Jyotirlinga was hidden in the well to protect it at the time of invasions by the Mughals, and other invaders. Once, the head priest had jumped into the well with the Shiv-ling to hide it from desecrators of the temple.'

'So the killer could have escaped via this well. Therefore, it must be connected to a tunnel to the outside. I'll have to check it out,' said Hawa Singh thoughtfully.

He removed his jacket, and said to Ruby, 'I have to inspect this well. Just make sure those policemen don't disturb the scene of the crime.'

Hawa Singh looked in the direction of the SSP and Baba Ramtirath, who were standing outside, nodded to them and jumped into the well.

The well was not too deep. The walls were cracked. He couldn't see any way out from there. He went down and almost hit the bottom. He came out of the water gasping for air. There was no way out.

He took another deep breath and dived in. He started to feel around the broken walls with his hands. The water was ice-cold and he was not able to hold his breath for long. He had to come up constantly and fill his lungs with fresh air each time.

Finally, his hands touched what looked like an iron lid against the wall. A trapdoor, rusted and heavy. He had to use all his strength to pull it open.

As he opened it, water gushed inside and he went with it. Hawa Singh swam through a channel and, after almost fifty metres, discovered that it opened out into a wider tunnel. The water had receded and Hawa Singh could stand up and walk through it.

It looked like an ancient passageway, built for the royal family and priests to move out safely if an attack took place. It was a long one, and there was the sound of water on all sides. It was also dark. Hawa Singh started to run.

A little ahead, he saw a gate on one side, jammed from years and years of rust and sand. At some places, water dripped from the ceiling. He couldn't understand what was above it and where the tunnel was leading to.

He started to run again. It took him a good fifteen minutes in the tunnel, and he knew that was pretty long. Finally, he came to an opening in the ground, gated with bars. He pushed it and, slowly, it opened. There was an incline that led up towards the ground.

The ground was wet. There was no chance they would get any footprints there. Pebbles from the river strewed his way. Nothing could be made out in that darkness.

He encountered another heavy iron grille, which he also removed. Beyond it, he found himself on solid ground. And then he saw that he was standing on the opposite bank of the Ganges. The tunnel had run under the Ganges all through the river's breadth. He looked behind him and saw Ramnagar Fort.

*

Hawa Singh took a boat to the ghats and it took him another twenty minutes to return to the temple.

Ruby, wearing latex gloves, was examining the body. She looked up at him and sighed with relief. Hawa Singh called out to the SSP, 'Inside the well there is a way that connects to a tunnel that runs right underneath the Ganges to the opposite bank.'

The SSP and the other policemen stared at him astonished.

'Yes, the killer used it to escape. That makes one thing clear—that the killer knows all the secret passages in this city pretty well. He has to be someone from Benares itself.'

'Someone who hates foreigners coming to his city,' added Ruby by his side.

Hawa Singh nodded, 'It could be. I want a team of forensics to go down into the tunnel and look for any prints, signs or clues we can get from there.'

'I'll get it done,' said the SSP.

Nobody else seemed to care that Hawa Singh was soaking wet and was shivering in the cold. Ruby got his jacket and put it around him. He shot her a grateful look. 'Thanks.'

The outpourings from his heart, just hours ago, had brought them together. They could communicate through their eyes.

Ruby pointed a gloved hand at the body and said, 'It's a similar cross. The body is smeared with ashes. It looks like a ritual. Apart from that, I don't see any signs of struggle on the corpse.'

'This time,' Hawa Singh reflected, 'the killer brought him right here, and killed him on the altar. It's like he was sacrificed to Lord Shiva.'

'Why did he close the door from inside? He could have easily walked away after killing him,' asked Ruby.

'He wanted to make a show of it. He wanted the entire crowd here, so they would get to know of the killing. Also, the body has been arranged. He is mocking us, taunting us.'

'According to FBI research, most killers return to the scene of the crime, to observe the police working. It could be that they want to see them helpless, and want to gloat over their act. It gives them a sense of power. Do you think this killer could also be here in the crowd watching us?'

Hawa Singh turned to look back at the massive crowd still standing at a distance. They were hoping that the body would be taken away and that they would be allowed their darshan.

'In this crowd, it could be almost anyone,' he replied to Ruby's question.

Ruby turned back towards the body and said, 'There is one more thing. The blood has not yet dried up.'

'The temple closes at 11 pm and opens at 2.30 am. The killer had enough time to play his game and arrange a spectacle for us,' said Hawa Singh.

The forensics team arrived. They went about their job—taking photographs, looking for finger- and fooprints, strands of hair, fibres from cloth, tissue samples or dust carried by feet.

Hawa Singh knew that they wouldn't find anything. Thousands came in here every day. The temple was more like an amphitheatre.

Ruby found that rigor mortis had already set in, in-the body. They picked up the bent-over body, the Cross sticking out from the back.

Hawa Singh called out to Gaya Prasad Sharma, the sub-inspector, and told him, 'Look around and see if anyone had ever met this man or knew him. Take his picture on your cell phone.'

Gaya Prasad looked shaken as he nervously took out his cell phone. Hawa Singh asked the forensics team to place the body on the stretcher. 'But let Gaya Prasad first take a picture of his face.'

As they laid the body face up on the stretcher, they saw a cavity in the region of the heart. The killer had again removed that organ. Under that a design had been drawn lower on the chest. Gaya Prasad was too nervous to notice it. He had not seen many faces of death. He took the picture with shaking hands and scurried off.

'What kind of pattern is that?' asked Ruby.

Hawa Singh looked at it and recognition hit him. It was probably drawn with a black marker. It was a kind of square below the chest of the victim. There were two diagonal lines inside the square and the middle points of each line were joined to the other, creating smaller blocks or houses.

'It's a horoscope chart,' said Hawa Singh.

But a greater horror awaited them.

CHAPTER 12

The air inside the SSP's office was heavy with smoke and nervous tension. Outside, the fog seemed to have cemented itself into a thick wall. A group of media persons had camped in the corridor waiting anxiously for the police to update them on their investigation.

SSP Neeraj Thakur had beads of sweat on his face. He was facing the toughest situation in his entire career.

'What are we going to tell these reporters?' asked the SSP agitatedly.

Hawa Singh, who was leaning calmly against a wall, said laconically, 'We'll tell them the usual—that the matter is under investigation, and that at this stage, everything cannot be divulged, for reasons of security.'

It was the standard police formula for extricating themselves from any sticky situation: half-truths.

The SSP nodded nervously and appeared to look appealingly at the large team of local police present in the room. 'The killer has struck again. He has created a spectacle for the entire city and media to watch. He seems to be a madman.'

Ruby took a step forward. 'Sir, according to FBI research, these are the signs of a serial-killer. There is a pattern in which he kills, and if he has struck twice, he will do so again.'

'What do you mean? That it will happen again? What are we doing here?' the SSP raised his voice in exasperation.

'While serial-killers take great care to conceal their identities by working in complete secrecy, they cannot resist showing off their strength and invincibility—and believe they can get away with it all. They could be anyone supposedly "normal"—an office worker popular with his colleagues, who laughs and jokes with them, takes them out to lunch, and then disappears on a killing spree. It's difficult to profile a serial-killer. They can range from being mentally deranged or be individuals who are motivated by everything from extreme hatred, to a desire to execute their own warped idea of justice and revenge—or pure fun,' said the experienced Ruby.

Sub-inspector Gaya Prasad Sharma, standing on the sidelines, softly interjected, 'But sir, the murder of Aghori Baba Tailanga Swami doesn't fit in with this.'

'Who the hell cares about the murder of an Aghori? We have two foreigners killed in our city. Their embassies and governments will hound us till we catch their killer—or killers. Right now I want all of you to concentrate only on the foreigners. The Aghori can wait,' said the SSP.

Hawa Singh, who had been listening intently, said, 'Okay, let's first look at what we have. In both the murders, the killer used a Cross. He took out both the victims' hearts and left the bodies where the public could see them.'

Ruby found a black marker, and made a short summary on a white board hanging on the wall. 'Holy Cross.' 'Hearts removed.' 'Bodies dumped at public places.'

'I want you all to come up with anything that comes to your head. Anything you think could connect to the murders,' said Hawa Singh.

'Ritual or sacrifice,' volunteered Ruby. Hawa Singh nodded and she added the point to the board.

'Sir, no fingerprints,' offered the sub-inspector, Gaya Prasad.

'Good, that's important. It shows the killer is not an ordinary madman, not a raving lunatic, but someone who plans things carefully.'

Ruby wrote it down. 'Like you said,' she reminded him, 'he could be a local, familiar with the city and the many holy sites'.

'Yes, definitely he is a local man.'

To this the SSP objected. 'What makes you so sure the murderer is a man?' he demanded to know. 'What if the killer is a female?'

Everyone turned to look at Hawa Singh. 'For me it has to be a man,' Hawa Singh replied, unperturbed. 'One thing is clear. The killer has to be physically very strong to carry out such murders. It would require a lot of strength to cut open the rib-cage, pull out the heart and then to stab the Cross into the body. Also, the killer arranged the body in both cases. Again, that would require physical strength.'

'The way the killer escaped from the well into the tunnel, and traversed the bottom of a wide river,' added Ruby. 'It has to be a man.'

Sub-inspector Gaya Prasad nervously raised his hand saying, 'The killer could be a Christian. After all, he used a Cross to kill.'

'Bloody idiot,' the SSP shot back. 'He drew a *horoscope chart* on the foreigner's chest! He has to be a Hindu.'

'He could very well be trying to deceive us, or mislead us in different directions,' put in Ruby. 'We should look into that possibility.'

Hawa Singh thoughtfully rubbed at his cold nose. 'In the first murder there was only a Cross, but in the second he added the horoscope chart. He is deliberately leaving contradictory clues for us. I believe him to be a Hindu.'

'What do you mean he is deliberately leaving clues?' asked the SSP, sharply.

Ruby indicated to Hawa Singh that she would do the explaining. 'The FBI have found that most serial-killers want to be found out. They want, in the end, for their faces to be revealed as the brains behind crimes that shook the population of an entire city, sometimes the nation. They take pride in these acts. They feel that they are smarter, far more intelligent than police detectives. For them it's like a game: "*Catch me if you can!*" Our killer has just started his game.'

'Don't keep saying that. I will not have any more murders here in Benares,' the SSP shouted in exasperation.

Hawa Singh felt one of his legs going to sleep. He had been standing in one place for too long. He shook it, and said, 'There's one more similarity we've missed out on. Both the victims are white foreigners.'

'We have still not identified the male victim,' Ruby reminded them. 'We don't even know who he is.'

Hawa Singh glanced at Gaya Prasad enquiringly.

'Sir, I have circulated the picture to all policemen on duty throughout the city,' the younger policeman spoke nervously.

'He must be staying at some hotel, guesthouse or a lodge. Just get cracking on all such places. There will be people who must have seen him in Benares. We have to identify him or we won't be able to move forward at all,' said Hawa Singh.

'We'll do our best, sir,' Gaya Prasad said meekly.

The SSP didn't relent. 'I don't want your best, Sharma!' he roared. 'I want information. Or consider yourself dismissed!'

Hawa Singh looked at the board, wondering what else he could be missing. 'One more thing,' he said. 'There seemed to be some connection to study of the stars in both cases. Eva is believed to have come here to study the *Bhrigu-Samhita*, being an astronomer herself. While for the male victim, we still don't know anything about him, there was the matter of the horoscope chart.'

'Anything else?' Ruby looked around from the board she was writing on.

There was a shrill sound of a cell phone ringing. It took a while for Hawa Singh to realize it was his own. He took it out and hit the answer button and hurriedly took the call. It was his father.

'Where the hell are you?' Fauja Singh shouted down the line. 'Are you aware that another foreigner was murdered in Benares? By the way, how's that CID girl? And why didn't you get me jalebis today, you good-for-nothing?'

The barrage of questions could be heard by all in the room. 'I'm busy with the case you're talking about,' Hawa Singh whispered back. 'Don't disturb me. I'll call you.'

'But do you even know anything about why the murders were committed?' the old man went on relentlessly. 'Everyone is talking about it! It seems the ghosts of our freedom fighters have come back to life and are killing all white foreigners, *one by one*!' bawled Fauja Singh.

'I'll meet you in the evening,' said Hawa Singh and cut the line. Seeing that all eyes were on him, he said embarrassedly, 'My father. You know how fathers are.'

The SSP paced up and down, fuming. 'Yes, it's all happening in Benares, in my city, the holiest of all holy places for Hindus.'

Hawa Singh looked at Ruby and she nodded and added the point to the board.

'Sir, both the places are pilgrimage sites for Hindus. First, the Ganges itself at Benares, and now the Kashi Vishwanath temple,' said Gaya Prasad Sharma.

'Thank you, Sharma,' acknowledged Hawa Singh. He looked around at the others. 'Have we missed anything else?'

Ruby read out the points from the board. 'The Holy Cross, hearts removed from bodies, bodies dumped at public places, the suggestion of ritual or sacrifice, no fingerprints, a careful planner behind it all, probably a local familiar with the city, male, physically strong, Hindu, victims white foreigners, one male and one female, astrology, astronomy, the *Bhrigu-Samhita*, and Hindu pilgrim sites in Benares.'

The SSP couldn't understand the point of the exercise. 'Okay, we know all this, but what's the use of it all? We are still at the same place where we began.'

Hawa Singh cleared his throat. 'We now have at least the profile of the killer. He has made one thing very clear, that he'll strike again. He is clearly very determined to carry on with whatever plan he has in mind. With whatever motive.'

'And what would that be?' asked the SSP.

'We don't know. It could be his simple hatred for whites or there could be something else that is deep-seated.'

'Sir, we should issue a warning to all foreigners,' Gaya Prasad broke in.

'Sharma, shut your bloody trap,' the SSP rounded on him. 'You want the entire city to be panic-stricken, living in abject fear of this killer? I would lose my job in a day's time, if that happened.'

Gaya Prasad looked at his feet, humiliated.

'There is one very important thing we missed. On the bodies of both the victims, there were no signs of struggle. It seems the killer befriended them and then seized the right moment and opportunity to kill them,' said Hawa Singh.

'You mean there could be people who might have seen the killer with the victims?' Ruby asked.

'Exactly. We have to hunt for this man quietly but aggressively,' said Hawa Singh.

The SSP gathered his thoughts and spoke in a calmer tone. 'Do you think this killer could have a criminal record?'

It was Ruby's turn to speak. 'Most serial-killers have no records of other crimes,' she said. 'However, like this one, they are cunning, careful, at the same time ruthless and devoid of emotion. They are focused when it comes to selecting and killing their victims. The FBI has a term for such killers—psychopaths.'

The SSP banged his fist on the table. 'So now we have a psychopath killer in the streets of Benares!'

'These psychopaths create their own rituals. The killer here has also created his own, with the Cross and now the horoscope chart. The ritual then becomes a framework. Fortunately for us, this proves their downfall. They often get trapped in their own framework,' said Hawa Singh. Deep inside, Hawa Singh knew that society would never be free of such lunatics, lurking in dark corners, with their dark minds.

A thought struck the SSP. 'What about the paper found in Eva's stomach?' he asked Hawa Singh.

'I think the killer forced her to swallow it.'

'What?'

'Yes, it was a paper with some mantras written on it. It was the mrityunjay-yantra given to Eva by Baba Ramtirath. By making her swallow it, the killer wanted us to find it and believe that nothing could protect his victims from him,' said Hawa Singh.

The Benares Police had never in their history encountered such a killer. They all had read about demons and asuras in mythology, but this one beat them all.

'There's just one more thing,' said Hawa Singh. 'I had found some red sand in Eva's hotel room and it seems that came from her own shoes when she visited Ramnagar Fort. The entire pathway from the main entry gate to the lobby there is covered in red sand.'

'When did you go into Eva's hotel room?' the SSP asked.

'Well, that was a long time back. Let's not go into it,' said Hawa Singh.

'What's happening here? Everyone has started his own investigation. Hawa Singh, this is not the way to work. I need to be informed about each and every move you plan to make.'

'Yes, sir,' agreed Hawa Singh. 'I would like to bring in Suryadev Singh and Abhay Narayan Singh for interrogation.'

'Are you crazy? Have you really lost your head? You want to bring in the king of Kashi and the state minister for questioning? There will be riots in Benares,' retorted the SSP.

Hawa Singh tried to keep his calm. 'On our visit to Suryadev Singh's bungalow, we found human parts preserved in jars in a cupboard there.'

The SSP looked at him with burning eyes. 'You call that a visit? You sneaked in—and for that I could have lost my job!'

Ruby broke in. 'We saw human heads, sawed-off hands, fingers and a heart. We need to bring that heart to test if it matches with any of the two victims.'

'Everyone in Benares knows about the body parts B.P Singh collected. The questioning cannot be carried out,' shouted the SSP.

'So, we just sit here and do nothing? Those are my suspects. The tunnel that I found opens onto the opposite bank of the Ganges, close to Ramnagar Fort. And when we met up with the Kashi Naresh, we saw he keeps his entire body covered—even his hands!'

The SSP looked at Hawa Singh and Ruby with astonishment, 'You went to question the Kashi Naresh?'

'It was a friendly meeting.'

'But everyone knows that the Kashi Naresh hardly meets anyone, and doesn't come out in public. You cannot point fingers at him just because a tunnel opens close to his fort. It's an ancient tunnel that anyone could have discovered and used. Don't create any more problems for me!'

By this time the reporters sitting out in the cold had become restless. They were pushing their way in towards the SSP's office and had started shouting slogans against the SSP and the Benares Police. The SSP was forced to call them in.

There was the usual round of questions, and half-baked answers.

One of the reporters pointed at Singh, saying, 'You have this officer from the Delhi crime branch who was once responsible for the death of his entire team, and also that of a reporter. He should be removed from this case.'

This brought out a hidden rage in Hawa Singh. 'What the hell have you guys done in life, apart from conjuring up lies and fabricating truths? I have a bullet right here in my head. How many of you have even got a pen-prick in your hand, forget the head or the heart?'

He got up and walked out.

The reporters insisted Hawa Singh apologize for his behaviour. They would never stand such highhandedness from the police. And they were going to publish that the police had failed in their job to catch the killer and were now teaching the press what to do.

The SSP sent ACP Shishir Jha after Hawa Singh.

'Sir, please, the reporters are getting angry. Just apologize to them once, and this matter will be over,' pleaded Shishir Jha.

'I will never apologize to these vultures. They are here for blood and they got it,' said Hawa Singh, as he walked away.

The SSP himself apologized on Hawa Singh's behalf, saying, 'There are times when he loses his head because of the bullet lodged inside it. Grant him that consideration.'

Soon, snacks and drinks were called in for the reporters, in a time-old effort to appease them. Later, the SSP handed out gifts. A bottle of scotch to each.

Hawa Singh tried to shake off his anger, and focus his thoughts on the killer. He would have to find other ways to get to Suryadev Singh and Kashi Naresh.

He decided to meet Pandit Shri Vishnu Shastri, the third person whose number was written down by Eva.

It was the word 'Sparrow' that still harrowed him.

CHAPTER 13

There was a certain restlessness and hunger inside him that he had not felt for a long time. The earlier pain—in his head and in his heart—had taken over all his faculties, and he had drifted listlessly from one case to the other. This particular case had given him a new lease of life. It was as if the very gods had pulled him to their land, and through death, were trying to revive him. He was filled with a purpose—to hunt the killer down.

He wanted to be in sync with him, the way he thought, the way he planned and the way he acted on those plans. But this killer was not giving him any leverage. Hawa Singh hoped he was not clutching at straws.

The killer was still just an idea, a shadow that disappeared into the fog, leaving no trace behind. He was playing an elaborate game of hide-and-seek. He was playing God—a destructive God.

The FBI taught its recruits that most serial-killers were apprehended when they wanted to be caught—and only then. They had laughed in the faces of the greatest of detectives and investigating officers. Hawa Singh didn't want to see that laughing face. He wanted to make its owner cry. He wanted to make him run. Run for his life.

Hawa Singh and Ruby Malik entered the sprawling campus of Benares Hindu University. They had come to meet Pandit Vishnu Shastri, one of the greatest scholars of Vedic astrology and Vedic mathematics.

BHU, Benares Hindu University, is one of the largest residential universities in Asia, with over 20,000 students. The university's main campus is spread over 1,300 acres and was built on land donated by the Kashi Naresh, the king of Benares.

There were many colleges in BHU but, right now, Hawa Singh was interested only in Sanskrit Vidya Dharma Vijnan Sankaya, one of the few colleges in the country teaching both astrology and the Vedas.

It was established in 1918 by the great Pandit Madan Mohan Malviyaji in order to realize the chief goal of this university, that is, to preserve and promote the studies of ancient Indian shastras, the Sanskrit language and culture, with the intention to bring about a fruitful dialogue between the East and the West. The Vedic texts taught here are in keeping with the traditional methods of hermeneutics as well as oral-cum-written tradition.

When they asked to meet Pandit Shastri, one of the students guided Hawa Singh and Ruby to the library, Shastri's choice of place, where he could sit enveloped by books and manuscripts. He loved the smell of old paper and ink emanating all around him from ancient scrolls and books. It was while sitting here that he made horoscopes for the country's top politicians, businessmen and actors. When it came to astrology, Shastri was the man to go to.

Pandit Vishnu Shastri was sitting with a pile of books and manuscripts in front of him. He looked about fifty-five years old and had a round, somewhat pock-marked, face. His moustache was thick and long, and his peppered hair gleamed with desi ghee. He wore a crisp kurta and white dhoti. There was a holy thread tied around his right wrist and a silver wristband with 'Om' inscribed on it.

He was lost in his calculations when Hawa Singh and Ruby approached him. They introduced themselves and Shastri asked them to sit.

Hawa Singh told him that he had found his personal number written on a piece of paper found in Eva's room, and about the dead woman's interest in astrology. He also told him about the second murder, in which a horoscope chart had featured, drawn on the victim's chest.

Pandit Vishnu Shastri looked thoughtful before he spoke. 'I remember that girl coming to me. She wanted to see the original manuscript of the *Bhrigu-Samhita* and some books on the history of Benares,' he said softly, reminiscently.

'You must have read about her murder in the papers. Why didn't you approach the police?' asked Hawa Singh

'I meet hundreds of people who come to consult me, just like that girl, or now you. I have also been travelling a lot over the last few days,' he said, as if absolving himself of blame.

Ruby listened quietly, her expert eyes focused on the grand Pandit Vishnu Shastri. She could see he cherished the moments when people came to consult him. In this digital age, the number of people interested in Vedic texts or mathematics had lessened. She asked him, 'Why do you think she was murdered?'

Shastri looked a bit uncomfortable. 'How would I know?' he asked back. 'She was beautiful, and because she was a foreigner, anyone could have tried to take advantage of her.'

Hawa Singh gathered that Shastri was not aware of the details of the murders. He changed the subject. 'What is so special about this *Bhrigu-Samhita* that so many of these foreigners want to study it?'

This was a subject that made the eyes of this master of his trade glow. Empowered with his knowledge, he said, '*Bhrigu-Samhita* was originally a massive database of the birth charts of millions and trillions of human beings. It deals with their life spans, their major achievements, as well as their losses. It also reveals a person's previous incarnations, and the ones to come. A permutation of more than forty-five million horoscope charts can be drawn from the calculations given in the book.'

'So where is the original manuscript?' asked Ruby.

Shastri smiled and said, 'Through the many invasions the country has witnessed, it seems to have been lost or taken away by the conquerors. In fact, the most unfortunate event was the destruction of the Nalanda university library by the then Muslim rulers, where several thousands of the horoscopes compiled by Maharishi Bhrigu had been stored. It is said that the library was so vast that, when it was set on fire, it burnt for more than three months. Now only a few fragments of the original horoscopes of *Bhrigu-Samhita* are left to the Brahmin community, which are now scattered over India.'

It didn't add up, thought Hawa Singh. If the killer was after the original manuscript of the *Bhrigu-Samhita*, why would he murder a foreigner who herself knew nothing of it? Or was he trying to safeguard the original manuscript?

But then, the greatest of Sanskrit scholars, and the Kashi Naresh himself, were not privy to its secrets. There were no answers, only more questions.

Hawa Singh took out a piece of paper and put it on the table. On it he had copied the horoscope chart drawn on the victim's body. He showed it to Shastri, saying, 'The killer drew this on the chest of his last victim. I know it's a horoscope chart, but please read it and tell us what it says.'

Shastri put on a pair of thick glasses and examined the chart with care. 'You know that a horoscope is drawn based on one's date of birth, time of birth and place of birth. By using these, the astrologers draw the positions of the planets, the zodiac and dashas. Astrologers looking at these planets, signs and house placements in your chart can read your personality, as well as life events and possibilities—both the good and the bad. They can even determine when the events will occur.'

'So what do you see in this chart?' asked Ruby.

'I see only death,' he said, looking up. 'I need to do a reverse calculation to get the dates and times. Just give me some time.'

With that Shastri got busy with his calculations. 'The killer was using Vedic mathematics and astrology to leave his signature,' reflected Hawa Singh and Ruby to themselves. It took a few minutes for Shastri to complete the calculations. 'I don't understand this,' he admitted. 'This horoscope shows that the person concerned would die on the coming 30 January. It also says this person will be killed in a mysterious way,' Shastri said.

'The killer has left a message for us that he will kill again on the 30th. Can you see if this person is a man or a woman?' Hawa Singh asked.

'I'm sorry, that cannot be gauged from this chart.'

Ruby almost shouted, 'Does this chart belong to a foreigner?'

Shastri looked again at the chart and said, 'Well, I can't say whether he or she is a foreigner, but definitely not of this holy land, Benares.'

'Are you sure about the date, 30 January?' Hawa Singh asked.

'My calculations are based on Vedic mathematics. They can never go wrong,' said Shastri austerely.

'We were right in thinking that the killer would strike again,' Ruby whispered, almost to herself. 'He had already chosen his target and drawn the horoscope chart of his next victim. We'll have to stop him this time.'

'Can you stop death?' Shastri snapped.

Hawa Singh and Ruby looked at him in bafflement. 'We can definitely stop the killer,' said Hawa Singh determinedly.

They picked up the piece of paper and were ready to leave when something struck Hawa Singh. 'One more thing,' he said, turning back to the professor. 'Does the word "Sparrow" mean anything to you?'

'Sparrow,' Shastri said reflectively, 'well, there is a Sparrow's Research and Analysis Wing for Mental Health here. In fact, it is funded by the royal family of Benares.'

'Actually,' Hawa Singh explained, 'Eva had written the word "Sparrow" on the same paper on which she wrote your number, along with that of Suryadev Singh and the Kashi Naresh. What could be the connection?'

'Maybe she planned to meet Manvendra Singh.'

'Who is that?' asked Ruby.

Shastri smiled. 'Manvendra Singh is one of the top scholars of the Vedas and Vedic astrology, and is also the younger brother of the Kashi Naresh. It was a case of a genius losing his mind. He lost his mental balance, and was admitted to the Sparrow institute two-and-a-half years back.'

'But we met with Abhay Narayan Singh, and he never mentioned it,' said Ruby.

'Kashi Naresh has cut off all relations with Manvendra since he went off and started living with the Aghoris on their cremation grounds. Manvedra wanted to learn tantra-mantra and all the secret knowledge of the Aghoris. He ate flesh from human carcasses with them. Slowly, he lost his mind. There were rumours that he had turned cannibal.'

'This Manvendra Singh is the key. We need to find him,' said Hawa Singh, after thanking Pandit Vishnu Shastri.

***

The TV media had splashed the news all over the city from its many local channels. From there it was picked by the national news channels all around the country.

The media had coined a name for the killer—'Butcher of Benares'.

The Butcher was now stalking the Ghost.

CHAPTER 14

He stood in the dense fog with his arms spread out wide. He felt invincible. He loved the name that the media had given him—the Butcher of Benares. He would have preferred to be called the God of Death, but this was close enough. Now people would talk about him, and speak his name in hushed whispers. They would spin stories around him. Experts would meet in panel discussions to analyze motives. He would definitely go down in history. He had an identity.

Not that anyone understood what he was doing. His motives were different. His purpose was big.

He had seen the tall police officer and that young FBI girl walking out of BHU. He knew they'd got his message. It was he who was making them run around in circles. Let them call him the Butcher; one day he'd tell them what was what. The story they had never heard.

He looked at the shining knife in his hand. It had a long, slender blade with an ivory handle, and had a Cross stamped in gold on it. It was a Russian knife, one that the KGB, the Red Army and now the Russian mafia used. This was one knife you could not buy. You had to earn it.

But he had neither bought the knife, nor earned it. He had it all right, and he was going to use it on the man with a bullet in his head—no ordinary knife would do the job. No one survives a cut from a Russian knife.

He planned to hold him by his neck, give it a slight twist, place the knife against his throat and slowly make a deep cut from left to right in the shape of a crescent moon. The heart would do the rest, pumping out blood in spurts.

It would make for great news, too. What would they call him then? Not that he had anything personal against the police officer—none whatever—but he was getting in the way. Deflecting him from his purpose.

His purpose.

The fog was really thick. It felt like ice. Thick and hard. Opaque. It gave him a perfect cover. The knife was ready. It positively danced in his hands.

Hawa Singh, walking through the fog, took out his broken cell phone preparing to inform the SSP about the importance of the date '30 January'. Ruby walked alongside as they moved away from the main road onto a narrow street. The Butcher was waiting for them.

He had seen the girl and liked her. He wondered whether he should kill her as well. Well, one at a time. First, the policeman had to go. He was a hindrance to the Butcher's lofty plans and had to be eliminated.

'Yes, Hawa Singh,' the SSP said as he answered the call.

'Sir, we have discovered something very important. The killer had left a message in the form of that horoscope chart. He will kill again.'

The Butcher could feel them coming towards him. He fingered the blade of his knife—*perfect*! Sharp enough to cut through the fog.

Hawa Singh came closer. Suddenly a fist hit his face. The phone fell from his hands and clattered away. Another blow to the jaw brought him to his knees.

And then he felt the long, sharp blade touching the base of his throat. Hawa Singh was no martial arts expert but he had wrestled in the grounds of top akharas in Delhi. There were a couple of tricky moves he knew well. And there was one rule he lived by—attack!

It was in a fraction of second that Hawa Singh grabbed the hand and twisted it. There was a pained cry and the knife around his neck lost its edge. It gave him enough time to haul himself up and whip out his .45 Colt.

He pointed the Colt in the thick air, blindly. One pull on the trigger could release a bullet that tore through the blanket of fog and hit its target.

He called out to Ruby to stay back. He sensed—rather than perceived—the knife slashing through the condensation towards him. He stepped aside but the Russian piece found a place to cut through. The knife gashed open the leather jacket and found his shoulder. Blood spurted out.

Hawa Singh felt warmth around his arm but didn't immediately realize he was bleeding. He waved the Colt in front of him frantically. He could hear the sounds of a bicycle bell. Must be a vendor or a milkman, he thought. There was also the laughter of children playing on the street. A housewife shouted from a balcony somewhere above to a vegetable-seller. A mother called out to her child to come home.

One wrong move of his finger on the trigger could prove disastrous.

The Butcher stood at a safe distance from him. He knew that his intended victim was taller than him, and more powerful. It was better to keep out of his range and pounce on him at a moment when he was caught unaware of the direction of his attacker. The fog was his ally. He smiled to himself. The Butcher had made his first cut.

Ruby called out, standing helplessly in the fog, 'Singh, are you okay?'

The Butcher grinned when he heard her squeaky voice—to him she sounded like a frightened mouse. Being a member of the FBI didn't make one immortal. There was a time to live and a time to die. And anyway, everyone finally died.

He had to make his move. It would be difficult to target the throat. But he knew there was another part of the body that was irreplaceable. The heart.

It is said a kitchen faucet would need to be turned on all the way for at least forty-five years to equal the amount of blood pumped by the heart in an average lifetime.

A cold wind came floating from over the Ganges, bringing more fog, what could be called a white darkness. Blindness.

This was the moment. The Butcher made his move, his knife poised. His was a practised hand and knew precisely the place that would let the slender knife move in without hindrance from the ribs.

The move was swift, with the arm stretched out full, and the shoulder providing ample power and thrust to it. The smile broadened on the Butcher's face.

It was in that fraction of a second that Hawa Singh saw the glint at the tip of the steel blade. Hawa Singh dodged aside, but the knife cut his chest open. It was Hawa Singh's turn to make a telling move. He grabbed at the hand that held the knife and directed a sturdy kick towards the knees of the owner. There was a cracking sound, and the knife clattered away on the ground.

Ruby was calling out for help, as she dialled the SSP's number from her cell phone.

Hawa Singh advanced to grab the attacker. The Butcher, fumbling for a new weapon, found a wooden plank and hit him on the head with it. Everything went black. Intense pain overwhelmed him. And then, his legs buckled under him. But he clung to his Colt, knowing it wouldn't betray him.

He was on his knees, pointing the Colt aimlessly. At a distance, the Butcher pulled himself upright. He had to get out now. The fog had swallowed his Russian friend.

There will be another time, another place, he vowed to himself. He was, after all, the Butcher. Indistinctly, he saw the nose of the Colt, searching for him. He hated guns.

Guns were responsible for more deaths than any other weapon. They killed, and there was nothing artistic or clever about them. It takes far, far more courage to wield a knife.

He could see Ruby frantically making calls, and Hawa Singh fighting to stay up on his knees. He knew all about him—he had made a study of his exploits. Not for nothing did they call him the Ghost.

It would take more than a Russian knife to get to him. But then, the Butcher promised himself, he would not disappoint. A crooked smile formed on the Butcher's face.

He dissolved into the fog.

CHAPTER 15

There was a combined sickening smell of spirit and vomit in the room. The white walls were stained, and cracks had formed, showing years of neglect. Electrical wires were crisscrossed by lizards chasing insects. Cobwebs awaited the survivors. The bins in the room overflowed with plastic, needles, left-over food and cotton swabs soaked in blood. It was cold and damp. A dreadful white glare from tubelights illuminated the room. It was not a place anyone would want to be in.

Hawa Singh was lying on a bed in the government hospital. He had had to have five stitches on his arm and another twelve on his chest. The Russian knife had found its way.

He opened his eyes, to see the SSP, Ruby and some others of his investigating team standing over his bed. 'Who was it? Do you think it was the killer? Did you see him?' A relentless barrage of questions came at him, fired by the SSP.

In here, there were no doctors or nurses to restrict the SSP. 'Please don't disturb the patient. He needs to rest,' they would have said. But there were hardly a handful of doctors for thousands of patients. Moreover, no one here would have dared to interrupt the SSP.

'Where's the knife?' Hawa Singh asked Ruby, fighting against his weakness from loss of blood.

'I have it.'

'Sir,' he turned to the SSP, 'send the knife to check for fingerprints. I couldn't see the attacker in the fog but I'm sure he was not wearing gloves.'

When the Butcher disappeared, Hawa Singh had managed to salvage the knife in the fog. Never one to carry a handkerchief—too girlish, he always thought—he had asked Ruby for hers. People around him had forever thought him to be shabby, rustic, and even uncouth. He had never bothered himself with their opinions. It was the Ghost that went into the darkness, into the fog, to fight, to spill his blood for them. To make them feel secure, and be free to mouth such comments about him. The darkness called to him again, and again, he had to be ready to obey its summons. Be ready to die. He always was.

Ruby gently touched the bandages on his arm. 'You think he was the killer?' she asked.

Hawa Singh struggled to a sitting position on the bed, resting against the meagre hospital pillows. 'Till now,' he managed, panting a little, 'the killer has been very secretive. He hasn't left any prints or clues. I don't understand why he would personally come out like this in the open, trying to kill me. Perhaps it was a hired hand.'

Ruby showed the knife to Hawa Singh. He studied it and said, 'This is no ordinary knife. It looks expensive and exclusive. There are very few people who could possess a weapon of this kind. It has the Cross embossed on its handle.'

'It looks Russian to me,' observed Ruby.

Hawa Singh turned his gaze to the SSP. 'More important than this, is the message that the killer left for us.'

Then he told them everything about the horoscope on the corpse of the dead man, and the hidden message that the next target would be killed on the coming 30 January.

Then SSP sat himself down on the wheeled steel stool beside Hawa Singh's bed. He was quiet, almost in a helpless manner. 'In less than two weeks, there have been three murders in Benares. Even if I don't count the murder of that Aghori, we still have two murders—of foreigners—on our hands. And now, this threat,' said the exhausted police chief.

'Don't look on it as a threat,' interpolated Hawa Singh. 'It's a clear message to us: "Stop me, if you can. But you cannot." He has already selected his next victim. He has planned it carefully, done research on the victim to the extent that he knows his/her birth date, birthplace and the time of birth, so that he can accurately make out the horoscope'.

'So what do we do?' asked the SSP in desperation.

'We need the entire police force on high alert. There should be policemen in mufti on the lookout. We have to prevent yet another killing,' said Ruby.

'She's right. One thing we've got to keep in mind is that both the last two victims were found at pilgrim sites. There is the probability he'll use another such site. What we don't know is whether he kills the victim at that spot, or after killing him or her, places the body there.'

'Do you have any idea how many such pilgrim sites there are in Benares?' asked the SSP exasperatedly, lighting a forbidden cigarette in the hospital room. 'The entire place is a centre of pilgrimage. How many places can we watch all that closely?' Everyone understood the extent of the pressure imposed on the SSP by politicians, various embassies and senior police brass, asking for immediate results to the investigations. But no one realized that results were a product of hard labour, toiling for days and queries into nothingness. How many of them had ever dealt with such a psychopath?

The SSP looked at Ruby. 'What does the FBI say, so far into this case?'

'We have to catch the killer before he strikes again, is what we feel,' she replied coolly. 'His message is that he has gained increasing confidence, to the point that he feels free to take on the entire police force. He has given us a clear date. But who the target will be, whether it will be male or female, is not clear. Also, there is nothing to go by to ascertain that it will be a white foreigner or someone else.'

Hawa Singh, trying to straighten up in bed, felt a painful tug at his stitches. Hearing his subdued cry, Ruby hurried to help him sit up straight. They looked at each other, then looked away. 'Okay, let's look at what we have in hand right now,' he said, breaking the air, heavy with tension.

'Yes,' the SSP said hurriedly, 'we got the autopsy report on the second victim found inside the Kashi Vishwanath temple. I almost forgot to mention it. It disclosed a similar modus operandi. The heart was removed and a Cross was placed in its stead. The ash smeared on the victim's body was found to be from the cremation grounds. It contained particles of bone ash and burnt human tissue.'

'The cremation grounds are the place where the Aghoris live,' put in Ruby.

Hawa Singh slowly nodded, lost in thought. His cerebral calculator was arriving at its own computations.

The human brain, as scientifically recorded, is the fattest organ in the body and consists of at least 60 per cent fat. And while one is awake, the brain generates between 10 and 23 watts of power—or enough energy to light up a bulb.

Hawa Singh was trying to energize the coils inside his brain and light up his thought bulb. 'Why would any Aghori target a foreigner?' he asked, finally.

'Who the hell knows why? These Aghoris do indulge in human sacrifices, and that is well known. Maybe they are targeting white foreigners for some special kind of ritual. We need to get cracking on them,' exploded the angry SSP.

Gaya Prasad Sharma, sub-inspector, who had been standing quietly near the door, said, 'Sir, I tried to talk to the Aghoris, to get the fingerprints of Neelambar Nath, to check against those found on the axe handle. They threw me out, and warned me that they would chop me into pieces if I ever dared to enter their grounds again.'

'I don't want you to waste your energy on the murder of that bloody Aghori,' riposted the increasingly heated SSP. 'Did you find anything about the second victim? Do we still have no idea who he was? Which country did he come from?'

'We are working on it, but now, with the murder being reported widely by the media, no one wants to come forward with information,' said Gaya Prasad.

A nurse came in to inject Hawa Singh with a painkiller. A drop of blood erupted where the needle went in, and she wiped it away with a cotton swab which she threw into an overflowing bin.

'When can I leave the hospital, nurse?' asked Hawa Singh.

'You'd better rest here for another week, or these wounds will not heal,' said the nurse tersely. She looked at the SSP, lowered her gaze and darted out of the room.

'So, now, we are one soldier down,' said the SSP.

'I'm not dead,' said Hawa Singh. 'These nurses don't know anything. I'll be out of here by morning tomorrow.'

The SSP nodded. He wanted him now, more than anyone else. Only a Ghost could track the Butcher.

'Gaya,' Hawa Singh now said to the younger policeman, 'we can't leave out anything. Go back to the Aghoris and tell them, if they don't help us, I'm going to go there and drag them to the police station. Also, take the prints of Baba Ramtirath and keep a close watch on the Naga sadhus.'

The SSP tried to protest. Then, he shrugged. 'Get it done, Sharma.'

Ruby re-entered the conversation. 'We need to have a foolproof plan for the 30th,' she said to Hawa Singh. 'Maybe we need to keep in mind that in the last two cases, the killer struck at night, or, to be precise, right before dawn.'

'Did forensics find anything inside the tunnel?' asked Hawa Singh.

The SSP sighed. 'Water had seeped in by then, and the entire tunnel was filled waist-up. No prints of any kind. They found other passages connecting the same tunnel to other places.'

'We need to keep an eye on that tunnel, said Hawa Singh. 'It's close to the ghats and the killer might be using it to escape.' He scratched his head, looked down at himself, and realized, with a jolt, that he couldn't find his Colt. He straightened up further and checked his back more thoroughly. It was not there.

'We have your horse,' said the SSP. 'Sharma, get it.'

Gaya Prasad took the Colt out from his own belt and handed it to the SSP. The senior policeman hefted it. 'Thank God you didn't fire it in the fog,' he smiled. 'It could have taken down a whole house,' he remarked, before handing it over to Hawa Singh. 'As an officer from out of state, you are not allowed to carry a weapon, and especially of this kind. Still, you may have it back. I know you'll need it. Just get me the killer.'

Hawa Singh took it and nodded at the SSP. 'We only have three days to the 30th. We'll need as many hands as we can use. There have to be policemen disguised as boatmen, pandits, vendors and beggars, whatever. Make sure all of them are armed. We are dealing with a madman who doesn't hesitate to kill,' he said grimly.

The SSP looked at him with an air of reassurance. 'Get some rest,' he said. 'I'll take care of everything.' With that, the SSP walked out of the hospital, followed by accompanying policemen.

Ruby was left in the room with Hawa Singh. She shifted to sit on his bed, and the coarse coir-filled mattress stabbed her like pins.

'This is a really bad bed,' she said with a grin.

'Welcome to Benares,' Hawa Singh smiled back at her.

She touched the bandages on his arm and chest tenderly. They didn't speak for a few minutes. Finally, Ruby broke the silence. 'You know I'm half-Pakistani.

My mother was from Pakistan, while my father was from the US, California. They fell in love and got married. I was born soon after. But when I was seven, my mother suddenly left me, my father and the US to return to her village in Pakistan. Since then, I have never heard from her. Now, everyone nevertheless calls me a "Paki".'

Hawa Singh reached for her hand. He could sense a similar pain inside her that he had hidden inside his heart. It seemed to connect them.

'There are times,' she continued slowly, 'when I dream about her holding my hand and walking on the beach beside our house. I remember her smiling playfully at me. Then, suddenly, she was gone.'

Hawa Singh reconnected with his own nightmares, his memories and a heart that cried without tears. They had both learnt to hide their pain.

Ruby leant her head on his chest. Hawa Singh flinched from the connection, and she moved away, startled. 'I'm so sorry,' she said contritely.

He smiled and brought her back close. She snuggled, gingerly this time, into his arms. In the comfort they brought each other, they forgot their nightmares and slept.

It was late in the night that Hawa Singh woke up. Something hammered against his head.

He remembered. He had seen that Russian knife earlier.

It had been part of a collection.

CHAPTER 16

This was when spirits roamed the land. It was perfect for the Ghost. Hawa Singh, with his jacket ripped through in several places, leaped astride an Enfield motorcycle and rode it through the dark. The bike was popularly called the 'Bullet'. He couldn't stay away from one.

The thumping beat of the bike matched his own heart's. His stitches hurt, and a dull pain assailed his head. The wind was icy-cold, and ahead of him there was fog, only fog. By now he had learnt its ways. One had to be slow, and steady, but keep moving. You had to become part of it, become one with it. Be the fog, itself.

He could hear dogs howling and a lone crow cawing in the dead of the night. It was said such animals could sense a spiritual presence. They had certainly sensed the Ghost.

The Bullet slowly moved ahead. He was able to discern a palatial bungalow floating ahead of the fog. The white marble edifice seemed almost to merge with it.

A few lights were on around the perimeter of the bungalow. There would definitely be dogs and guards.

Hawa Singh left the bike at a distance away from the bungalow and quietly merged with the fog. He approached close to the walls of the bungalow. He had seen the guards, all armed with rifles, close to the gate, sitting around a bonfire. They all looked drunk.

Any dogs in sight were chained. But no one dared to sneak into Suryadev Singh's house. Ever. Hawa Singh was going to do it. Again.

He realized that the wires running over the wall had high-voltage current running through them. They could fry an elephant. It was impossible to cut through them. He looked around and saw a crow sitting high atop one of the electric wires. It cawed, looking in his direction.

He took off his now tattered leather jacket and flung it at the wires. Nothing happened. He pulled it down with an available stick of wood and wrapped it in a bigger bundle of material—anything he could find around him. The jacket touched the wire. He slowly pushed it up and slid under it. He started to move to the other side of the wall, the crow keeping a constant eye on him. Crows liked the dead—or the dying.

The Ghost had gotten in.

The house inside appeared totally dark. The doors and windows were locked fast. The Ghost decided to first climb to the roof and then move in. He moved carefully from one window sill to the other, and from one drainpipe to the next. Until, finally, he was on the rooftop.

The door to the stairs below was locked. He didn't want to attract the guards. The dogs had been set free and were circling the house frantically, looking towards the roof. The guards disregarded their attention. No one could possibly get directly to Suryadev Singh's rooftop.

One of the guards consoled himself against the ominous barking of the dogs, chanting words from the *Hanuman Chalisa*, hoping they had merely sensed a harmless spirit circling the house. He was right, in his way.

Hawa Singh traversed the rooftop terrace, hunting for a place that would let him in below. There was none. Spotting a large balcony, he decided to get down somehow to it, before planning his next step. He hung from the parapet of the roof, letting his entire height reduce the distance, and then let go. With a light thud, he was there.

The dogs surged below, barking their throats off. Enormous searchlights were switched on to sweep the garden. Guards spread everywhere, their guns ready. Not that they could see much, in that fog.

In the balcony just above, the windows were covered by a strong iron grille. They were locked from the inside and were probably unbreakable. Hawa Singh sought with his hands at the corners of the iron grille and realized that it was screwed into the wooden frame. He took out his Swiss knife and unscrewed it.

Many householders had suffered from this mistake of simple carpentry. Hawa Singh removed the grille easily, and set it aside. There was a windowpane to tackle, next. He'd have to break the glass.

Hawa Singh took out his leather jacket and again folded it into a bundle. He surveyed the glass pane, his blood still trickling down from his arm to his fingers.

The dogs were still barking, and the lone crow cawing, when Hawa Singh placed the bundled leather jacket against the glass, and hit it with his elbow.

He carefully pulled away the long shards of glass that emerged from the small explosion he'd caused. They had left a big-enough hole. He put his hand in and slid open the bolt. The Ghost skimmed smoothly inside the house.

A lone dog barked, and barked. The guards searched, vainly, for an intruder in the dark. The crow blinked, still watching the figure moving inside the house.

Hawa Singh could sense that there was no one home. The absence of people created a vacuum in a place, and the air felt stale. The furniture felt dead and the artworks hung like dead pieces on the walls. The presence of inmates made all the difference. The house breathed and felt like it was living. Everything came alive.

Hawa Singh could feel the cold air creeping in through the cracked glass pane. With that, the fog, too, snaked in and drifted into the room like smoke. He focused his thoughts, trying to remember the exact place where he had last seen the knives.

He swiftly and silently climbed up the stairs. Once he was in the corridor, he spotted the right door.

Hawa Singh pulled down the sleeve of his leather jacket over his palm to cover any fingerprints and slowly applied pressure to the knob. The door opened; he stepped in, feeling the soft carpet under his feet.

By then his eyes had adjusted well to the dark. He could see the Cross hanging on the wall. It was kind of silver, with some letters engraved on it. There were three doves drawn across the Cross.

It was an Armenian Cross, with Armenian inscriptions on it—probably of sixth-century vintage. The three doves represented the Father, Son and Holy Spirit. It was one of the only three such Armenian Crosses in the world. It was worth a few millions.

He turned to view the guns on the walls. There was a huge painting hanging from the wall facing the door. He couldn't make head or tail of it. There were geometrical patterns, and an eye, staring at him. He saw a name underneath, Picasso. Must be from Jharkhand, he thought.

He bent closer to the remembered drawers and opened them. He saw the gleaming knives. It was obvious they belonged to different countries and different time periods. Expensive. Exclusive.

He noticed one of the slots was empty. Now, he got it all clear in his head. This was the very slot where he saw that Russian blade that had sliced at him.

Who could it be? Suryadev Singh or Prashant? thought Hawa Singh. He closed the drawer and left the room, walking purposefully toward the sound-proof one. Who would want a sound-proof room in their house? And for what purpose?' he continued to wonder.

Well, it could be multi-purpose, he answered himself in his head. A room from which no sound escapes—no one hears anything, no one sees anything, nothing emerges from it. Deadly.

How funny it is that our own thoughts become questions—and then go on to supply the answers.

Hawa Singh relied on his brain—or what was left of it. This made him a part of an exclusive club. It was not scientists or top IT professionals who were cerebral. It was such policemen—and taxi drivers who were famous for knowing all the streets by heart—who had a larger-than-normal hippocampus. They were the ones who memorized more and more information daily, causing their brains to expand and grow.

Nevertheless, Hawa Singh was still not comfortable with computers. He hesitated even to press a delete button, afraid he'd lose an entire file of information. He still preferred to use pen and paper. And he didn't have an email account.

'Why is everyone so obsessed with communication nowadays?' he often asked his puzzled self. He had known people who got stressed because they hadn't received mail recently, or whose photos on Facebook had not been 'liked'. He'd much rather cut himself out of the picture. The fewer the people around him, the happier he'd be. He'd rather feel free to hug his private—very precious—memories to himself. He didn't want to share them. Or seek people's approval of them.

He reached the heavy door of the sound-proof room. Again using his sleeve, he opened the door, and smelt stale air, faux leather, plastic, paint and spirits. An almost hospital smell.

The room indicated a disordered mind. Someone who was fanatical about tidiness, order, sound levels, the kind of people and things he wanted around him. Basically, a mentally disordered person desperately seeking order in the house.

Hawa Singh moved to the shelves displaying body parts pickled in alcohol. He looked at one grinning head with its eyes bulging out. A hand—sawed off at the wrist—with its fingers stretched out, trying to hold onto something, perhaps a last grip on life. An eye, gouged out with a knife, floating in yet another jar, like a playful marble.

What makes people like B.P Singh and Suryadev keep these body parts as souvenirs, he asked himself again, sickened to the core. Do they really feel proud of their actions? Does all this give them a junkie's high? Maybe, the high a cold-blooded killer gets from the kill, was of a different, even more compulsive kind. Perhaps, that is why he commits one murder after another, till he himself is killed.'

Ruby had told him such habitual assassins began to regard themselves as artists, who created a world and space for themselves. They were the kings of their world, close to God Himself. They believed they held command over life—and therefore death—the continual pattern of the universe.

'Rats. They are just like rats that come out of their holes and then scurry back to hide in. My role is to smoke them out and end their menace,' Hawa Singh had told Ruby.

He liked talking to her, discussing his life with her. He had told her about Kavita. She had told him all about her life. He felt so calm in her presence. They had held each other in each other's arms, and slept together, but they hadn't felt the need to take things to another level. He didn't want to mar the purity of this relationship.

So, was making love an impure act, something that was dirty? Or do I feel it would be cheating on Kavita? He tortured himself with self-doubt.

Then he slapped his forehead. What the hell was happening to him? Why did all these thoughts keep coming back? Focus, man. Focus.

He then looked at the jar that had held a human heart. He remembered clearly that the last time he'd been there, there was one heart in it. Now, there were two.

Eva and the other victim had had their hearts wrenched out.

He brought down some of the jars and placed them on a table. There would be no way to ascertain the human identity of the hearts, except by matching tissue.

The jars were pretty heavy, filled to the brim with formalin. It wouldn't be possible to move out swiftly, carrying them. And he could hardly pocket their contents.

He removed the lids of the jars and bent close to them. The smell of alcohol and dead flesh penetrated his nostrils. He was overcome by nausea, close to puking, when he hurriedly opened a window and sucked in the fresh air.

The dogs kept on barking. The crows got louder. He was left with one last option. He took out his Swiss knife, made fine cuts in both hearts and took out portions of tissue, placing them in a plastic zip-lock pouch that he always carried on him. Adding a little alcohol from the jars, he zipped them shut.

He would have to slip out the same way he had come in. The dogs now sounded like they had been unleashed. He looked at the still-open jar with the floating hand. Its smell attracted the dogs, who came running into the room towards it.

Hawa Singh used that distraction to escape into the fog, bound over the wall and under the wires. The guards heard only a thumping sound in the distance. A crow flew into the dark sky. The Ghost was gone.

CHAPTER 17

28 January.

The shards of sunlight came cascading down through the fat clouds, overcoming their gloom. It was a bright morning, as if God Himself was bestowing a blessing on Benares. The pilgrims took exhilarated dips in the Ganges while, behind them the temple bells rang joyously and sweet incense wafted through the air. The sounds of ghungroos, tabla and music emanated from the houses lining the streets as dance students practised Kathak. The sweetshops displayed freshly made laddus, jalebis, and kachoris. It was a heady mix in the city. Benares, the beautiful.

Hawa Singh and Ruby Malik stood in the warm sunlight, staring at the large board that read 'Sparrow's Research and Analysis Wing for Mental Health'. A few sparrows flitted in the nearby trees. They could easily represent the fleeting moods that gave wings to the imagination of the patients within. Those had been categorized as 'abnormal' people.

It was a red-and-white brick building. The structure looked very European; the board said the building had been designed by Ted Johnson, a British architect. There were many windows in the front, opening out on the large open space where Hawa Singh and Ruby stood. A few eyes seemed to be examining them secretly. And not just those of the sparrows.

They moved to a gravel path, which crunched under their feet. Hawa Singh loved that sound. The circuitous path led them to a long corridor with white pillars on both sides. The floor was squeaky clean. The walls looked freshly painted. The air was fresh. They saw a woman scrubbing the already clean steps going up.

Hawa Singh was wearing his trademark jacket over a t-shirt and a fresh pair of jeans. Finally. Ruby had bought him a new shirt, a pair of jeans and a few t-shirts. He never wore shirts. The stitches on his chest and arm had dried and now pulled at his skin, uncomfortable and itchy. He made a determined effort to forget them. Forgetting was bliss.

Ruby smiled at the woman cleaning the stairs, who stared at her. Hawa Singh pointed out the signage on a board: 'Chief Medical Officer, First Floor'. They walked up the stairs.

The woman mumbled to no one in particular. 'They have come to take him away. But they will all die. It's written in their horoscopes.'

They reached the first floor and walked through the next corridor looking for another signboard. There was no staff member around. At the far end of the corridor there was a man staring out at a tree, smiling. 'The blue sparrow will come today, and then I'll be free,' he repeated over and over again to himself. 'I'll be free.'

Ruby pointed out a room with a nameplate outside that read 'CMO, Sudha Krishnamurthy'. They knocked on the door. A woman dressed in a white saree answered it and stood regarding them quizzically.

'We are from the police and would like to meet the CMO. It's very important,' said Hawa Singh.

The woman looked at Ruby with a questioning eyebrow. 'She, too, is with the police,' said Hawa Singh

The woman nodded. 'The CMO is busy at a morning meeting. You'll have to wait for a while,' she said, and shut the door.

Hawa Singh and Ruby were left standing where they were. They exchanged glances and shrugged.

Hawa Singh turned away from the door, adjusted the Colt in his waistband and tried to plan his next move. He had handed over the specimen samples from the two hearts to the medics. He was told that they didn't have the expertise and equipment to analyze the tissues, so the specimens would have to be sent to Delhi. It would take a week or ten days for the reports to back come to them.

His thoughts were racing to find ways to trap the killer. Somehow, he felt he had slipped so far. There was something that was just not fitting into the larger picture. There were only questions. He needed more answers. He hoped the Sparrow would provide them all.

Ruby spoke out her own thoughts softly. 'It has to be that Prashant,' she whispered close to him.' The missing knife and the two hearts clearly point to him. His father is too old to have committed those murders. I am sure the prints on the knife will also be his.'

Hawa Singh was quiet. He had never heard of mafia men killing for the sheer pleasure of it—they always had a motive to kill. But then Prashant Singh was a deranged man. He would fit in nicely at the Sparrow facility. All locked up. He had a reason to attack Hawa Singh. He was out there and could very well be the killer.

Hawa Singh knew society would never be free of its lunatic fringe. There would always be crazy people out there—till such time as they could contain their madness no longer, and spilled out like blood in the streets.

He was lost in his thoughts when the woman came out of the room and addressed them. 'Madam has asked for you to come in.'

They walked into the room. It was a simple office with the shelves of one wall filled with medical books. There was a file cabinet with many drawers. There was no air-conditioner or heater. It felt cold. A printer worked tirelessly, throwing out black-and-white prints.

Sudha Krishnamurthy sat behind a wooden desk peering into an old PC. She looked up at them and said, 'So sorry to keep you waiting.'

She had a gentle smile. She looked about fifty and her hair was greying. She was wearing a silk saree. He noticed that her voice was soft and husky. She wore an old cardigan with a shawl wrapped around her. There was not much jewellery, just the plain diamond earrings worn by many south Indian women.

The way she blinked her eyes, the smile and her slightly bent posture all reminded him of Kavita's mother. Her parents blamed him for Kavita's death and had left Delhi to settle down in Chennai. They had neither met nor spoken since.

Hawa Singh did the introductions. He told Sudha Krishnamurthy all about the murder of Eva and the subsequent foreigner who was killed. He was trying to establish to himself that that would be the way to extract more information about Sparrow, and whether Eva had wanted to contact the brother of the Kashi Naresh, who was admitted there.

'You must be referring to Manvendra Singh,' said Sudha in her husky voice. 'He is a very interesting case. A genius gone wrong. A human being turned into a cannibal.'

'What really is the problem with him?' asked Ruby.

Sudha smiled. 'In here we work with the tools of psychotherapy and psychoanalysis. Manvendra Singh's is a case of schizophrenia. He started with experiencing hallucinations, delusions, and disorganized thinking and speech. He left the fort and started living with the Aghoris where he tasted human flesh. Research has shown that cannibalism causes euphoria, once the person turns their fantasy into reality. When cannibals finally act on their fantasies and hunt down a victim, the feeling they get from eating flesh releases dopamine in the brain. That gives them a high, which they want to feel again. The cannibal's mind then becomes conditioned to seeking out more and more human flesh to eat, and they also begin to thrive on the process of hunting down a victim.'

'So did he attack any living person?' asked Hawa Singh.

Sudha nodded with a sigh. 'Many times. It was in fact his own brother, Abhay, who brought him here for a cure. Manvendra had at many times attacked the guards at the fort and bitten off their ears or noses. In one instance, he bit off a large chunk of flesh from a tourist's face. Abhay attempted to control him, but one day Manvendra turned on him, too, and bit off his finger. Finally, he had to be admitted here.'

Ruby shook her head. 'It's crazy and unbelievable.'

'You'll have to see him to believe it,' spoke Sudha.

'What do you mean?' asked Hawa Singh.

Sudha replied grimly. 'He even tried to eat himself.'

Hawa Singh took in a startled gasp of air and then slowly exhaled. 'Do you think,' he continued with his questions, 'that these people might prefer to eat specific body parts? Like the heart?'

'Well, it is believed that by eating someone's heart, you add that person's life to your own longevity. There are certain sects that believe that if you sacrifice eleven human beings and eat their hearts, it will make you immortal.'

'Eleven,' repeated Ruby in a daze, her eyes wide.

Hawa Singh had never entertained the possibility that he would encounter cannibals in Benares.

Sudha broke the silence. 'I would like to help you as much as I can. It would be better that you meet him yourself.'

The very thought of seeing a living cannibal, who might at any moment attack her, frightened Ruby. Hawa Singh looked at her and nodded reassuringly.

Sudha pressed the buzzer on her desk and another doctor hurried in.

'This is Doctor Binod Pradhan,' she said. 'He is one of the senior psychologists here. He'll take you to the patient,' she smiled at Binod. In a very soft but authoritative tone, she added, 'Binod, this gentleman and lady are here to meet Manvendra Singh. They're from the police. Please assist them.'

A bead of sweat trickled down Binod Pradhan's forehead. He stared at Sudha and then at Ruby and Hawa Singh, saying, 'Have you told them about him?'

'Yes, I have. They are working on a case. Don't keep them waiting.'

Doctor Binod Pradhan nodded resignedly. 'Please come with me.'

He led them through the corridor into a narrow pathway with rooms on both sides. The white painted doors looked heavy. They could hear some soft voices coming from inside. There was someone singing a classical raag.

Binod smiled for the first time, wryly. 'We mostly get cases of talented individuals who have lost their minds. We have musicians, singers, dancers, writers, painters—even mathematicians and doctors.'

He laughed a little loudly. When the laughter echoed against the walls, he quickly suppressed it.

There were a few burly men around, dressed in whites. Binod led Hawa Singh and Ruby to a door.

'We have reached his room,' he told them. Let me warn you right now, please do not try to go near him or touch him. He might attack you. Or he might be very gentle and nice to you. Those are all tricks played by such minds to lull victims into a false sense of security. The craving is still there. The flesh is stronger than the spirit. The craving of the flesh turns them into monsters—and sometimes into most loving creatures.'

Hawa Singh and Ruby nodded at his warning.

'Welcome to hell,' said Binod, and opened the door.

A human figure sat inside, his face to the wall. Long hair fell to his sides. The white walls were covered by many hand-drawn diagrams he was presently adding to. There were planets, stars, what looked like a kind of solar system, and many charts of horoscopes.

'Manvendra,' Binod tried to distract him from his ceaseless drawing, 'look, you have guests. Won't you say hello to them?'

The man didn't react and continued to draw on the wall.

'Manvendra Singh,' Binod mused, 'brother to the Kashi Naresh and the greatest exponent of astrology and Vedic mathematics, now locked up in here plays with a mind that played with him. Life is cruel.'

'Life is pure bliss, Binod. Life is a blessing,' Manvendra suddenly broke in.

It was like a snake hissing and talking at the same time. A voice that hunted and killed for prey.

'You can add more meaning to your life with simple acts,' said Manvendra, finally turning around to face the rest.

Ruby gave out a shriek and clung to Hawa Singh, hiding her face in his shoulder.

'Ah, lady,' Manvendra said, observing her reaction. 'Life has many faces, and each face has many facets. You will have to learn to look at each of them. Each of them hides a different story. A story of its own.'

'By the way, you are very beautiful. I like your earlobes. They look so pink and soft and they stand out from your face. If you permit, may I feel them.'

Hawa Singh marvelled at the man's grotesque appearance. There were long, deep cuts from his left eye down to his chin. Another tore through the nose and the cheek. One of the earlobes looked like it had been chewed away. The skin had folded up around it. The upper lip was torn, showing off his sharp, almost pointed canines. A large chunk of flesh close to the jawbone was missing, only a thin layer of tissue covering the bone.

Ruby held on to Hawa Singh tightly.

'It seems I have frightened the lady. Don't worry, I won't really scare you. Why don't you give *me* a hug?'

Hawa Singh gently nudged Ruby behind him, blocking the mad man's view. He directly addressed the spectacle before him. 'Did you know Eva Marie Cassidy, a US citizen who worked at the Vatican?' he barked. 'Did she ever meet with you?'

'Eva, Eva, Eva... another beautiful lady. I would have loved to bite into those luscious cheeks. I heard that someone wanted to meet me—many do. But then they all run away.'

Manvendra shook his head remonstratively at Hawa Singh. 'You don't seem to be one of those. What happened to your head? You seem to be just like me. The entire body feels useless once this powerhouse fails,' he said, tapping his temple. 'One short circuit here leads to failure. You've got the mark of a genius on your head.'

Binod snapped sternly, 'It's useless talking to him. You won't get anything out of him. He just rambles and makes up stories.'

There was a loud hissing sound and Manvendra attacked Binod with lightning speed. He stopped right behind a red line drawn across the room, and emitted a cry.

Hawa Singh noticed the chain tied to Manvendra's feet that allowed him only that much mobility. If it was not for the chain, he would have torn off Binod's face.

Manvendra growled like a hungry wolf spotting its prey. The inability to reach his intended victim added to his snarling rage.

Hawa Singh put his arm around Ruby and said, 'Let's go.'

Manvendra started to laugh, 'You won't be able to stop anything you are trying to stop. It lies in the heart. You have to tear it open and bring out the life.'

He continued to laugh maniacally.

Binod shut the door. The laughter muffled. It turned to sobs. Wails.

The cannibal cried his own heart out.

CHAPTER 18

The bazaars of Benares were actually at their colourful best in the evening. The tungsten bulbs hanging from red and blue coiled wires threw off a golden hue, touching the shining brassware, silk sarees, bangles and brightly coloured fabrics on offer with magic.

The two walked from the Town Hall, through a market, past the Goshala, a charitable sanctuary for stray cows. From there, they took a cycle-rickshaw, rode through the main market of the city to reach the Chowk.

From the Chowk, they walked again through yet another market, this one devoted to articles required at showy weddings, the Kachori Galli and into Khoa Galli, the lane that sells milk products—flavoured yoghurt, paneer and condensed, sweetened milk. They were silent throughout. Each was trying to sort out the many questions that assailed them with a million 'Whos?', 'Whys?' and 'Hows?

Night was returning to the city. So was the fog. But the sky was still clear. Hawa Singh and Ruby hoped to see the stars after so many fogged-out days.

They moved into a lane with shops selling gleaming brassware. They heard sounds of metal being beaten and shaped into Hindu icons, figurines, decorative flying swans and lamps. Finer and more complex sounds emerged from the knots of craftsmen as they painstakingly engraved metaware—to sell them off as antiques to the many gormless foreign tourists who knew no better.

The narrow lane had a warm and sharp smell of molten brass, fire and coal. Hawa Singh stopped at an old wooden door painted patchily in blue. Where the paint had peeled away, there was half-eroded wood. A heavy iron latch chain hung on it. Hawa Singh held the chain and rapped on the door.

There was the sound of heavy footsteps approaching the door. A small crack appeared as it opened slightly and an eye examined them through it. Then the door was flung open and Gaya Prasad Sharma, sub-inspector, cut them a smart salute. He led them to a small dingy room, filled with more junk than brassware. An oil lamp stood on a rickety wooden table, casting long shadows across the dusty floor.

He had called Hawa Singh to this place to interrogate a man who was caught selling a passport. The passport had the picture of the white man who was found murdered inside Kashi Vishwanath Temple.

Gaya handed the passport to Hawa Singh. It read: 'Name: Brian Johnson. Age: 39 years. Nationality: British. Occupation: Archaeologist'. It provided an address in London.

'Sir,' began Gaya Prasad, 'I have already spoken to the British High Commission and they have confirmed his identity. He worked as an archaeologist with Allen Archaeology, a firm based in London. Brian came to

India two weeks back. He landed in New Delhi and from there travelled to Jaipur and Jodhpur before coming to Benares.'

Hawa Singh snapped out directions to Ruby. 'Contact this London firm and get all the information we need about this Brian Johnson.'

He turned to look at the man crouching in the corner. His hands were tied with a rope. He was of medium height, dark-skinned, frail, with thinning hair. The hands looked rough, even from a distance; the hands of a manual labourer. The feet were dirty, the heels cracked and the toenails broken. Clearly, he was a foot soldier. The clothes were of cheap, shabby material. There was no wrist-watch. He was wearing torn rubber slippers with visibly worn-out soles. Definitely a poor man. One compelled to resort to desperate measures just to eat.

'I have tried everything but he is not willing to reveal any information,' said Gaya Prasad.

Hawa Singh bent closer to the man and looked him in the eye. 'We don't have enough time to play quiz rounds with you. If you tell us everything, I'll let you go. Otherwise, it will be your body next floating in the Ganges.'

'I have not done anything. I found this passport, on the roadside,' the wretch whimpered.

Hawa Singh was about to slap him hard when Ruby stopped him. The expert FBI interrogator wanted to try out her special set of skills. She began, in a sweet and calm tone, 'Look, we are here to help you. For that you'll have to help us.' Gaya translated it for him.

He cried out again, 'Madam, I don't know anything. I'm telling the truth. I found it on the roadside.'

Hawa Singh and Gaya Prasad looked at each other in perplexion.

Ruby bent closer to him to study his body language. She could see that the man was terrified. His mind was racing to find concocted stories to save his skin.

She had read somewhere that Buddha described the mind as being filled with drunken monkeys who jumped, screeched, and chatted endlessly. Fear, according to Buddha, was an especially loud monkey. Buddha taught meditation as a way to tame the 'drunken monkeys' in the mind. This man was one crazed monkey.

Ruby handed him a bottle of mineral water. 'Drink this. You'll feel better.' He gulped down the water thirstily, but did not shift his gaze from her.

'Now tell me. Did you know this man?'

He spurted out the water from his mouth onto Ruby's face, shouting, 'Bloody bitch, get away from me! I don't want to answer any questions.'

Hawa Singh administered a sharp kick to the man's ribs. He cried out in pain. 'I know the right way to handle him,' Hawa Singh said.

Hawa Singh looked around the room and saw a rusted half-broken steel blade on a shelf. He picked it up and looked at its sharp edge. He sat on his haunches, looking at the man as he played with the blade in his hands. 'Do you see this?'

The man nodded nervously.

Hawa Singh put the blade right against his jugular. 'It'll take just one cut here to drain out all the blood in your body.' Hawa Singh moved his hand slightly, and a fine cut emerged on the throat. It bled immediately.

'Sirji, please, I don't want to die. Don't do this to me,' the man begged.

'Okay, first tell me your name,' asked Hawa Singh.

'Kanhaiya, sirji.'

Hawa Singh smiled and looked around at Ruby and Gaya. 'That's a nice name, isn't it? But our Kanhaiya is not looking like our laughing Love God, so I'm going to make him smile. Let's widen his mouth.'

Hawa Singh caught at the hair of the half-kneeling man, jerking his head back and putting the edge of the blade to his cheek. 'Can you feel it, Kanhaiya? How about having a permanently broad smile?'

Kanhaiya peed in his pants. Ruby backed away, holding her nose as the trail of urine meandered towards her.

'So, first, you spat water at her face and now you have spoilt madam's shoes. I told you I don't have enough time. So tell me, truly, how did you get the passport?' Hawa Singh increased the pressure of the blade. A thin trail of blood emerged.

'Sirji, I'm just a travel guide and take tourists around the place. I met Brian saab when he came to Benares and took him on a tour,' Kanhaiya babbled in terror.

Hawa Singh stood up with a sigh. This was a side of Hawa Singh that Ruby had not seen before. She tried to take control of the situation.

'Which places did you take Brian saab to?' asked Ruby.

Kanhaiya looked dumbfounded, and Gaya repeated the question in Hindi. 'I'm telling you the truth,' protested the man, in tears. 'I didn't kill him. I had nothing to do with it.'

'Who killed him?' asked Hawa Singh.

'I have no idea, sirji. I met him at the Benares airport and we started on the tour from there. He was more interested in historical sites. So I took him straight to Bodhgaya.'

Gaya Prasad glanced ironically at Hawa Singh and asked, 'You took him out of Benares the very day he landed here?'

'Yes, sir, I'm telling the truth. I swear by Mother Ganges. We took a taxi and went directly to see the Bodhi temple.'

'Sir, that is a 2,500-year-old temple in Gaya,' Gaya Prasad broke in helpfully. 'It's where Gautam Buddha found enlightenment under the sacred tree, which is there in the same temple complex.'

'Brian saab clicked many pictures at the temple,' Kanhaiya seemed to be eager to reveal all now, in a rush, to make up for his earlier reticence, and fearing sustained torture. 'We stayed there at a guesthouse. The next morning I took him to Nalanda. He seemed to be more interested in the ways our ancestors studied stars and the planets.'

Ruby voiced her thoughts out loud. 'That's another connection to astronomy,' she said.

'What did you do in Nalanda?' asked Hawa Singh.

'Sirji, I told him whatever I had mugged up as a tourist. He wanted to go deeper into the ruins and study them closely.'

'What did you tell him?'

'That Nalanda was one of the world's first residential universities from the fifth century AD to 1197 AD,' Kanhaiya rattled off obligingly. In its heyday, it accommodated over 10,000 students and 2,000 teachers. The university was considered an architectural masterpiece, and was marked by a lofty wall and a magnificent gate. Nalanda had eight separate compounds and ten temples, along with many other meditation halls and classrooms. On the grounds were lakes and parks. The library was located in a nine-storeyed building where copies of texts were meticulously reproduced. The subjects taught at Nalanda University covered every field of learning, and it attracted pupils and scholars from Korea, Japan, China, Tibet, Indonesia, Persia and Turkey.'

Kanhaiya took in a deep breath and continued, 'The library of Nalanda, also known as Dharma Gunj (Mountain of Truth) was the most renowned repository of Hindu and Buddhist knowledge in the world at the time. Its collection was said to comprise hundreds of thousands of volumes, so extensive that it burned for approximately more than three months when set aflame by Turkish invaders. And almost 90 per cent of Nalanda still remains unexcavated.'

Hawa Singh smiled with satisfaction at Ruby. *Now,* the man was talking. Ruby knew that when the mind recalls a memory, it's not the original memory. In fact, the act of remembering is an act of creative re-imagination. The put-together memory doesn't just have a few holes; it also has some entirely new bits pasted in.

She looked closely at Kanhaiya and knew the man was not lying any more. He was not in a position to. The blade had done the trick.

'So how long did you stay in Nalanda?' asked Ruby.

Gaya translated for Kanhaiya's benefit.

'We were there for the next three days, going up and down from Bodh Gaya. Brian wanted to get permission from the government officials to excavate the remaining site of Nalanda. He told them that his firm in London specialized in this kind of work. He was looking for a contract from the state government. He was refused.'

'When did you return to Benares?' asked Hawa Singh.

'Sirji, we came back on 20 January. Brian had heard about the murder of the foreign woman and was afraid for his own life. He didn't want to stay in a lodge or guesthouse. We had become good friends, so I invited him to stay with me in my room.'

'Brian was staying with you?' asked Ruby, surprised.

'Yes,' said Kanhaiya, shortly. 'I took him all around Benares. He checked out temples and many ghats. He loved the markets. He seemed to be working on some project that he didn't share with me. It was totally secret.'

'And after what happened, you didn't say a word of this to the police?' said Hawa Singh.

'I was scared that the police would arrest me for killing him. I swear by Mother Ganges and Vishnuji. I didn't do it.'

'What about Brian's luggage and clothes? Have you sold them too?' asked Hawa Singh.

'Sir, I have everything confiscated, and have gone through each item,' the sub-inspector reassured him. There are clothes, a camera, a few travel books, tickets, and a diary in which he wrote about his travel experiences. You can go through them all,' said Gaya Prasad.

Hawa Singh nodded thoughtfully and then asked, 'By the way, did you manage to get prints from the knife?'

'We got a set of prints and they don't match with any in our records.'

'One thing is clear,' interposed Ruby. 'That the killer has no past criminal records. He could be anyone here—a milkman, a guard at the king's Fort, a policeman, a government official, postman or a delivery boy. The probabilities are infinite.'

Kanhaiya, still crouching in the corner, whimpered, 'Sirji, please can I go now?'

'First, I want to ask you something,' replied Hawa Singh. 'Since you are a local guide, you must know everything about Benares. Do you know of a tunnel that runs under the Ganges right up to Ramnagar Fort?'

'I can guarantee you, saab, there is no such tunnel. There's nothing in this Benares that can escape the eyes of Kanhaiya.'

Hawa Singh nodded, looking meaningfully at Ruby and Gaya Prasad. 'Okay, I'll let you go. From now on you will be working for the police. You will not leave Benares till I allow you to. And you'll do exactly what I tell you to do.'

Kanhaiya nervously nodded.

'I need to know the names of each and every person whom Brian met in Benares. And I want it all quickly.'

Kanhaiya nodded, his eyes filled with fear.

'Now get up and leave.'

Kanhaiya slowly got up. He stepped on his own puddle of urine. He cursed and walked out with a hand on his cheek. He could still feel the sharp metal. The image of the zig-zag cut on the head of his interrogator danced inside his head. The steely eyes had meant each and every word.

Kanhaiya fled without another word.

Ruby was flipping through Brian's passport. She saw the visa stamp of India. She turned back to a page earlier and scrutinized the stamp on it as well. It was of the Vatican City.

Ruby showed Hawa Singh the passport entry, adding, a little unnecessarily, 'Look at this. Brian Johnson came to India from the Vatican City.'

The Vatican. Benares. The two Holy Cities, thought Hawa Singh. What could be the real connection?

Darkness now galloped in from all sides to conquer this one.

Hawa Singh looked at his watch.

It was 7.40 pm, 28 January.

CHAPTER 19

In the street illuminated by lights from many shops, he could see the pair of heavily shod feet walking ahead on the fractured broken road. The soles of the shoes were encrusted by mud and were close to worn out. The leather on the upper soles was intact, however, and looked good. He would have loved to skin the owner—as the leather must once have been.

He didn't concentrate on the female walking close to the man he was following with his telescopic sight. He focused, instead, on the long and obviously muscular legs of her companion. He could size up, from afar, the strong calves, flexible knee joints and the powerful thighs. A crooked smile appeared on his lips.

He watched intently—he couldn't afford to lose him. He moved his sights up and saw, again, the broadness of the policeman's back. The leather jacket. The man loved leather. Skin. The watcher had sliced through that second skin into the man's own, once. Oh, the thrill and lingering excitement of that experience!

He now directed his vision to the nape of the man's neck. That was a good spot—but not a great one, when you needed to kill with one shot. He moved the cross-hairs upwards to Hawa Singh's head. Ah. *Perfect!*

He was holding a SVD, a Snaiperskaya Vintovka Dragunova, a rifle popular with snipers. It had been designed in 1958 by the Soviet Union for sudden and secret assassinations. Only a few of the assassins remained in the Russia after the USSR had broken up and divided into many countries. The rifle used 7.62x54R ammunition and was equipped with a ten-round magazine. He had had the latest Russian telescopic sight fixed to the weapon to make it even more accurate in its aim and surer in its power to kill.

He had a great love for all things Russian. He believed their products possessed a solidity others lacked. He thought of all those Russian trucks, tanks, jeeps, guns, binoculars, telescopes, their knives, their jackets, boots, caps and all. Everything looked so effective. Filled with life. And promising death.

He could see Hawa Singh walking away into the fading light. Still, he told himself, he was sure he could easily hit his aim from this distance. Back in the USSR, snipers were chosen from personnel who did well in terms of rifle marksmanship. Those special ones were estimated to have a 50-per-cent probability of hitting a man-sized target at a distance of 800 metres, 80 per cent at a distance of 500 metres and 90 per cent at a distance of 200 metres.

He knew he was one of those skilled ones.

His index finger curled tighter around the trigger, even though his knuckles were going tense and white in the cold. There was a slight wind, but that didn't blow away the fog. Wait, his target may soon be lost in it—there was so little remaining light! The would-be assassin was perched on the rooftop of a building and could see him up to a distance of more than 300 metres. Which, he calculated backward, still meant a more-or-less 90-per-cent sure shot. He still had the cross-hairs fixed on the head.

One soft squeeze on the trigger would blow it into smithereens. The target suddenly, and unaccountably, stopped. He was, unbelievably, turning around.

What happened? Has he sensed me? he thought.

Hawa Singh looked directly up towards the rooftop. To the man with the telescopic sights, it was like he was looking right into the watcher's eyes.

The finger on the trigger jammed. He gritted his teeth in frustration.

He watched him turning away again, back in the old direction. Now was the time. He looked even more carefully through the telescopic sight.

Hawa Singh had disappeared into the rolling fog.

He lowered the rifle and smiled. *These guns are for my collection alone,* he consoled himself. *I wouldn't have killed you with this. It would have happened too easily. Too quickly.*

The Butcher watched the fog settling over the tree tops, surrounding the electric poles, round the street dogs, sadhus and beggars. It took various shapes. It circled the little boy shivering on the roadside and curled around a stray cat for warmth.

He heard the sharp shriek of an eagle high up in the sky, and looked up. The eagle was hardly visible. At this distance the Russians would have accepted a reduction to a 40-per-cent probability of hitting such a target. He looked through his telescopic sight. The finger caressed the trigger.

Squeeze it, he urged himself.

For someone as special as him, surely it would be 100 per cent?

They should have given me a different name, thought the Butcher.

The 'Artist of Benares', perhaps?

CHAPTER 20

Hawa Singh glanced up at the wall clock. It read 10.30 pm. They had been waiting for more than one hour, fortifying themselves on masala tea at the lounge of Ramnagar Fort. Ruby was tense, as her immediate boss at the FBI had asked for a detailed report and her progress in the case. She knew she had not made much.

She paced up and down the room in her thigh-length winter boots. Outside, it was icy-cold. The dark water of the Ganges appeared frozen in the moonlight. The Fort itself, uphill, looked eerie, like a haunted castle in a film. There was no sign—yet—of the Kashi Naresh, Abhay Narayan Singh.

Ruby looked at the walls, hung with countless antique guns and weapons. There was something perverse about accumulating so many pieces of death and destruction, it seemed to her. Why would their ancestral collectors find any glory in killing or maiming?

Hawa Singh sat quietly, sipping on his tea. It was his fifth cup. With every sip, he knew his personal clock was ticking.

It was not till fifteen minutes later that he and Ruby were escorted by two armed guards into an area that looked like a workshop. Amazed, they saw there, nothing but clocks. The walls held big, small, hand-painted, wooden, metal and every other kind of timepiece conceivable. Many had pendulums swinging. There were clocks on tables and clocks hanging by hooks from the ceiling that measured from four to seven feet in height. The sound of their combined ticking was the only thing that could be heard in that ghostly silence.

Ruby and Hawa felt suspended in time. They'd thought they were short of time, but here it seemed to be in abundance.

'Oh, I'm so sorry to keep you waiting!' said Abhay, as he emerged from behind the curtain of clocks.

They shook hands. Hawa Singh noticed that the Kashi Naresh still wore gloves, and that his entire body remained covered, aside from his face. 'Welcome. Although, I was working on some very intricate parts of a new clock and didn't want to be disturbed,' he said suavely.

They walked to the operational area of this time warp. A large clock, with exposed parts, was hanging from a hook attached to the ceiling. It looked like a body cut open for surgery.

Abhay was enjoying their look of wonder. 'You must be curious about all these clocks,' he smiled. 'This is my passion. I make clocks. Most of these are handmade. I learnt the art of clock-manufacturing from our royal clockmaker, who designed the astrological clock you saw in Saraswati Bhawan.'

'Well, there were some questions,' said Hawa Singh, 'so I thought I'd meet you here personally.'

Abhay raised a finger. 'Just a minute. I need to adjust something.' He picked up a tiny instrument and slowly tightened a screw. Then he stood back and looked at the clock before him with almost paternal pride. 'This is my masterpiece. This is going to become known as the best astrological and astronomical clock in our country.'

Hawa Singh and Ruby tensed at something he'd said, but he continued implacably. 'I have designed it after the Prague Astronomical Clock, in the capital of the Czech Republic. That had been installed in 1410, making it the third-oldest astronomical clock in the world. I offered to buy it but the Czech authorities refused. So I decided to make one myself.' He paused to stroke the clock face. 'Look at this. Just like the one in Prague, this one is also composed of three main components: the astronomical dial, representing the positions of the Sun and Moon in the sky and displaying various astronomical details. The calendar dial, the one with the medallions, represents the months, and the many sculptures show the time. The background to the astronomical dial represents the standing Earth and sky, and around those are the four main moving components: the zodiacal ring, an outer rotating ring, an icon representing the Sun, and an icon representing the Moon.'

Abhay paused to smile proudly again, and then went on. 'The blue circle directly in the centre represents the Earth and the upper blue is the portion of the sky which is above the horizon. The golden Roman numbers at the outer edge of the blue circle are the timescale of a normal twenty-four-hour day and indicate time. Isn't it wonderful?' Abhay said excitedly.

'That's really fantastic. But we were wondering, can we talk now?' Ruby cut him off.

'So you were not impressed,' laughed Abhay. 'Okay, shoot.'

'Last time we met,' said Hawa Singh, relieved to be able to speak his mind at last, 'you didn't tell us about your brother'.

'Well, you never asked.'

'I did mention the Sparrow but you refused to acknowledge it,' said Hawa Singh a little sharply.

Abhay sighed heavily. 'The royal family has broken all ties with Manvendra. He has turned worse than an animal.'

Ruby tried to gauge the extent of his fear. 'Did he ever attack you?' she asked, her head to one side.

Abhay stared back at her, long and hard. 'He chewed off my finger,' he said finally.

'It's hard to believe that a man would do that to another man,' said Ruby.

'Could we see that hand, please?' Hawa Singh asked.

Abhay was quiet. His eyes twitched. There was a hint of nervousness that he tried to hide. He turned away, looking at the clock. Hawa Singh and Ruby stood there waiting.

Abhay brushed imaginary dust off the clock. Then he turned back to them. Quietly, he removed his glove.

His entire hand was covered by scabs, where the skin had folded thickly. One of the fingers was missing. It was a horrible sight.

'You can see for yourself. The other hand also has a curse on it,' said Abhay, removing the glove off it. It, too, was covered with scabs and ghastly boils.

'Curse?' asked Hawa Singh.

'I was cursed with this disease. I went from the US to the best doctors in Europe. They told me I had a rare skin disease that cannot be treated. In fact they don't even have a name for it. It has started to spread all over my body.'

Hawa Singh and Ruby were quiet. Ruby felt the bile rise in her throat, and longed to spit it out.

Abhay put on his gloves again saying, 'Imagine, I can't touch anything, without my gloves on. Even in the dark, women can feel my diseased skin, and don't want to touch it. Even prostitutes have refused to come to the Fort. And day after day, I have to look at people with normal, healthy skin. It fills me with hatred.'

They were all silent. The sound of ticking filled the space between them. 'I'm a creator,' said Abhay, with a sudden revival of his earlier mood. 'I create time. Isn't this clock a marvel? I am working on it so it will also calculate the exact time of the day from sunrise and sunset. I have used the calculations of Vedic mathematics.'

'It shows your genius,'observed Ruby.

Abhay looked at her and smiled bitterly. 'Really? But still you won't sleep with me.'

Then he laughed out loud. 'I am just whiling away my time on all this. The simplest of pleasures have been taken away from me. Some holy men have told me that it is all karma catching up with me. I have to pay the debt for whatever I did in my previous lives. *Pay off the debt.* My foot!' cried out Abhay.

His eyes filled suddenly with tears, and he turned around to hide them. The kings of Benares never cried.

Ruby took a deep breath. 'Did this man ever come to meet you?' she asked, showing Abhay the picture of Brian Johnson displayed on her touch screen phone. The tiny gadget was a sophisticated one. Hawa Singh had once tried to use it but his thick fingers kept pressing all the wrong keys and slipping away.

'Why do you show me pictures of a white person? Man or woman, they do something to me. To my skin,' said Abhay.

Hawa Singh cleared his throat and spoke in his heavy baritone.'This is Brian Johnson, who was killed inside the Kashi Vishwanath temple.'

'Brian...' Abhay tried to recall. 'I did hear about the second murder but never knew who he was.'

'We have found two of those killed were connected to the Vatican. We are still working on that,' said Ruby.

'Vatican, yes, now I remember. He did come to meet me.'

Ruby was all ears, her eyes wide at this discovery. 'He told me that he was some kind of archaeologist and wanted me to grant his firm a contract to excavate around the Fort area.'

'Why?' asked Hawa Singh.

'He said that they had studied some satellite pictures and done some research which revealed that there could be something major hidden under the Fort.'

'Like what?' Ruby asked.

'He seemed to be more interested in old manuscripts that would give an idea about the earlier inhabitants,' said Abhay Narayan Singh.

'Did he ever mention the *Bhrigu-Samhita*?' asked Hawa Singh.

The very mention of the word froze them all. Only the ticking broke the silence for a while.

'I see what you mean,' Abhay finally said slowly and thoughtfully. 'We did speak about archaeology, astronomy and astrology. He looked very interested in the ancient Vedic science of astrology but he never mentioned the name, "*Bhrigu-Samhita*".

'We have to explore this connection with the Vatican,' said Hawa Singh. 'These people seem to have unearthed some secret that the Vatican didn't want to come to light. It's the Vatican that had them killed in Benares.' He looked at the gigantic clock behind Ruby. It showed 12 am. Midnight.

It took a second to change it. 29 January was upon them.

CHAPTER 21

7 am. 29 January

The fog now looked like a cement wall around the SSP's office. The policemen standing on guard outside shivered, despite their winter uniforms and the heavy woollen mufflers around their heads and ears. Their teeth chattered and it was hard to breathe. They had to fight to keep their eyes open. It had been more than thirty-six hours since any of them had last slept. All leave had been cancelled. All hands had to be on deck.

Their fingers were numb. It was unlikely they would find purchase on the triggers of the rifles were danger to suddenly appear. It was the perfect time for dark souls to emerge and lay siege.

Inside the SSP's office, fingers curled around mugs of hot tea. Only a few of the officers had had their quota of full eight hours' sleep. They were not used to working for such long hours. None of them seemed to have any pointers to the killer—apart from reciting a litany of his crimes.

Earlier, Hawa Singh had hardly closed his eyes for two hours. He had stretched out on the bed in Ruby's room, while she cleaned his wounds and put white medical tape in the form of crosses over the cuts on his chest and on his arm. Later, the faint tap-tapping of the keys on her laptop lulled him to sleep. He was dimly conscious of having held her hand as he lay exhausted, she beside him. Just doing that had eased his pain, within and without. These simple gestures of love and caring were somehow lost in the world outside their little room, with its demands of cold connectivity, craving and frustrated longing. Ruby brought him back in touch with his own humanity.

Then, as always, he woke up in the pre-drawn and accompanied Ruby back to their headquarters.

Now, he stood in the SSP's office, facing a giant map of Benares. The SSP, Ruby and some other senior officers watched as he pinned on it small triangular flags representing each ghat in the city, and saffron flags for all important temples. There were some hundred ghats in Benares and Ruby prepared a list of them alphabetically. Her meticulous work included the name of every ghat: from 'A' for Mata Anandamai, right down to 'V' for Vijayanagaram.

Two armed policemen were assigned to patrol each ghat. Their names had been written alongside. They were given strict orders to keep out all beggars, urchins, sadhus, pandits, vendors, boatmen, flower-sellers from the ghats, from night to the next morning. There was another instruction, 'No one will speak to the media.'

There were more than 23,000 temples in Benares. Given the paucity of personnel, Hawa Singh had chosen the ones that attracted the highest number of worshippers.

The one that grabbed his attention the most was the Sankat Mochan Hanuman, one of the most revered temples of the god, situated by the Assi river. It is believed that this site was where the medieval saint Tulsidas had a vision of Hanuman. Thousands flock to the temple on Tuesdays and Saturdays, the days associated with Hanuman.

This was the same temple that had suffered the brunt of a terrorist attack on 7 March 2006. In the attack, one of the three explosions had hit the temple while the evening *aarti* ceremony was in progress, and many devotees were injured.

Two other temples were also earmarked by Hawa Singh—Durga Mandir, built about 500 years ago, and Durga Kund, built in the eighteenth century. The latter was built in the Nagara architectural style, characterized by its colour—the ochre-red sacred to the goddess—and its multi-tiered spires. There is a rectangular pond there, where, on the annual celebrations of Naag Panchami, the god Vishnu is depicted reclining on his serpent Shesha Naag. It was the presence of the pond that alerted Hawa Singh. The last victim had been found inside a temple where a well permitted the killer to escape right across the Ganges via a tunnel below. Couldn't the pond be hiding similar underground secrets that would provide a waterway route to the expected assassin?

And then there were the temples dedicated to Annapurna, the goddess of food, located close to the Kashi Vishwanath, and the Sankatha, close to Sindhia Ghat, dedicated to the goddess of remedy. The last had a large sculpture of a lion, and a cluster of nine smaller structures, shrines of the nine planets.

The last two to catch Hawa Singh's eye was the ancient Kalabhairav, near the Head Post Office at Visheshar Ganj, dedicated to the *kotwal*, or guardian, of Benares, and the Shiva temple, Mrithyunjay Mahadev, which also had a well believed to be fed by several underground streams, and having curative powers.

'We have to concentrate on all these sites and round up all the suspects,' Hawa Singh told his men. 'The fog could be the killer's biggest ally, but we have to beat it, to beat him.'

'I can't let this go wrong. The image of the entire police force is at stake.' The SSP felt it was his turn to address the assembled policemen.

Hawa Singh responded dryly, 'I don't work to protect the image of the police. I work to prevent crime and apprehend those who commit it.' The SSP opened his mouth to say something, but then closed it with some effort and turned away.

'What did you find out about the second victim?' asked Neeraj Thakur.

Ruby looked questioningly at Hawa Singh, and he nodded his permission. She was free to share the details. 'We know his name—Brian Johnson, a British citizen,' she began. 'He was an archaeologist with a London firm. His last assignment, before he came to India, was at the Vatican.'

'Sir, this Vatican is up to something. Both victims had a connection to it,' ACP Shishir Jha put in.

'I have checked with the Vatican but they don't seem to be responding,' Ruby went further. In the case of Brian, I have found that he was sent by his firm, Allen Archaeology, to work on a secret excavation inside the Vatican City. Brian was working along with Israeli archaeologists in a mission to prove the authenticity of biblical place names. The Israeli archaeologists have recovered a seal containing the oldest mention of Bethlehem ever found. It dates back 2,700 years. The Bible mentions Bethlehem, and so this finding is proof that the city did indeed exist at the time. The seal, 1.5 cm long, was found in the City of David, a huge archaeological site just outside the walls of Jerusalem, where it is believed King David built his palace. The Vatican subsequently invited the archaeologists to conduct secret excavations in the Vatican City too. It is not known exactly where they were working in the Vatican, as that had been kept secret. However, Brian, who was researching with the team, seemed to have developed a deep interest in Vedic astrology as well. He came to Benares and met with Abhay Narayan Singh.'

Silence fell like a curtain in the SSP's office—they could hardly hear one another breathe. Hawa Singh was the first to break it. 'There is something about the Kashi Naresh that connects him to the killer. Both the victims had met him. He has a vast storehouse of antiques and ancient manuscripts that the victims were probably interested in delving into,' he said.

'Are you suspecting him to be the killer?' the SSP asked Hawa Singh.

'Yes, I am. He is on top of my list,' said Hawa Singh.

Sub-inspector Gaya Prasad Sharma, who had hitherto hardly spoken a word, spoke up. 'Sir,' he interposed, 'I have checked the prints found on the knife. They are not in any records. I even sent them to the National Crime Records Bureau but there, too, they couldn't find a match.'

Hawa Singh nodded thoughtfully and said, 'What about the thumbprint that was found on the axe that killed Tailanga Swami?'

'We managed to get the prints of Baba Ramtirath, the Naga leader, and Neelambar Nath, the new Aghori Swami, but none of them match to the print found on the axe.'

Hawa Singh scratched at his heavy stubble. 'Do one more thing,' he said. 'Match the print on the axe and the one on the knife.' When he caught the look of shock on Ruby's face, he went on to explain, in his usual terse way, 'The probabilities are infinite. I'm just trying to narrow them down,' said Hawa Singh.

CHAPTER 22

The qualities essential to a policeman are a systematic mind, logical thought process, and a good memory for details. But above all, he has to be a dogged individual, never one to give up.

Hawa Singh had not become a policeman to catch young lovers romancing in parks, to guard corrupt politicians or to rain blows on protesting innocent masses. He didn't carry the bullet in his head for nothing. He was there to get the true criminals, the ones who committed violent crimes and threatened the very fabric of society.

The Butcher of Benares had to be stopped in his tracks.

He walked into Mukti Bhawan and saw his father, Fauja Singh, sitting unclothed in his room, smeared with ashes. He was staring at the wall and chanting 'Om Namo Narayana'.

Hawa Singh rushed to him. 'Do you want to die naked?' he shouted into his father's ear.

Fauja Singh turned to look at him with a smile. 'It's not my time yet.' He resumed staring at the wall and continued with the chanting.

Hawa Singh had heard that Benares does lots of crazy things to people. Many foreigners had given up their bright careers to settle down on the banks of the Ganges as sadhus, some of them with the Naga sadhus and the Aghoris. There were those who had given away their vast fortunes in charity in search of God.

In their search for moksha, they had lost their Ferraris, their big homes and their yachts. They'd left behind loving families and lovers. They'd discarded expensive clothes to become naked fakirs.

Hawa Singh knew Benares exercised a similar pull on his father. Fauja Singh had tried all the various alternative medicines available in the temple city, stopped to consult wayside astrologers on his future, even had predictions picked out by parrots, sacred bulls, tarot-card readers and the pandits on the banks of the river. He loved to be in the company of mystics. No doubt some charlatan had now advised him to strip himself of clothes, and turn to chanting.

Hawa Singh picked up the tattered blanket and put it around Fauja Singh. The man continued to chant and stare. Hawa Singh looked in the direction that his father was staring, and suddenly, the wall seemed to rush at him. He felt the bullet pricking at his brain. He saw a shape that he had seen earlier—a rectangle with its diagonals intersecting each other and the mid-points of each line connecting with the other. It was the shape of a horoscope.

It was drawn on the wall with charcoal, its thick black lines standing out. He peered at it more closely, and saw letters and numbers written inside it. He saw the number '3'. The bottom loop curved up and then came down to cross the arc. He had seen the same loop in another horoscope drawn on the body of Brian Johnson.

Fauja Singh looked up from his staring. 'A Naga sadhu came to me and drew that chart,' he said slowly. 'He told me that I still have many more years to live.'

Hawa Singh was increasingly certain the chart was drawn by the same hand that drew the chart on Brian's body. The Butcher. The killer had actually come right up to his father and left his stamp on the wall.

One thing was clear: the killer was watching his every move. He was there somewhere, close by. Someone who would trail him, attack him in the fog and look for the right moment to kill him.

He'd been racking his brains to ascertain who could be the next victim. Now, he felt he was that person. The killer seemed to be a step ahead of him all the time. Who was this killer and what did he want?

Fauja Singh was looking at him, bemused. 'Those doctors had told me that my heart would soon stop working. I came to Benares to get moksha—but what if I actually don't die?' he asked.

'Who was this man that came in and drew this chart?' asked Hawa Singh in turn.

'I have already told you he was a Naga sadhu. He was totally naked and smeared with ashes. He carried a long trishul. His hair was long and knotted.'

'Are you sure that he was a Naga? Aghoris have a similar appearance.'

'He looked like a Naga to me. The Aghoris only know tantra-mantra. It's the Nagas who understand the finer aspects of the Vedas and Vedic astrology. He gave me these ashes and told me to chant prayers.'

'You must have noticed something peculiar about him. His eyes, height, weight, any mark on body?' asked Hawa Singh.

Fauja Singh shook his head and wrapped the blanket tightly around him. Then, he said with a sigh, 'Well, he looked lean, of medium height, he spoke softly and there was something about his eyes.'

'Eyes, what do you mean?'

'The colour was different.'

'What colour?'

'I don't remember.'

'If you saw him again, would you recognize him?' asked Hawa Singh.

'Yes, I would.'

'Try and focus. Were his eyes blue?'

Fauja thought hard. 'Yes,' he said finally, 'they were blue'.

CHAPTER 23

The cold smile on his face was reflected in the coldness of his deep blue eyes. Baba Ramtirath, the leader of the Naga sadhus, and Shri Mahant of the World Council for Nagas, sat in front of Hawa Singh with the calmness of a psychopath. If looks could tell, he was the picture of a coldblooded killer.

With years of living with the Naga sadhus, he was fluent in Hindi and Sanskrit, and one of the greatest exponents in Benares of Vedic literature and astrology. He was associated with black magic and was believed to possess the power to kill anyone in any part of the world by sorcery alone.

There was a close-knit coterie of naked trishul-wielding giants who protected him and would kill for him. His body language was relaxed, despite the repeated threats the Aghoris had made to throw him and his people out of Benares.

Hawa Singh had come to him with his father, Ruby, Sub-Inspector Gaya Prasad and some armed personnel in tow. One doesn't take chances with Naga sadhus. You never knew when the naked sadhus of the Himalayas would rise up in anger. And they were always armed.

'Look at this man carefully,' Hawa Singh told his father. 'Was he the same person who came in and drew the chart on your wall?'

Baba Ramtirath sat there with a smile. Ruby felt nervous in the crowd of naked armed men. She couldn't distinguish one from the other—their faces and bodies were unrecognizable behind the ashes. She looked at Gaya Prasad and he nodded at her in assurance that all was under control.

Fauja Singh said apologetically, 'This one has a beard. The sadhu who came to Mukti Bhawan was clean-shaven. Nor did he wear glasses, like this one here.'

'You never told me that he was clean-shaven!' Hawa Singh protested.

'You never asked,' said his father, closing his eyes in concentration.

'It happens,' intervened Baba Ramtirath. 'When you look too hard, you don't see it. You have to loosen up and let the force guide you.'

Hawa Singh opened his eyes and looked at him.

'At times it is as simple as that—and as complicated,' continued Baba Ramtirath. 'You are now just like us, a sadhu, and a naked fakir, who has given up everything and dedicated his entire life for a purpose, for something. You are as transparent as our naked bodies, as truthful as the truth of Shiva.'

'And I'm just a bull-headed policeman, who believes in the best outcome,' retorted Hawa Singh.

'Har Har Mahadev,' smiled Baba Ramtirath.

Ruby glanced at the giants standing in a circle around their leader. She had a feeling that the men believed in, and would die for their leader. They were fearless warriors and yet the most peaceful sadhus. This was one more paradox to add to the many about Benares.

'Har Har Mahadev is not a war-cry,' Baba Ramtirath told those assembled around him. 'It's the essence of all Vedas and of Hinduism itself. It simply means that God, or Mahadev, lives in each one of us. We are a part of Him. We have come from Him and life is a journey back to Him.'

'Then why am I not getting moksha? Why is death not coming to me?' pleaded Fauja Singh.

Baba Ramtirath smiled his response. 'Nothing happens without God's will. You'll have to surrender to His will, and His will will be yours.'

Hawa Singh wondered, not for the first time, whether the man before him was a genuine sadhu or just another trickster. 'We need to take a look at all the Naga sadhus in turn,' he said aloud. 'I suspect that one of them could be the killer.'

'You are free to do as you please. Now that I have realized your father is just one of us.'

Hawa Singh took his father from one sadhu to the other, showing him their ash-covered faces. 'Closely examine the eyes. See if anyone of them was the man I'm looking for,' he instructed his father.

Fauja went around, and then gave up. 'I don't think it was anyone of them,' he told his son. 'They all look big and strong. He was of medium height and lanky-looking.'

'Why don't you check with the Aghoris,' suggested Baba Ramtirath. 'They look very much like us.'

Hawa Singh nodded.

'But there's one more thing,' stipulated the sadhu. 'I can't keep all these other sadhus waiting here. They all want to go to Allahabad for their bath in the Sangam, the confluence of the Ganga, Yamuna and Saraswati.'

'We can't let *you* leave, Baba Ramtirath,' said Ruby decisively.

'Don't worry, I'm not going anywhere,' the head of the sadhus assured her. 'My close circle of eleven disciples will remain with me, too, but the rest will leave.'

The mention of the number eleven caught Hawa Singh's ears. 'What's the significance of the number eleven?' he asked.

'It has a special place in Hinduism,' replied Baba Ramtirath. 'In systems such as astrology and basic numerology, eleven is considered to be a Master Number. Eleven can also represent sin, transgression and peril. Ten being the perfect number, eleven represents the exceeding of both. It is interesting to note that eleven, when broken down—one plus one is equal to two—comprises the two of duality. This Master Number is of the super-intellect or genius. Black and white are two colours of eleven, signifying truth, latent and active, hidden and revealed.'

Hawa Singh looked at him dourly. There were no blacks and whites for him. Everything seemed hidden. *His* job was to reveal. He called Gaya Prasad over. 'Make sure to get the fingerprints of all these sadhus before they leave Benares.'

'It will be done, sir,' the younger officer replied.

'Baba Ramtirath, along with his eleven disciples, will stay here. Keep a close watch on them,' further instructed Hawa Singh.

The calm blue eyes looked like sparkling marbles studded on a cold face.

*

Hawa Singh took his father to meet Neelambar Nath and the Aghoris. They made their rounds once more, but Fauja Singh was certain that none of the sadhus there remotely resembled the man who had visited him.

Hawa Singh told Gaya Prasad to get the fingerprints of all the Aghoris in Neelambar Nath's group. He didn't want to leave any stone unturned.

Later, he sat with Ruby in her room enumerating the possibilities. It helped them clear their minds and come up with newer ideas about their investigation. Ruby Malik, trained though she was in the interrogation techniques of the FBI, found herself at a loss trying to comprehend who was lying and who was not. At the FBI they used truth serums, polygraph tests, chemical gases and other innovative techniques to extract the truth. She realized that men like Baba Ramtirath had a certain degree of control over their minds, and none of those techniques would decipher the truth.

She had been taught that about half of all crime commited is under genetic control. Environmental factors such as parenting, poverty and discrimination account for the other half. In other words, nature and nurture are both important in developing the mind. However, the mind of a psychopath was totally different.

She had observed the Aghoris and instantly known that they were not professional criminals or psychopaths. But they were men of faith—and faith could lead men to do strange things. For them anything was possible. They lived to uphold the name of God. In the deep recesses of their minds, they heard God's voice—or that's what they said—and acted upon it.

The killer could well be acting on such a voice. He might believe that he was the messenger of God and fulfilling His will. It was like a task for them ordained by the divine will. Once the task was finished they would disappear. It would be almost impossible to track down such killers.

'One thing is certain,' Ruby told Hawa Singh. 'This killer is not at all what we so far thought him to be. At times, I actually feel we are looking in the wrong direction altogether.' Hawa Singh was quiet. Somewhere deep down he could feel a worry gnaw away at him.

He knew that the killer was playing a nasty game with him, now hiding, then confronting him. He'd been sure that the killer was a local from Benares. And yet, he'd come right up to his father. And shown him his blue eyes.

'He must have been wearing coloured contact lenses,' Hawa Singh mumbled to Ruby.

'Are you sure?'

'Yes, he loves to taunt us. Enjoys misleading us.'

"What if he really has blue eyes? It would be easy to close in on him,' said Ruby.

'That's exactly what he wanted to do. Point us in the wrong direction.'

Meanwhile, the hands on an unseen clock raced around to complete their lap.

7 pm. 29 January.

CHAPTER 24

It was 10.30 pm by the time the policemen took their posts at the hundred ghats and many temples. All the vagabonds were removed from the sites. A curious journalist from a local Hindi newspaper tried to question the SSP on the sudden police bandobast. The SSP told him that it was just a police exercise in security measures.

However, the SSP was nervous. What if those reporters added two and two and came up with five?

'You cannot help it,' Hawa Singh told him. 'Those people always write what they want to. Let them create stories. We have other things to do.'

Hawa Singh went with Ruby to the Dashashwamedh Ghat. For him, this was the key location. The first body was found here and the second victim was found inside Vishwanath temple—also close to this ghat. Somehow, he knew that the killer would strike in the vicinity.

Each of the police personnel was equipped with a wireless radio, to communicate with the rest in an emergency. Every half hour Hawa Singh would himself take reports from coded teams. No names on the wireless.

'It is possible that the killer listens to all our communication on the same radio frequency,' Hawa Singh had told the SSP.

For this Hawa Singh advised total silence on the wireless. Apart from him no one else would speak—unless they had the target in sight, or needed back-up. None of the usual police chatter over the frequency.

Ruby shivered on the steps of the ghat. The darkness was impenetrable. The only sounds were of waves lapping at the steps below and street dogs howling in the night. The sight of their breath condensing in front of their faces frightened the policemen. It could be their last.

The SSP had given Ruby a Beretta, which she had placed in the inside pocket of her jacket. It was a semi-automatic M 1923 model, a standard service pistol for the Italian Army from 1923 up to 1945. The pistol had a 4-inch barrel with a 7-shot detachable magazine. It had grooves for a shoulder holster machined into the bottom of the grip frame. It was one of those pistols the police had seized from some arms dealers.

Ruby was more used to the big M 9 pistol, a standard issue for the US Army, with its nine-inch barrel. The M 1923 looked too small to her. Still, it was something.

They were not wearing gloves as that would make it difficult to draw their guns and shoot. The cold had frozen their fingers—Ruby had to keep rubbing her hands to warm them.

At 11 pm Hawa Singh made a check with all the posts, using the code assigned to each. It was all clear so far. Their hour had not come. They were not even sure when the killer would strike—the pattern only suggested that he would kill before dawn.

Hawa Singh's chest and arm felt better with the tapes Ruby had placed on them. But for the first time—in a long, long time—he was terrified. The darkness was more than darkness. The fog looked thicker than snow.

He walked close to Ruby as they strode up and down the ghat. He nodded once or twice at her, intimating that things were under control. In the darkness, he tried to peer into her eyes. They reminded him of Kavita's. He felt for, and caressed, her cheek. There was a certain unspoken assurance in that gesture. That he was there. That he'd take care of her. What else did a girl need?

The clock hands completed their lap. It was midnight. And another step took them into a fresh new day.

30 January.

The day of the dead.

*

He stood on high ground, surveying the little he could see of the scene below him. Dear friends. He had earlier watched Hawa Singh and that FBI girl on the ghat. And also several other armed policemen. Benares that night had turned into a fortress. He liked this Hawa Singh. The man was a fighter.

He smiled, thinking, 'Friends, can you stop me any more than you can stop the darkness or the fog? I appear and disappear just like them, at my will.'

They had no idea who he was. He could have been one of those many reporters who daily queue outside the SSP office for juicy stories. Or he could be one of the policemen himself.

He wanted to laugh. As those foolish policemen tried to hunt him down, they forgot the basic tenets of Vedic astrology. How many more signs did they want? Should he shout down to them? '*Look, here I am*!' An expert astrologer can never go wrong. If the chart indicates death, even God will have to back off.

He spread his hands out to the welcome night. 'Ah, my Benares, they don't know anything! They don't want to know anything. The Ganges knows, but she can't speak out. Blood will flow, like her. Blood that will cleanse everything.'

He looked at the Cross in his hands. 'First, they crucified you and then they started worshipping you. What kind of God are you? You couldn't even defend yourself. So how can you defend the one that your Cross is going to kill? O Lord, protect the ones who are going to die!' He nearly laughed out loud.

He removed the blue contact lenses from his eyes. The deep black eyes now matched the darkness.

CHAPTER 25

It was a narrow confined space and he thrashed around it in a frenzy. He had scrambled up and down it on all fours, but it was walled in on all sides. He had been in many such spaces before, but he'd always managed to find his way out. Odd. *He had to escape! He desperately wanted to meet his family. Surely they were out there, somewhere?*

But even his limited faculties told him he had no options. He smashed his body again against the solid mass surrounding him. There was one thing his scrambled brain registered: he would never succeed like this.

If people could only see him now, he would have become a source of humour. Videos of him would have been shared on the social networking sites. Live humour today, after all, was derived from the misfortune of others. Compassion, love and romance were mocked at and pushed to the confines of cinema.

He felt broken and defeated, and a terrible sadness engulfed him. Soon the struggle would be over. It was becoming difficult to breathe. The darkness danced around him and was closing in on him. He clawed at the walls, his fingers torn and bleeding.

And then he realized he did indeed have a last option. He would chew through the wall with his own sharp teeth. He was a rat. He could find his way out of anywhere.

Rats have excellent memories. Once they learnt a path—even through copper and aluminium—they never forget it. He started biting on the cold wall. Surprisingly, it started to flake off easily. He chewed at a fragment of it. It tasted a lot like flesh—only a little different. If he went on biting, tearing and cutting, he'd make a big enough hole to get out.

Rats love being in a group of their own species, eating, playing and sleeping curled up inside each other. When rats don't have company they feel lonely and desperately anxious. A group of rats is often called a 'mischief'.

*

It was around 5 am on 30 January that the police control room got the call. Hawa Singh along with a sizeable force had been patrolling the entire night and everything seemed to be under control until the icy dawn. The Butcher had kept his word.

Hawa Singh was in one of the numerous streets checking with the policemen blocking the narrow alleyways when he got the message on wireless. He drove through the deserted vegetable market in Rajendra Prasad Ghat, next to the Dashashwamedh. He stopped at an old building, the Man Mandir, erected by Maharaja Man Singh of Amber in around 1600. They jumped from the police jeep and ran up the stone steps to its terrace.

It was on this terrace that Maharaja Savai Jai Singh II, the then Maharaja of Jaipur, had constructed an observatory. It was popularly called the Jantar-Mantar—much like similarly called observatories in Delhi and Jaipur. Jai Singh had been a great admirer of science and technology, but his reigning passion had been astronomy.

Hawa Singh reached the head of the stairs and immediately saw the body lying there. The sight froze all those who followed in his wake. Despite all the precautions they had taken, the Butcher had had his way after all.

They moved closer and saw the Cross sticking out from the chest of the corpse. Ruby pulled on her latex gloves before touching the body. The policemen switched on their heavy torches. It was the body of a male, smeared with ashes.

Ruby made a closer examination. 'There is a deep cavity in the upper left of the torso,' she informed the rest. 'It's clear that the heart has been removed.'

Hawa Singh turned away, looking at the Ganges flowing peacefully below. 'The killer didn't break his pattern,' he said heavily. 'We failed to look into the pattern. We forgot that astrology and astronomy went together. He still operated close to the Dashaswamedh Ghat, but we ignored such an important site right next to it.' Hawa Singh kicked at a wall with frustration.

Ruby continued with her examination. 'Just like in the others,' she told the men around her, 'there are no marks of any struggle. The body is naked. The man looks strong, heavy and tall, approximately six feet and three inches. It would be difficult for anyone to kill such a strong man without a fight.'

Hawa Singh came closer. He noticed what seemed like movement under the body. Everyone's eyes glued themselves to the phenomenon. The gap in the body widened, and two beady eyes, followed by a small, furry body with a tail, emerged, looking inquisitively at the men pointing beams of light at it. The rat, fattened with blood and tissue, had fought its way out. It left a big hole in the stomach.

While the men stood there, paralysed with shock, Hawa Singh and Ruby wondered the same thing: 'Had the killer planned to put that rat in a hole under the body, knowing it would gorge on it and gouge its way out? Had he wanted to make the sight more gruesome than it already was?'

They turned the body over with some effort, heavy and grown stiff already. There were no more signs on it except for the opening in the back that the rat had made to escape. But there was a hole in the cement in which the rat had been trapped for a while. Hawa Singh crouched and played a torch on it. There was the expected blood and tissue around the cement hole.

And just next to it, the faint lines of a horoscope chart.

A note for the next kill.

Hawa Singh turned around and shouted, 'Get Pandit Vishnu Shastri here, right now.'

Sub-inspector Gaya Prasad ran down the steps, sensing the urgency. This was not the time for questions, arguments and discussions.

The old, by-now-familiar pain shot through Hawa Singh's head. He knew he might black out at any moment. He sat down to rest against the wall, holding his head in his hands, as if it was not a part of his body, and yet connected agonizingly to it.

Seeing him crumple, Ruby rushed to him and handed him two aspirins from his pocket, forcing him to gulp them down without water.

'You sit here till your head feels better,' she said, briskly taking charge. 'I'll keep up with the investigation.' Hawa Singh tried to nod, but his head threatened to explode with that small movement.

Ruby, the interrogator, took over. She looked around and asked, 'Okay, first tell me, who made the call to the police?'

One of the police officers pushed forward a dark-skinned, heavy-built, altogether tough-looking man, 'Madam, this is the Dom Raja, Sanjeet Choudhary. He made the call.'

Ruby walked up to the Dom Raja and looked directly into his eyes. She was looking for that slight flicker of the eyelids, the nervousness, the quivering of lips, and the hesitation in speech that indicated a liar.

'Madam,' Sanjeet Choudhary spoke with some fear, 'I received a call on my cell phone about an unidentified body lying here in Jantar-Mantar. The caller told me to collect the body before sunrise. So I hurried right up here and saw this. I knew it was the work of that Butcher. I have read about it in the newspapers. I didn't touch anything and made the call to the police.'

'Good,' said Ruby, approvingly.

'What do you Doms do?' Hawa Singh couldn't resist calling out, despite the pain.

'We are a community who are the cremators of the dead,' he replied with pride, 'and the keepers of the sacred fire in cremation grounds, which is never allowed to die down.'

Even more proudly, he added, 'We are the descendants of Kalu Dom, who worked as a cremation undertaker during the regime of Raja Harishchandra.'

'What time did you get the call?' Ruby resumed her questions.

Sanjeet Choudhary took out a cheap cell phone and checked the log for received calls, saying, 'It was 2.45 am.'

'But you made the call to the police only after 4.30 am. What took you so long?' asked Ruby.

'Madam, every day we get such calls and the pyres keep burning all through the night. I was supervising a cremation and could leave only after 4 am.'

'Trace the number from which the call was made,' Ruby told the still silent policemen.

Hawa Singh asked to be shown the Dom Raja's cell phone. He checked the number and said, 'This seems to be a public phone. We would never trace the killer from this. Still, try and follow up.'

They sat there discussing the many possibilities of the killer's leads. One of the policemen brought up some tea. Anything hot was welcome in that weather. Hawa Singh took out his flask and sipped on the whisky. The pain was slowly subsiding. He felt better.

Hawa Singh let the Dom Raja go with a curt instruction not to leave Benares and specifically not to speak about the incident to anyone. Not a word to the media.

The body was being wrapped prior to being hoisted away when Ruby called out to them to stop. She had noticed a tattoo on the arm of the dead man. She snatched a torch and cast the beam of light on the tattoo. There was a numeral and, above it, was the shape of wings stretched out from a parachute. And right above them was a crown and a lion standing over it.

She gave a soft whistle and looked in Hawa Singh's direction. 'He belonged to the British Paratroopers, one of the best combat forces in the world!' she exclaimed.

Hawa Singh came for a closer look. He was not proficient in the emblems of armed forces, especially those of foreign ones. Ruby pointed again to the tattoo. 'This is the insignia of the British Paratroopers,' she repeated. 'The numbers, like the one here, are personal codes and the year shows that he was part of the 2003 war in Iraq.' She shook her head in puzzlement. 'The question is, what was he doing in Benares? And how the hell did this killer manage to kill an army commando?'

Ruby made one more comprehensive check of the body. 'There is no sign of poisoning, orally or by injection or dart gun—just as there was none in the other cases,' she said. She checked in between the fingers, toes, the nape of the neck, all crevices, but there was nothing. Only when she was convinced that there was nothing more to look for, did she let them take the body away for post mortem at the government hospital.

It was another half-an-hour before Pandit Vishnu Shastri arrived, with Sub-Inspector Gaya Prasad Sharma. Hawa Singh shook hands with him and apologized for summoning him at that hour.

Vishnu Shastri saw the bloodstains and asked, 'Has he struck again?' Hawa Singh silently nodded.

Vishnu Shastri paled and shivered—one could tell it was not from the cold. It was fear that had turned his face white. He gathered himself and said, 'This is the perfect place, where astronomy meets astrology. This Jantar-Mantar was built to measure local time, the Sun's declination, altitude, the declination of the stars and planets, and to determine eclipses. It incorporates multiple structures of unique forms, each with a specialized function for astronomical measurement.'

Hawa Singh pointed to the place where the body was found. 'The body was lying there,' he said, rather more simply.

'That's the Samrat Yantra,' said Vishnu Shastri. 'Look carefully, it is a giant triangle that is basically an equal-hour sundial. It is 70 feet high, 114 feet long at the base, and 10 feet thick. It has a 128-foot-long hypotenuse that is parallel to the Earth's axis, and points towards the North Pole. On either side of the triangle is a quadrant with graduations indicating hours, minutes and seconds. At the time of the Samrat Yantra's construction, sundials already existed, but the Samrat Yantra turned the basic sundial into a precision tool for measuring declination and other related coordinates of various heavenly bodies.'

Shastri paused for breath and went on. 'There are other instruments here, just as precise.'

'How is it all connected to the murders?' asked Ruby.

'Well, the main purpose of this Jantar-Mantar was to cast horoscopes.'

There was a stunned silence. The night around them was surrendering to the rising sun, although the cold wouldn't let up.

Hawa Singh went into self-control mode and pointed at the floor of the terrace where the body had just lain. 'Shastriji,' he reminded the scholar, 'you missed the chart drawn there. That, too, will need some calculations.'

Vishnu Shastri peered hard downwards and, slowly, the lines stood out to be deciphered. He saw the numbers in the houses. He trembled at the thought of forecasting another horror.

It took him a few minutes to make a few mental calculations, but they appeared to puzzle him. He looked up at Hawa Singh and said, 'It's the horoscope of a policeman.'

'What?'

'Acoording my calculation, the birth date of the person should be 15 September 1974.'

Hawa Singh looked at him aghast. 'That's my birth date.'

'Well, according to the horoscope you are the next victim,' said Shastri.

*

The man again struck a match that flared briefly in the surrounding fog. Hawa Singh had been observing him from the terrace on Man Mahal. The man had been there since they climbed up to Jantar-Mantar. It reminded him of Ruby's theory that most serial-killers come back to the scene of the crime to enjoy the sight of police personnel desperately at work on something they knew nothing of. It gave them a perverse sense of power over others.

The Ghost decided, once more, to vanish into mist. Only to re-appear at Dashashwamedh Ghat.

He could again see the golden domes of Kashi Vishwanath temple reaching for the sky. The morning's aarti was in progress. Shiva had made peace with Benares.

The man was at a distance of about 100 metres when Hawa Singh took out his Colt and removed the safety catch. Then, he strode towards the figure.

At that moment, the man turned and saw him coming towards him. He started to run. Hawa Singh chased him as he ran into a street and from there into a narrow drain. Hawa Singh never took his eyes off him, but all he could see was his fleeing back.

The drain led to an open sewer. Hawa Singh hesitated. Something told him there could be a trap ahead. But he knew he had to jump into whatever lay ahead—if he wanted to catch the Butcher. He jumped.

He could hear the footsteps of the man running ahead. Hawa Singh followed him as the sewer took many bends. Hawa Singh suspected that it would lead them directly into the river. He was ready for the fall.

He heard a heavy iron gate flung open and his prey enter it. Hawa Singh ran after him.

It was so easy to bait these policemen, the Butcher thought as he ran ahead, smiling. His plan was so simple, and working so beautifully. He could hear the footsteps running behind him and he led them directly on deliberately.

Hawa Singh slowly realized that he was in the same tunnel that ran underneath the Ganges across its width. And he knew that the Butcher had planned for a long while to bring him there.

Overwhelmed, Hawa Singh saw a giant wall of water rushing towards him. He turned and ran back, to see another wall of water approaching from the other direction. The Butcher had opened the sluices from both sides—sluices installed four hundred years ago to trap enemy forces—to let the water in. As they engulfed him, Hawa Singh lost his footing.

He scrambled up against the force, but the water had already risen to his chin and soon would go over his head. There was only one thing that he could resort to, his .45 Colt. He raised it and fired at the ceiling of the tunnel. Loose plaster tore off it and the bullet ricocheted under water. He fired again, at another angle. The roof didn't seem to budge. In fury, he emptied all the bullets into the roof.

Nothing happened.

The water crossed his nose and was soon over his head. He had spent all his firepower and was sapped of all energy. There was hardly any air left in his lungs. The darkness seemed to overtake him. He never thought it would be all over like this. A fleeting image of Kavita danced in front of his eyes. He closed them.

The sound of rumbling came to his ears. The roof gave way and parted. The holy Ganges wrapped Hawa Singh in her arms and drew him upwards. He kicked his legs frantically, and broke the surface.

He looked at life again.

CHAPTER 26

In the near distance, as he emerged, he could see a figure pacing about, and heard an agitated shouting. It was Fauja Singh, who was furious and tearful on seeing his son come out of the watery grave.

'This police job is not a profession, it's a curse,' he cried. 'We didn't come to Benares to get caught in other people's cases. This is not your job, Hawa. I don't care whether I die or not, we're going to leave this place!'

By the time Hawa Singh had come out of the cold river waters, he was terribly tired and water had seeped into his lungs. He fell unconscious on the ghat. Luckily, Fauja Singh, too, was there for his morning prayers, and he had called out to nearby policemen.

Fauja Singh looked around at the police officers and shouted, 'You all are useless! There is only one killer out there and none of you can catch him. Are you going to let my son die?'

Hawa Singh looked up at him and Fauja Singh nodded in resignation. 'Okay, do what you want,' he said irritably. 'I'm going to take my *jal-samadhi* in the Ganges.' Having got that off his chest, and after making sure his son was looked after, he stalked off angrily.

Hawa Singh sat inside the SSP's office, sipping on dark rum. A medic worked on the reopened cuts on his chest and arm. Hawa Singh was wrapped in a dirty old blanket as they hadn't found fresh clothes to fit his unusually large frame. His body still glistened with the cold water of the Ganges. He had finally had his holy dip.

The SSP and several other officers stood around mutely, as if in a vacuum. Ruby was in a corner, caught up in an alien world, dismayed at the helpless faces she saw around her. There was only so much she could do. She knew in her heart and in her trained mind that if there was anyone who could stop the Butcher, it was only Hawa Singh.

The sharpest knife couldn't have cut through the stasis in the room. Everyone there had lost all basic sense to think, look ahead and prepare. Failure held them in its grip.

SSP Neeraj Thakur picked up a paperweight in his anger and threw it at the wall. 'It's all over,' he raged. 'The politicians and the media will roast me alive. I'm done for.'

Hawa Singh and Ruby sought each other's eyes at the same time. They had developed a common wavelength.

Hawa Singh took another sip of rum. 'Just like in the other murders,' he said impassively, 'the killer had premeditated my death in a cold and calculated way.'

No one in the room reacted. It was like they all had fallen into a state of coma. They could hear everything, all right, but could not react to any comment.

Do they have a term for mental paralysis? Hawa Singh asked himself. If there was, it would describe what he was looking at today. He tried to shake them out of their catatonia. 'He has already attacked me once, with a knife, but this was unimaginable.'

The SSP limited himself to nodding, in a worried way.

Hawa Singh showed them a cigarette stub. 'I found this on the steps of the ghat. There were at least ten similar stubs all around the ghat. I suspect the killer always smokes a rolled-up cigarette like this one. Only hard-core smokers smoke this stuff. It contains ganja.'

Sub-inspector Gaya Prasad Sharma came out of his stunned silence. 'Sir, ganja is very popular here in Benares. Most foreigners smoke it. The Naga sadhus, the Aghoris, the beggars and hundreds of other sadhus living close to the ghats smoke it.'

Hawa Singh nodded in agreement. 'The killer seems to be a chain-smoker. He won't be buying ganja from street peddlers. We need to catch the big ones.' *The science of deduction*, he reminded himself. *One needs to look into the invisible and slowly retrace one's steps. The links will emerge.*

The SSP paced the room. 'What about this latest victim?' he demanded to know. 'Do we have any information on him?'

He was all ears when Ruby replied, 'The tattoo on the victim's arm confirmed that he was a British Paratrooper. I checked with them, giving them the number tattooed on his arm and they mailed me some information on him. His name was Tom Barry and he took active part in the 2003 Iraq war. After that, he seemed to have gone through severe psychological problems. In 2008, he left the British Army and joined the Vatican Guards.'

The very name of the Vatican revitalized the room. Hawa Singh gulped down the remaining rum in the steel mug. *The art of listening: do nothing but listen. It is a process of gathering information, and then sorting it out to uncover the hidden.*

Ruby went on. 'Just to tell you, the Swiss Guards are the oldest standing army in the world. Their main role is to protect the Pope. Tom Barry was offered the post of their new Anti-Terror Unit by the Chief of the Vatican Police Force, Camillo Cilsin, after two attacks on Pope Benedict during Christmas Eve Midnight Mass at St Peter's Basilica in 2007. Tom's role was clear. To prevent any further attacks on the Vatican and the Pope. He was working in close co-operation with the Interpol to catch the masterminds of the attacks on the Pope. However, no progress was made and they could not apprehend anyone.'

'What was he doing here in Benares?' shouted the SSP.

'I have no idea,' admitted Ruby. 'His murder, too, was connected to the Vatican—just like those of the last two victims. Apart from that, there's nothing more we know.'

Hawa Singh wrapped the blanket closer around him and said, 'These murders have a connection with astronomy too. The first victim, Eva, worked at the Vatican Observatory. Do we have something on that?'

Ruby pulled out a file saying, 'Only this morning, I received a dossier on that from the FBI. I will give you the basic activities of that Observatory.'

She read out, 'The Vatican Observatory is one of the oldest astronomical research institutions in the world. The Church has had long-standing interests in astronomy, due to the astronomical basis of the calendar by which holy days such as Easter are determined. For instance, the Gregorian Calendar, promulgated in 1582 by Pope Gregory XIII, was developed by the Jesuit mathematician, Christoph Clavius at the Collegio Romano, from astronomical data.'

She looked around and continued, 'In fact, Nicolaus Copernicus was a Renaissance astronomer and Catholic clergyman who was the first person to formulate a comprehensive heliocentric cosmology which displaced the Earth from the centre of the universe. Later, in 1633, Galileo was convicted for grave suspicion of heresy for following the position of Copernicus, which is contrary to the true sense and authority of the Holy Scriptures.

'In the nineteenth century, as the Church came to face severe criticism for its stand from the scientific community, it turned Galileo into a hero. The Church came out with a declaration that supported Galileo's theory that the Sun is the centre of our solar system and the Earth revolves around it.

'The Vatican claims that many other Jesuits contributed to the development of pendulum clocks, pantographs, barometers, reflecting telescopes and microscopes, and to scientific fields as various as magnetism, optics and electricity. They spotted, for instance, in some cases before anyone else, the coloured bands on Jupiter's surface, the Andromeda nebula and Saturn's rings.

'Pope John Paul II said, "Through the pursuit of a scientific understanding of the universe, something of the Creator of the universe is discovered. Faith and science are not irreconcilable. Faith and reason are the two wings on which the human spirit takes flight."

'Pope Benedict XVI reaffirmed that, saying, "There is no contradiction between what we know through our faith and what we can learn through science.'

Ruby looked up and saw that none of the police officers had understood much about it. The SSP was fuming. It all sounded like poppycock to him.

There was one idea Hawa Singh latched on to: 'Just like astrology and astronomy went hand-in-hand, the Vatican brought faith and science together. It was all a long-drawn battle to prove the authenticity of the Bible, and that God exists.'

The Vatican.

Benares.

The Butcher.

'Okay, so now the question is, why is the killer targeting all these people connected to the Vatican?' he asked, at last.

Ruby knotted her eyebrows. 'It could be his deep-seated hatred for the Vatican, for Christianity. The use of the Holy Cross as a profane weapon indicates that.'

'What else?'

'It could be his hatred for white skin,' suggested Gaya Prasad.

'What about the connection to the Vatican?'

'There are many who come here to study the ancient scriptures,' the SSP ventured. 'It's not unusual that many come from the Vatican. It was evident in their interest in the *Bhrigu-Samhita*.'

'What do you mean?'

'Well, it could be that there is no connection to the Vatican. The killer just targets white Christians,' said the SSP.

'We still need to find all about Tom Barry. The place where he was staying and the places he visited in Benares. The people he met and everything he did here,' said Hawa Singh.

Ruby cleared her throat, trying to get attention, and said, 'Let's not forget that the hearts of all the victims were removed. It looked like a kind of ritualistic killing.'

Hawa Singh was at once reminded of the cannibal. *The heart functioned in spite of the brain's death. The heart was controlled by something more major.*

The SSP turned to Hawa Singh. 'What about that Dom who discovered the body?' he asked.

'I have spoken to him. He got a call from a public telephone about the body. Have we got any details on that?' Hawa Singh looked around.

'Yes, sir,' Gaya Prasad said with alacrity. 'The telephone number has been traced to a public telephone at the railway station. We tried to speak to many passengers who were sleeping there, but they hadn't noticed anyone in the booth.'

'Don't take this Dom at face value,' cautioned the SSP. 'These Doms rule the cremation grounds of Benares. They have a deep relation with the Aghoris. Many of the Doms are filthy-rich and drive Mercedes cars. They are shady people.'

The loud ringtone broke the perfectly measured silence of the room. It was Gaya Prasad's cell phone. He hesitantly took the call.

Gaya looked up with an ashen face. 'Sir, forensics have checked the fingerprints on the knife and the thumbprint on the axe.'

'And?' Hawa Singh looked up, attentively.

'Both prints are of the same person.'

Ruby's mouth was half-open as she looked at Hawa Singh. The SSP and other officers seemed to have returned to their coma.

'So the Butcher also killed Tailanga Swami,' concluded Hawa Singh.

'But why did he break the pattern?' Ruby asked, still at a loss. 'Or was it just to confuse us?'

'No, the pattern never broke. We failed to see it. In all the murders, he left the Cross behind. In the case of Tailanga Swami, he left the axe. The Cross and the axe had one thing in common. The wood,' said Hawa Singh.

'Is it possible that the axe's handle and the Cross were made of the same wood?' asked Ruby with renewed excitement.

'Yes, it's possible. We need to check on that.'

CHAPTER 27

Hawa Singh and Ruby sat inside the Sparrow building in Sudha Krishnamurthy's office. Sudha was drinking tea and coughing badly. She wore three sweaters, one over the other, the inner one a full neck. Over them all she wore another elegant silk saree. There were, in addition, a shawl over her shoulders and a woollen muffler covering her ears and most of her head. She looked like a rabbit, with her nose sticking out and her lips twitching.

'I can't stand this cold,' she complained. 'I am more used to Chennai weather—this winter is too harsh for me.'

Hawa Singh nodded with a smile. He was back in his wet jacket and a fresh pair of jeans and t-shirt bought for him by Ruby. Ruby was dressed in her best dark-grey suit with knee-length boots. Her Beretta M-1923 snuggled in her shoulder holster.

Hawa Singh glanced at the family photograph on the desk, and Sudha noticed the look. 'That's my family,' she smiled. 'My husband passed away before I came here to Sparrow. My son is a software engineer in the US. I decided to devote my own life to the care of the mentally ill.'

'There are very few people like you,' said Ruby.

'We all need to find a reason to live,' said Sudha.

Hawa Singh cleared his throat. 'There are certain things that I wanted to understand from the psychological point of view. I'm just a policeman and I have my limitations. I wanted to know about serial-killers. I mean the way they think and act.'

Sudha sat back in her chair comfortably. Ruby could see that Sudha was a confident and competent woman who prided herself on the knowledge of her subject. The glittering eyes were enough to tell that Sudha now held the commanding position in the room. The brows arching upward, and the thin smile on her lips amounted almost to condescension.

There were hundreds of such men and women who toil away in such dark and damp rooms, unheard, unseen, almost invisible to society. It was only natural to feel important when someone actually knocked at their doors to seek advice.

Sudha began in her soft, husky voice. 'There are still conflicting views on the reasons that make one a serial-killer. It could be a traumatic childhood or the effect of violence around an individual. They are generally described as possessing IQs in the normal-to-bright range, but often have trouble keeping their jobs and tend to work in menial ones.'

Ruby looked at Hawa Singh meaningfully. The FBI had already taught her all this.

Sudha took another sip of her ginger tea. 'There are some who are termed psychopaths. They lack empathy and guilt, are egocentric and impulsive, and theoretically do not conform to social, moral and legal norms. Instead, psychopaths often follow a distinct set of rules which they have created for themselves. They may appear to be normal and are often quite charming, a state of adaptation that psychiatrists call the "mask of sanity".'

'The Butcher seems to have all the characteristics of a psychopath,' said Hawa Singh.

'Don't tell me he has killed again!' said a shocked Sudha.

Hawa Singh looked at Ruby, and with a sigh, said, 'No, but we want to be prepared.'

Sudha nodded to indicate she understood the situation. 'Most serial-killers exhibit degrees of ASPD, Anti-Social Personality Disorder,' she continued. 'However, they often know how to hide many of these characteristics in order to blend with the rest of society. Serial-killer Ed Kemper in the US became particularly notorious for doing this, when he tricked psychiatrists into believing he was cured, seven years after being admitted to the Atascadero State Hospital for the murders of his two grandparents. Three years after his release, Kemper went on to murder at least eight additional victims.'

Ruby gave a whistle although she had heard the story umpteen times.

'The serial-killer begins as no different to any other individual who seeks approval from parents, sexual partners, or others. This need for approval is what influences children to attempt to develop social relationships with their family and peers. But if they are rejected or neglected, they cease to do so. This is because of the drastic lowering of their self-esteem, and their search for an alternate fantasy world in which they are the ones in control.'

'So, control over others is what motivates a serial-killer?' asked Hawa Singh.

Sudha coughed loudly, then sipped again at her tea. 'In psychology, the motives of serial-killers are generally placed in four categories: visionary, mission-oriented, hedonistic, and power or control. However, the motives of any given killer may display a considerable overlap among these categories. The visionary serial-killers suffer from psychotic breaks with reality, sometimes believing they are another person, or are compelled to murder by entities such as the Devil or God.'

'The Butcher seems to think of himself as God,' remarked Ruby.

'The mission-oriented killers typically justify their acts as ridding the world of a certain type of person perceived as undesirable—such as homosexuals, prostitutes, or people of different ethnicity or religion. However, they are generally not psychotic. Some see themselves as attempting to change society, often to cure a societal ill.'

'I could see the Butcher as being one of those, too,' said Hawa Singh.

Sudha seemed to ignore the interruption. 'The hedonistic serial-killer seeks thrills, and derives pleasure from killing, seeing people as expendable means to his goal. They could be driven by lust, a desire for excitement, or comfort.'

'The killer in this case seems to have a mission, and considers himself to be the hand of God,' Hawa Singh reasoned. 'That proves, even further, that he is deeply religious. Maybe he also leads a solitary life and doesn't have a stable job.'

'I think that sums it up,' said Sudha, rubbing her cold hands.

'I haven't personally dealt with serial-killers in Delhi,' Hawa Singh told Sudha hesitantly. 'This is my first such case.'

'History is full of serial-killers,' Sudha informed him. 'Liu Pengli of China, cousin of the Han Emperor Jing, would go out on marauding expeditions with twenty or thirty slaves or criminals. They would murder people, seizing their belongings, for sheer sport. Eventually, it was discovered that he had murdered at least 100 people. The officials of the court requested that Liu Pengli be executed. However, the emperor could not bear to have his own cousin killed, so Liu Pengli was demoted to the status of commoner and banished.'

'That's some relief,' said Hawa Singh, half-jokingly.

'There's more,' said Sudha. 'In the fifteenth century, one of the wealthiest men in Europe and a former companion-in-arms of Joan of Arc, Gilles de Rais, sexually assaulted and killed peasant children, mainly boys, whom he had abducted from the surrounding villages and taken to his castle. It is estimated that his victims numbered over 800. The Hungarian aristocrat Elizabeth Báthory allegedly tortured and killed as many as 650 girls and young women before her arrest in 1610.'

'I have read,' Ruby chipped in, 'that Thug Behram, a gang leader of the Indian Thuggee cult of assassins, has been tagged to be the world's most prolific serial-killer. He was believed to have murdered 931 victims by strangling them with a ceremonial cloth between 1790 and 1830. According to some estimates, the Thuggees murdered 1 million people between 1740 and 1840.'

'You must be aware of,' added Sudha in her turn, 'the famous and yet unidentified killer known as Jack the Ripper. He killed at least five prostitutes, and possibly more, in London in 1888. Those crimes gained enormous press attention because London was the world's greatest centre of power at the time, so having such dramatic murders of financially destitute women in the midst of such wealth focused the news media's attention on the plight of the urban poor, and gained coverage worldwide. He has also been called the most famous serial-killer of all time.'

'They all seem to have had really sick minds,' said Hawa Singh with undisguised disgust.

'Most of them were caught only after they had already done the damage,' went on Sudha, undeterred. 'While many great investigators and detectives like you toiled in the dark searching for them.'

'And all the time, those serial-killers were there right under their noses!' marvelled Hawa Singh. 'Like you said, these serial-killers were masked men. Normal people wearing masks.'

'You could say that,' said Sudha dryly.

Ruby looked thoughtful and asked, 'What about ritual killings or human sacrifices?'

Sudha rubbed her nose. 'Many ritual murders involve the idea of human sacrifice, usually for religious reasons. Human sacrifice is a feature of some, but not all, occult belief systems. The word "occult" means hidden and because of its very nature, this kind of ritual killing can be hard to investigate.

'Even more difficult for forensic psychiatrists are those cases where a murder has been committed by a true believer who considers murder to be a sacred act of sacrifice. Such deaths tend to occur outdoors in a designated sacred area on a significant date. Generally, such acts are blood rituals involving a knife. Depending on the belief system involved, the killing may involve a rapid slitting of the throat, or be slower and more torturous.'

'In the case of the Butcher,' supplied Hawa Singh, 'his first victim was killed on Makar Sakranti, 14 January—but then, the other dates don't seem to have any significance.'

'Well, Makar Sakranti is an auspicious day and maybe the killer believed it to be the start of a long pending work that he intends to finish.'

'You mean he kicked off the series on that "auspicious" day?' asked Ruby in disbelief.

'It seems so.'

They sat for a while in silence, Sudha still smiling gently. Ruby pitied her helplessness. There was only so much a psychologist could do.

Hawa Singh finally straightened up in his chair and asked, 'How is Manvendra keeping?'

The skin below an eye of Sudha twitched slightly. It was a sign of nervousness, thought Ruby, as she observed it keenly. Is she hiding something?

'It's difficult to tell,' Sudha said. 'There are days when it seems that he has improved a lot, and then there are times when it seems all our hard work has gone down the drain. It's like trying to reform a man-eater,' said Sudha.

'Man-eaters are finally shot dead,' said Hawa Singh nonchalantly.

'That doesn't cure anything. We at Sparrow's believe in providing holistic mental health and care. I can only hope for the best.'

Ruby could see that Sudha had relaxed again. The brief tic under her eye had stopped. Perfectly understandable. Not many people questioned her about the cannibal.

'Can we see him?' asked Hawa Singh.

Suddenly, Sudha was on guard. 'You want to see him *again*?'

'Yes, if you don't have a problem with that.'

Sudha raised her hands, signifying no objection. She summoned Dr Binod Pradhan, who once more took Hawa Singh and Ruby to meet the king's brother.

As Dr Binod Pradhan opened the door to the cell, a heavy pungent draught came from the room. Manvendra was sitting in a corner sheathed by thick smoke. Hawa Singh saw that he was smoking a rolled-up joint. The smell was definitely of marijuana. He turned to look at Dr Pradhan questioningly.

Dr Pradhan waved the smoke away from his own nostrils and said, 'We use marijuana as a medicine to calm down such patients. And especially in his case, it has proved very effective.'

'You are turning him into an addict,' said Ruby.

'No, we monitor the doses. Earlier, we used to give it to him in his food but he threw it around. It seems he enjoys smoking it.'

'What if he burns himself?'

Dr Pradhan chuckled, looking at the monstrous face of Manvendra Singh behind the cloud of smoke, 'You think he can harm himself any more than he already has?'

Hawa Singh's own head was buzzing. Was it possible that this Manvendra got out and went on his spree of killings? he wondered. No, he discarded the thought, it would be impossible for him to move beyond those doors.

The cannibal looked at him and smiled. 'You need a big heart, sharp mind and clear eyes to look through the fog,' he intoned.

CHAPTER 28

He sat alone, admiring the Colt in his hand. He had opened it up, piece-by-piece, greased, re-assembled and loaded it. It was the revolver Hawa Singh kept with him at all times—the one that the policeman shot his way out of the tunnel with. The one he'd lost in the river.

Nothing is ever lost in the Ganges.

He had paid five hundred rupees to one of the little boys who dived deep into the river to look for coins thrown by devotees. On his fifth dive down, a little boy had found the gun for him. The look of the Butcher—and the money, of course—was enough to keep his little mouth shut forever.

It is said that children can recognize the face of danger.

He rested the Colt on his lap and caressed it. Should he use it to blow the man's brains out, or just his heart? He laughed at the thought that Hawa Singh already had a bullet waiting in his head.

The room was quiet. A few birds chirped outside on the branches. The din of traffic was far, far away. He could hear his own heartbeat. A cold gust of the ever-present wind blasted in through the window. The paper on the table before him rustled with it.

These were his most precious moments when he could be all alone with himself. He loved his solitude. In solitude he was with his God. The silence *was* God. It was not an absence of sound, but the presence of the Omnipresent, Par Brahma.

Those policemen didn't understand him. He was not the Butcher the media proclaimed him to be. He had a purpose. If only they recognized his purpose; they, too, might join him in savagery.

'Yes, I did kill Tailanga Swami, the Aghori leader. It was all so simple. He knew about me, had seen me, and wanted to expose me. He had to be stopped,' he almost whispered to himself.

The purpose behind an act was bigger than the individual who carried it out. So many people led purposeless lives. He had seen them going about their daily business, leading a rats' race, only to glean a few grains, to squander it all on their petty wants, their greedy desires, their needless gadgets and vulgar statements of style. And they called *him* mad!

But he was no messiah, to gently convert society to its real purpose. He was not there to change the course of history, or re-write it. He was going to end the chapter.

If that made him a Butcher, so be it.

'Oh Lord, forgive them, for they know not what they do.'

CHAPTER 29

It was late evening and the Ganges seemed to suck out all sunlight. The sun hung limply in the sky, ready for a dip in the holy river, which already glittered with it. There was hope against hope the next day would be brighter and sunnier. But the winter, despite the weatherman's forecast, was getting more and more severe. The fog was thicker than ever before. The quickly ensuing darkness turned out to be blacker than black.

Hawa Singh had left Ruby at her hotel room to co-ordinate with the local police, gather all the forensic reports and make a point-by-point report of the investigation. He was out in the cold, walking towards Manikarnika Ghat. He could see shops lined with items used during cremation rites—ghee, timber, offerings and white cloth. This was the bazaar of the dead.

While funeral pyres are usually lit a little distance from the heart of towns, as they are considered inauspicious, this doesn't hold true in Benares, where Manikarnika is situated quite in the middle of the town itself. This is precisely because the entire city of Benares is considered the 'Maha-Shamashan' or the 'Great Cremation Ground'.

The ghat was crowded with mourners and Doms. There were a few foreign visitors, who found the spectacle of burning the dead fascinating, even amusing. They stood at a distance, watching the rituals and discreetly taking pictures on their digital cameras.

Hawa Singh was looking for the Dom Raja, Sanjeet Choudhary. A little ahead he could see a group of Aghori sadhus absorbed in their rituals. They were sharing a longish chunk of flesh. It looked like a half-burnt human leg.

There were over thirty pyres burning at the same time. The best place to be in this harsh winter. The flames leapt up in the sky and above them was smoke. Above them all was the circle of crows.

Crows are excitable birds. They react to hunger and invasion by vigorously vocalizing their feelings. They display happiness, anger and sadness.

They also share an excellent memory. They're masters at stashing food in caches, moving it sometimes two or three times in a day, and remembering exactly where they last placed it. For their size, they have the largest brains of all birds—except some parrots. Their brain-to-body ratio is equivalent to that of a chimpanzee's and amazingly, not far off that of a human's.

The air was filled with the smell of burning human flesh and bones, mixed with ghee and other herb potions poured on the dead. There were sounds of bones cracking and wood splintering. A few laments could be heard of grieving relatives, along with the chanting of mantras. Ash flew around, making the air thick.

Hawa Singh moved between the pyres and finally spotted Dom Raja supervising a cremation. He was covered with ash. The combination of his naturally dark complexion and the ash covering him lent him an eerie appearance. All the Doms looked the same, while cremating the dead. Theirs was one of the oldest professions practised in Benares. They said it was even older than prostitution.

The sun finally submerged itself in the Ganges. The river shone blackly and inked all of Benares with its now uniform hue. Night fell.

Sanjeet, Dom Raja, called to his men, 'I'm going to the *dawakhaana*. I'll be back later.'

It sounded like an ordinary chore he had to carry out at the chemists', so no one took any real notice of his departure. Dom Raja wiped the ashes from his face and walked away. This time, Hawa Singh followed him.

He tailed him through narrow streets and bazaars till they came to a temple. Sanjeet went behind it into a small broken-down brick structure, plastered with mud. There was a small iron door to it, and a dirty little board hung over it—'Dawakhaana', it read.

Hawa Singh followed him inside, to be met with a mist of heavy smoke. He could smell ganja and knew at once that this was one of the opium dens of Benares.

There were many locals, labourers, a few foreigners who had gone there to experiment with local drugs, a couple of eunuchs who tried to extract money from the smokers. Hidden in the crowd was Kanhaiya. Hawa Singh at once recognized the tourist guide who had taken Brian Johnson, the archaeologist, to Gaya, and later tried to sell his passport.

Dom Raja took his regular chillum and began to smoke. His eyes became droopy and he was soon lost in the embrace of marijuana. A loud Bollywood song started playing in the background. A few locals, all of them drugged, started to swing and sing along.

Sanjeet saw Hawa Singh walking towards him, but didn't react. He held out his chillum instead to Hawa Singh with a big smile.

Hawa Singh went straight up to Kanhaiya and sat close to him, putting his arm, as if with affection, around Kanhaiya's neck. Kanhaiya looked up and tried to run, but he needed a bull's strength to escape that grip.

'Kanhaiya, you disappeared. I asked you not to leave Benares,' said Hawa Singh, tightening his arm around the guide's neck.

'Sirji,' Kanhaiya stuttered wildly, 'I never left.'

'I asked you for something else. I wanted you to find out about all the people that Brian met in Benares.'

Kanhaiya licked his lips in fear. Hawa Singh tightened his hold further, causing Kanhaiya to squeal in pain.

'It doesn't take much time to die. I'll make sure you are cremated on Harishchandra Ghat. You will go directly to heaven. Find moksha.'

'I don't want to die, sir, and that's why I cannot open my mouth.'

'Your choice, Kanhaiya,' said Hawa Singh, evenly.

As his grip turned into a vice, Kanhaiya was soon out of breath and started to flail his legs. 'I'll tell you,' he cried.

None of the visitors to the opium room noticed them. Hawa Singh acted like he was playing a game with a long-lost friend. He laughed and thrust the chillum at Kanhaiya's mouth.

'Last chance, Kanhaiya. I want only the truth.'

Kanhaiya licked his lips, took a long drag on the chillum and exhaled the dense, acrid smoke. He leaned closer to Hawa Singh, his eyes darting round the room to make sure there was no one watching them, and whispered hoarsely, 'Sirji, Brian had met with Prashant Singh, Suryadev's son.'

Hawa Singh sat there in the swirling smoke. He was sure the madman with a love for peculiar souvenirs was involved in the killings, somehow. 'I'll check on him myself,' he told Kanhaiya.

The wretch swallowed uneasily, his Adam's apple bobbing nervously up and down. 'Just don't go there today,' he managed to gasp. 'If you step in, they will kill you.'

CHAPTER 30

The white marble bungalow floated like an iceberg in a sea of mist. There were a few trucks lined up outside, waiting to be let in. He could see the barbed wire barricade above the wall had been raised further, since the time he had jumped in.

There had been talk that Suryadev Singh had discovered the loss of one of his precious souvenirs—a human hand—from its jar. The guards on duty had told some strangers over a desultory chat that the dogs found one on the lawn and had ripped it to shreds. Those guards were never seen again.

Hawa Singh moved steadily through the thick bushes lining the wall. He sneaked a lift from one of the trucks going in, clinging to the underside of the chassis, and was safely home.

He saw a crowd of human bodies out in the chilling night. There were shivering naked boys and girls, and another group of totally nude women who tried to hide their shame with their hands. A group of naked men stood apart quietly.

There was something about being naked in public. It stripped one of all humanity and showcased one as a piece of meat. It was like severing a person's soul from his or her human body, leaving a shell of flesh and bone.

Hawa Singh ran out to take cover behind the wall. From there he studied the place. There were armed guards all over, and the trucks were bringing in masses of more men, women and children. The guards forced them to strip and stand out in the open. There was no chance he would make it himself, out of there, alive.

He was unarmed in hostile territory. He missed the Colt. He turned away in pity when the guards beat the naked women into standing straight in the cold, and in their shame. He realized the bullies wouldn't hesitate to shoot any of these innocents who didn't toe their line.

He saw one of the guards pinching the nipple of a young woman. She resisted and he butted her with his rifle. She was bleeding from her head and could hardly stand. The other women rushed to help her to her feet.

The helplessness of one kind of people brought out the animal in the other.

The Ghost quickly merged into the darkness, and waited.

The gate was closed to the stripped-down human mass. The doors of the living room opened and Prashant Singh stepped grandly out. He was dressed in finery. His shoes gleamed in the darkness. He carried a horse whip in one hand.

Prashant walked up to the group of children. He examining them one by one pointed at the chosen ones with his whip. Those little ones were asked to stand aside.

From there, Prashant walked up to the mass of women and pointed at the stronger-looking ones. He moved on to the men and asked them to turn, show their legs and backs. This time, too, he chose the sturdiest.

Then, Prashant addressed them all coolly. 'All the chosen ones will work at our coal mines while the others will work at the collieries, loading coal.'

These were workers illegally rounded up from villages in UP and Bihar to work at Suryadev Singh's mines. They would be paid minimum wages and forced to work long hours. They didn't figure in any official government count and no one bothered if they went missing.

'Enough of all this!' shouted one of the desperate men. 'You killed my son and now you want to kill us!' Hearing this, the guards rushed up and threw him to the ground. Prashant took the rifle from one of the guards and pointed it at the man.

'Once you come to me, you all become my slaves. Only your death can free you,' said Prashant calmly.

The men, women and children cowered under his words with wide open eyes. They no longer had any voice of their own. They were just pairs of hands and legs and uncomplaining backs to carry the burdens of the coal mafioso.

Prashant tightened a finger around his gun—and a shot rang out in the air. Hawa Singh had snatched a rifle from one of the guards and aimed it straight at Prashant. The bullet ripped through his hand, flinging his gun, useless now, to the ground. Then, Hawa Singh came forward so he could be seen.

'Kill him!' Prashant screamed at the guards. There was a volley of shots around Hawa Singh, but he had already run and ducked behind a wall. He aimed and shot down two guards running towards him. From there he ran behind the line of trees, bullets whining after him.

Prashant said under his breath, 'Bloody Hawa Singh! You won't get out of here alive.'

Hawa Singh fired, killing another guard, and sprinted to one of the cars. It was Prashant's favourite car, a red Ferrari.

Hawa Singh got in to it and sped it around the grounds firing without cease. The mass of men, women and children huddled together in fear, surrounded by gunfire and death.

The guards riddled the Ferrari with their shots, infuriating Prashant further. He grabbed the nearest gun and fired another volley of shots at Hawa Singh. In his attempt to manoeuvre the car, Hawa Singh rammed it into one of the trucks. The Ferrari turned into pulp.

It took fifteen minutes for the police vans to arrive and another half-hour to break through the heavy gates of the bungalow. Hawa Singh had called up Sub-inspector Gaya Prasad from one the cell phones dropped by the guards running helter-skelter.

While he waited for relief, Hawa Singh had rapidly set fire to two of the trucks standing in line, all the while narrowly dodging a hail of bullets that whistled close past his ears. There was one that sliced his cheek open, leaving a fine line of blood.

The police surrounded the entire place. Hawa Singh held Prashant by his collar and threw him into the police jeep. He instructed Gaya Prasad to ensure a safe passage to all the would-be victims back to their villages.

The Ghost had a lot to say to the Madman.

Hawa Singh sat in the jeep and barked a further order to Gaya Prasad before departing. 'Sharma, I want that Kanhaiya in the police headquarters. Right now!'

The jeep moved out of the bungalow, Prashant bellowing impotent curses from its floorboards. Even as it was leaving, the media vans rushed in, mouths open to grab their greedy bytes.

Even before the premeditated and thoroughly timed attack, Hawa Singh had brought in the newshounds to the police station and presented them with the story of their lives. Many careers—journalistic and otherwise—would be made out of it. The pictures of the unclothed mass of people, the illegal guns, dead bodies and burning trucks would make for a great front-page splash.

The hounds attacked the place with their cameras and pens. They surrounded Sub-Inspector Gaya Prasad Sharma, the new national hero.

'It's only in B-grade films and comic books that the police posse arrives late. As soon as we got the information, the police team barged in and took control of the situation,' Gaya Prasad proudly told the reporters and cameramen jostling for his attention.

Flashes. More bytes. Furious scribbling. Camera. Action.

Story.

*

'I'm not the Butcher!' shouted Prashant Singh for the hundredth time. But there was no one there to listen. He turned around to see the still silent figure of Hawa Singh. One moment, he was nowhere to be seen, and now he was there. Prashant was confused.

Some said that Hawa Singh knew the art of standing inside a room, having already shut the door behind him, and at the same time knocked on it from the outside.

*

'Where have you brought me? I want to be taken to a police station,' protested Prashant.

It was a room filled with cardboard boxes, dusty sacks, broken parts of vehicles, old furniture and a pile of old newspapers. The slightest movement made the dust fly up. The walls were damp and there were no windows. A heavy door was locked from inside. No way out.

Hawa Singh hadn't taken him to the station. He had dumped him like a sack of coals instead, in a warehouse close to the police headquarters. He knew Suryadev would try to have political pressure applied from higher-ups to get his son released.

But this way, there was no official record of his arrest. Prashant Singh would remain in public oblivion. Till Hawa Singh decided to bring him out.

'Now tell me all that you said again,' said Hawa Singh.

Prashant said, through bared teeth, 'Just wait till my dad gets to know about this. You'll be cremated right here in Benares.'

Hawa Singh smiled affably and counted off the facts on his long fingers. 'First, the knife with which I was attacked in the mist came from your personal collection of antiques. Second, there were two human hearts in jars placed on convenient shelves in that cupboard in your palatial house. Tell me, where's the third?'

Prashant laughed humourlessly. 'Oh, so he has struck again? Which means you found out fuck all about his identity and decided I'd make a nice scapegoat. I'll say it again. I'm not the Butcher.'

'What about the two hearts in the jars?'

'Those were collected by my grandfather, B.P Singh. I have nothing to do with them and I have no idea whom they belong to,' shouted Prashant.

'The archaeologist from London, Brian Johnson, met with you. And then, he too, was killed. Do you know anything about that?'

'Just because I met someone, and he happened to die soon after, doesn't mean that I killed him. I met him at an auction in New Delhi. He was an archaeologist, a historian, and showed an interest in my collection.'

'How come the knife was missing from your place?'

'Someone could have stolen it.'

'You mean it's so easy to break into your heavily guarded bungalow?'

'If you broke in, anyone could,' was the insolent answer. Hawa Singh greeted that with a short laugh.

'Who is more religious, you or Suryadev Singh?'

It was Prashant's turn to laugh. 'Don't give me all that psychobabble. I've told you I'm not the killer.'

There was a knock on the door, a coded one that Hawa Singh recognized. He opened it, and Ruby walked in.

Prashant leered at her. 'The FBI sure has some awesome agents,' he observed, looking her up and down.

Ruby ignored him and took out a file from her briefcase. 'We matched the prints on the knife and on the axe with Prashant's fingerprints,' she detachedly announced to Hawa Singh. 'They don't match.'

Hawa Singh nodded without expression, his mind immediately abuzz with new considerations.

'We have also got the report about the specimen that you sent to Delhi. The tissue doesn't match that of the first two victims. The report says that the specimen belonged to the heart of some wild animal, probably a wild boar.'

Prashant roared triumphantly. 'See, I told you. Now you have nothing against me.'

'I had asked Gaya Prasad to bring in Kanhaiya,' Hawa Singh said to Ruby. It was a rhetorical question.

Ruby looked at him with wide eyes. 'Kanhaiya is dead. On my way here, Sharma informed me that he found him with his throat slit from ear to ear and his tongue cut out. It's sort of a punishment for opening his mouth.'

This time the Madman laughed hysterically.

CHAPTER 31

Suryadev Singh couldn't remember a more dismal, grey and depressing dawn in his life. The newspapers and television channels carried the news of the massacre inside his bungalow. The stories that emerged described him as a mafia don—there was no shred of doubt that his political image had been ripped apart. There were exposés on his illegal businesses—unlicensed coal mining, smuggling of arms, trafficking of men and women, enforced child labour under the most appalling conditions and past incidents of mining accidents due to sheer and callous negligence.

A few of the villagers who were interviewed testified against the Singhs, saying, 'Both Suryadev Singh and his son Prashant killed innocent tribal people and burnt their villages to take over any land that bore promise of deposits of coal and other minerals.'

Shortly after, Hawa Singh formally arrested Prashant Singh and let the newshounds loose on him. Prashant cowered behind a conveniently produced head-wrapping while the flash bulbs gleefully feasted on every feature of his that was visible. Suryadev Singh, similarly hooded, was arrested, too, and dismissed from his political party. The reign of the top coal mafioso had come to an end, said the media with absolute certitude.

Hawa Singh knew better. He couldn't recall that a single politician had ever been convicted in his country. Even if the crimes were heinous, the bigwigs always found ways to wriggle out of the grip of the law. All this show of arrest and imprisonment was a smokescreen for the people and the media. Once they got hooked to another scam or scandal, the politicians quietly came out of the woodwork—their prisons. Many went to 'recover' on long vacations in Europe and came back to make public appearances as totally reformed men.

It was hoping against all hope that the prison walls would keep Suryadev Singh long enough inside. Hawa Singh was no optimist, not after all those years of being a policeman. He'd learnt, the hard way, that the judiciary of the country was in a shambles. The laws of the country were more than a century old, formatted by the British Government. The judges were piled with hundreds and hundreds of cases which took years before they could be heard. There was no time for justice, quickly delivered. The country seemed to be hanging on that last thin thread—*Ram bharose*, God's will.

It was the media, if any, who, pronounced judgements now, right or wrong. But Hawa Singh acknowledged that the press, just like the police, were a necessary evil. They were both watchdogs. Watchdogs—often ill-equipped—of an increasingly frustrated and frequently violent society which had begun to take serious note of the goings-on around them.

Or begun not to care.

Hawa Singh thought of Kanhaiya. No one knew about his family. Where had he come from? Had he any relatives? A home? A life? Nothing. He was only twenty-three years old—and dead.

Kanhaiya was one of the millions who spent their entire lives as vagabonds, seeking shelter in railway stations, in street corners, on traffic dividers and under bridges, abused physically and psychologically from their infancy to their usually unnoticed death.

Deprived of food, education or means of livelihood, they turn to delinquency. Those 'rescued' in their early years find themselves serving futile terms in juvenile homes under even more appalling conditions and, by the time they are adults, have turned into monsters.

And none of us cares enough, thought Hawa Singh bitterly. It is we who breed criminals. It is society itself that has become their secret sanctuary, from which they will emerge at will only to wreak revenge and havoc back on it.

*

As if the prevailing chaos wasn't enough, a guesthouse owner in Benares had come forward to report that one of his foreign guests had gone missing. Hawa Singh and Ruby hurried to the two-storeyed, bright-yellow building close to the banks of Ganges. The sign outside said 'Rudraksha Guesthouse'.

The owner, Brahm Dev, an ex-wrestler as it turned out, was a devotee of Hanuman and had vowed to lead a celibate life. He was of stocky build and small height, five feet three inches in all. He had read about the murders of white foreigners and didn't want to invite trouble.

When his guest didn't return the night before, he lodged a police complaint.

He handed the guest's passport to Hawa Singh. It read, Name: Tom Barry; Age: 42 years; Occupation: Swiss Guard. His home address was in the town of Milton Keynes, in the UK.

They climbed the stairs to his room, a sparsely furnished bed-sit with white walls that looked newly painted, with a couple of framed pictures of the Kashi Vishwanath temple and the evening aarti at Dashashwamedh Ghat. There was a wooden cupboard. The bedsheets smelled as if they had been freshly ironed. A curtain printed with red flowers and green leaves hung from the single window. There was no air-conditioning. Altogether a cheap, functional room.

Ruby looked around with her trained eyes. Hawa Singh opened the cupboard. There was a bulging rucksack in it. A few clothes hung on the hangers. A jacket and a pair of track pants were folded and kept on a shelf. There was a pair of heavy army boots. A travel book. A Swiss knife.

Hawa Singh rummaged through the rucksack and took out few more clothes and books. The subjects ranged from travel, Benares, astronomy, Vedic astrology to the Holy Bible.

He put down the books in a row on the bed. Both Hawa Singh and Ruby knew there was a connection there, but what exactly, they couldn't say.

Hawa Singh turned to look into the toilet. There were the usual men's toiletries: a shaving kit, aftershave, hair cream, a deodorant and a lighter. There were a few cigarette stubs lying on the floor. He picked one up and saw it was from a rolled cigarette. He smelt it. Ganja.

Hawa Singh handed the butts to Ruby who placed them in the evidence pouch she carried. The stubs looked similar to the one Hawa Singh had found at Dashashwamedh Ghat. He remembered that similar stubs had been found in the room of the first victim, Eva Marie Cassidy.

He looked at Ruby curiously. 'Is it possible that the killer met with all his victims on an occasion or occasions *before* he killed them?'

'It's a possibility,' said Ruby.

'So why are these cigarettes to be found only inside the toilet?'

'Maybe they cleaned up the room and threw them here.'

Hawa Singh said, 'Or the killer came to meet his victims personally. It was he who may have smoked them. Maybe he had come here too.'

He called up Brahm Dev and asked for CCTV footage. There was none in the guesthouse.

'Do you remember anyone who came to meet Mr Barry in his room?' asked Hawa Singh.

'Yes, I remember a sadhu with long hair who had come here. Other than he, I didn't see anyone,' said Brahm Dev, shakily.

Hawa Singh thanked him and let him go.

'In Benares, a sadhu's is the easiest disguise to assume. No one would know who he really was,' conjectured Hawa Singh.

'One thing is clear,' said Ruby with conviction. 'That the killer goes about in disguise. He came to meet your father as a Naga sadhu, and maybe to meet Tom Barry disguised as another kind of sadhu.'

'Maybe he is there right in front of us every day and we have not been able to identify him.'

'That's very possible,' said Ruby.

Hawa Singh searched the room thoroughly. The shelves. Under the bed. Under the mattress. Between pillows. Inside drawers. Inside the boots.

He found a digital camera in one of the pockets of the rucksack. He checked, but there was not a single photo. It looked as if everything had been deleted.

He handed it to Ruby saying, 'See if we can retrieve some pictures from it.'

They stood near the door, taking a last look at the room, ensuring they hadn't overlooked anything. Ruby looked again at the books lined up on the bed.

She noticed a page-marker sticking out of the Bible. She opened to the page and pulled it out. It was a long strip of white paper with clear writing on it in blue ink. Ruby turned and showed it to Hawa Singh.

He read: *Bhrigu-Samhita*.

CHAPTER 32

Hawa Singh shook his head to rid himself of the jumble of thoughts rattling in it. The water rippled under them as Ruby sat close to him in a rowing boat. Sitting opposite them were the two opposing spiritual forces in Benares, Baba Ramtirath, the leader of the Naga sadhus, and Neelambar Nath, the new leader of the Aghoris. Hawa Singh had picked them up from Dashashwamedh Ghat.

In the middle of the Ganges, they were on neutral ground. Rowing the boat were a brawny Naga sadhu and an Aghori, who manned either side. Baba Ramtirath was, as usual, wearing rimless glasses over his blue eyes, and nothing else. Neelambar Nath wore a grimy, ash-smeared loincloth.

There was a boat to their left rowed by ten Naga sadhus who never left their leader's side. They all held tridents in their hands and their long matted hair flew in the wind. Their eyes were set on Hawa Singh and the Aghoris.

To the right was another boat, carrying a group of Aghoris armed with swords and tridents. They, too, had pledged their lives to protect their leader.

Hawa Singh had not bothered to call in any policemen. He wanted the Nagas and the Aghoris to trust him, and thereby enlist their aid. Ruby Malik was there to study them, analyse them and, as had become their protocol, provide support to Hawa Singh.

By now the SSP had given full rein to Hawa Singh to conduct his own investigation. Neeraj Thakur was too busy trying to butter up his seniors in Delhi and retain his job.

Hawa Singh looked over at Baba Ramtirath who was smoking a chillum that exuded fumes of ganja. He was one of the very few foreigners to be commanding such a high religious position among all the Hindu sects. 'You are one of the most important exponents of Vedic astrology here,' Hawa Singh said to him. 'What could possibly be hidden in that manuscript to get the Vatican so interested?'

Baba Ramtirath took a deep breath of fresh air and bent to dabble a hand in the water. 'The *Bhrigu-Samhita* is as mysterious as this river. The Ganges is called the mother of all rivers, and the *Bhrigu-Samhita* is the mother of all astrological texts in the world.'

Ruby noticed that Baba Ramtirath was as poised as a yogi. There was not a hint of a dent in his implacable calm. In contrast, Neelambar Nath appeared positively fidgety. His eyes wavered from side to side. They kept turning, as if for reassurance, in the direction of his followers in the boat alongside. He looked like he had something to hide.

Baba Ramtirath went on. 'As you know, the *Bhrigu-Samhita* was compiled a few thousand years ago. The original text might contain things unknown to most that caught the interest of the Vatican. But I, for one, am not aware of any such thing. As I already told you, the original manuscript was lost to antiquity.' He took a dismissive drag at his chillum. A direct hit.

Ruby took over. 'The killer used a wooden Cross,' she addressed no one in particular, 'and smeared ashes from cremation grounds on all his victims. He also took out their hearts. All this seems connected to the Aghoris.'

Neelambar Nath looked furious. 'Are you telling me I'm the killer?' he almost shouted. 'I have had enough of this. You forced me into giving my fingerprints. You interrogated the Aghoris and inspected our resting places. You have found nothing to link us to the murders.'

'There's another kind of link,' interjected Hawa Singh.

'What?'

'We have found that the Butcher also killed Tailanga Swami,' said Hawa Singh.

This shook Neelambar Nath and even Baba Ramtirath looked startled. Ruby noticed the changes in their body language. Was it possible that they both knew the Butcher? And were afraid of him?

'Swamiji was killed by an axe while—' spluttered Neelambar Nath.

Ruby cut him off. 'We are sure of what we're saying. Also, the wood used to make the Cross and the wood used in the axe's handle come from the same place, from the cremation ground. The wood used for cremation.'

'Your fingerprints may not match but all other factors point to the Aghoris and the cremation grounds,' pitched in Hawa Singh.

Perhaps it was only a cold draft of wind over the Ganges that made Neelambar Nath shiver, because he went on gamely. 'There are many others who work at the cremation grounds. Like the Doms. I'm *sure* that none of the Aghoris is the Butcher.'

Ruby noticed that Neelambar spoke with a certain confidence that usually goes with telling the truth. She looked at Hawa Singh and the unspoken words in the slight flutter of her eyes were enough for him to get the point.

One of the many things that niggled at Hawa Singh's mind was that none of the victims had any signs of struggle on their bodies. Still, the Butcher managed to wrench out their hearts and kill them. *Without facing the slightest resistance?*

In the case of Prashant Singh, he knew that Prashant loved to inflict pain, and was what some called a sadist. He enjoyed hitting, whipping and slashing people and revelled in their cries of anguish and writhing and pleas—till he triumphantly shot them between the eyes.

But the Butcher was a man who was evidently in control of his mind and senses. He calculated as precisely as a mathematician. At the same time, he was deeply and unshakably religious.

Hawa Singh had another question for Baba Ramtirath. 'Is there any way that such murders can be committed without the slightest struggle or fight?'

'I know what you mean. I have read in the papers about the absence of such telling signs on the bodies found. Well, there is one possibility.'

They were all ears. Even Ruby's watchful effort to register any other reaction, however slight, met with no result.

'There is an ancient Indian form of martial art known as Marma-Adi, as old as the Vedas and the *Bhrigu-Samhita* itself. During the Vedic ages, this art was known to kings and warriors, and was put to practice in the battlefields. Marma-Adi is the science of manipulating *marmas*, or the vital points in a human body. These are nerve junctures located close to the skin's surface. The human body contains 107 marma points which, when struck accurately, induce insensibility. Like if *lohit*, a marma point on the leg, is struck, it results in paralysis. Striking another point in the region of the neck can cause unconsciousness.'

'*None* of the Aghoris, including myself, know of this,' Neelambar Nath broke in excitedly, as if a point had been made. 'We are not into martial arts. We only do tantra-mantra and black magic.'

'Who are the practitioners of this art?' Ruby asked Baba Ramtirath.

'Marma-Adi is now a near-extinct science,' replied the blue-eyed sadhu. 'It lives on only in a few remote corners of the place of its origin. Even in this age of technology, Marma-Adi has remained a tradition shrouded in mystery.'

Total silence greeted this revelation. There was only the creak of the oars, the gurgle of the river, the peal of temple bells, and the occasional splash of boys diving for coins in the Ganges. A sparrow chirped between flitting from one boat to the other.

Hawa Singh noticed that the distance between the boats of the Naga sadhus and the Aghoris, now just a little ahead of theirs, had reduced. There was heavy tension in that little distance. They looked ready to kill each other.

Hawa Singh turned to Baba Ramtirath. 'Do you know of someone, particularly in Benares, who practises this martial art?'

'I know of only such one person in Benares.'

'Who's that?' Ruby asked.

'That's me,' said Baba Ramtirath, his blue eyes shining serenely.

CHAPTER 33

The night sky was so clear, and the stars were shining so brightly—it was almost an astronomical miracle at this time of the year. Below, the Ganges looked like a black road, gently meandering with the city lights dotting its sides.

Ramnagar Fort stood like a benevolent guard over the city of Benares. The moon was a big, bright spotlight on the Fort. On its terrace stood the Kashi Naresh, Maharaja Abhay Narayan Singh, looking through his telescope at the vast spectacle of the skies.

It was a Russian-made LS110, a classic Newtonian telescope, named after Sir Isaac Newton, its seventeenth-century inventor. It had a large aperture—110 mm—to achieve high resolution and very bright images, and long focal length to achieve high-power magnifications, without making the telescope too cumbrous. One of the great advantages of the LS110 was its light-gathering power. It delivered stunning views of even very remote galaxies and nebulae.

Abhay smiled with satisfaction as he looked through the telescope. He had many tools, devices and machines by Russian manufacturers, but he believed that it was with this telescope that the Russians achieved perfection.

He looked and, at low-to-medium power, the moonscape became a fabulously intricate panorama of craters, rays and rills. He set it on higher powers and explored the individual crater systems in detail.

It was as if God had chosen to bless Benares tonight with such a clear sky in winter. Abhay observed the cloud belts of Jupiter with their ever-changing detail. He looked at the four main moons of Jupiter, orbiting the giant planet, and sometimes casting shadows onto Jupiter's dense atmosphere. He looked at Saturn's magnificent system of rings and its famous moon, Titan.

Hawa Singh and Ruby Malik came up on the terrace. This time, they luckily didn't have to wait. The air was wintry all right, but there was not much wind.

'Ah, so the police are back in my home,' said Abhay, looking up from his favourite pastime.

'You seem to have a great interest in astronomy,' Hawa Singh said.

'Yes, apart from clock-making, I love to observe the skies. It makes me realize that I may be King, but I'm actually just a tiny speck in the universe. Our family has always had a deep interest in astronomy. You do know, our day-to-day lives are still linked closely to astronomy? And that it has been a continuing hobby, indeed an obsession, of mankind since earliest civilization?'

Hawa Singh observed that Abhay was wearing a windcheater under his long coat that was zipped high up his neck. He had his habitual gloves on, and wore elevated boots. There was a woollen cap on his head that covered his ears. The only visible part of his body, as always, was his face.

'Every time we meet, I notice that you observe me with the eye of a hawk—or should I say policeman?' said Abhay.

Hawa Singh smiled. 'As a policeman, you get wired to that sort of behaviour.'

Ruby took off her gloves. Abhay looked at her hands, long and white, ending in slender manicured fingers. He marvelled at her long slender neck, her firm chin, the high cheekbones catching the moonlight, the sculpted silhouette of her head and body turned slightly away from him.

Beautiful.

And he was ugliness personified.

'Is it my interest in astronomy that has brought you here?' he asked with sarcasm.

'As a matter of fact, it is,' replied Ruby coolly. 'That, and its link with astrology.'

For a moment he had been transfixed by her loveliness, but he quickly recovered himself. 'Are you referring to the latest case at Jantar-Mantar?' he asked, moving away.

Ruby looked at Hawa Singh, amazed.

'You might be successful in hiding it from the media,' said Abhay smoothly, 'but remember, I'm the Kashi Naresh, the King of Benares. Nothing is hidden from me.'

Abhay sat down on one the chairs placed around a table. He gestured politely towards the others. After the two had taken their seats, he poured scotch into large-bowled tumblers of cut glass and handed them around. 'Cheers to the Butcher of Benares!' said Abhay.

They stopped, their drinks halfway to their lips as they stared at him in astonishment. *Was the man quite mad?*

He looked at them and laughed in merriment. 'Look at your faces! You were paralyzed by fear because you've failed to nab him! Oh, I am worried too, but at the same time slightly excited, in a way. At last, *something* is happening in Benares. It's such a dull place, otherwise! You visitors come and take your customary dip in the Ganges, go to the temples, watch the evening aarti, do some pooja—and the pilgrimage is over. The Butcher has changed everything.'

Hawa Singh raised his glass slightly and took a sip.

'So what kind of an astronomer are you?' asked Ruby.

Abhay shook his head in self-deprecation. 'Oh, I'm just an amateur, or more specifically, you could call me an archaeo-astronomer.'

'What does that mean?'

Abhay took another sip from his glass. 'It's basically someone who studies ancient cultures and their practices of astronomy.'

Ruby was studying him constantly. He turned to show her he was aware of her intense gaze, and beamed genially at her. 'There have been found, all over the world, many mysterious ruins of ancient monuments with astronomical significance—like the Stonehenge in England and Carnac in France, the pyramids of Giza in Egypt and the Yucatán. They mark the same kind of commitment that transported us to the moon and our spacecraft to the surface of Mars. You can call them neolithic computers or astronomical devices.'

Hawa Singh looked around at the vast spread of darkness, the sky above dotted with stars and the telescope pointing up towards the gods.

Abhay went on, 'Few people realize that the seven days of the week—Sunday to Saturday—were originally named after an astronomical source. Ironically, they derive from the time of Ptolemy in the second century AD and his incorrect theory that the Sun, Moon and five planets revolved around the Earth. Thus were the days named after the Sun or Sol (Sunday), the Moon or Luna (Monday), Mars or Mardi (Tuesday), Mercury or Mercurious (Wednesday), Jupiter or Jeudi (Thursday), Venus or Vendredi (Friday) and Saturn or Saturnus (Saturday).'

'Do you think,' asked Hawa Singh, 'that astronomy could have any bearing on the dates of the recent murders?'

Abhay, who was still looking at Ruby, suddenly turned his face away. 'I have not been able to ascertain the significance of those dates or even days.'

Ruby could feel her body gaining warmth as the whisky went down. 'There have been theories,' she said 'that sacrificing eleven human beings can transfer their life energy into the killer. Do you know anything about this?'

Abhay looked at her with piercing eyes and said with gritted teeth, 'I have no idea about such theories.'

'What do you think of human sacrifice?' asked Hawa Singh.

'I'm totally against them.'

'You said that the killings had added a sort of excitement to this otherwise peaceful city. Do you feel sympathetic to this Butcher?'

'Are you trying to corner me into some sort of verbal duel here?' Abhay Singh said at a high decibel.

Ruby saw in the light of the moon that his eyes had widened in rage. She said gently, 'We just wanted to know your outlook on it.'

He looked back at her and his smile returned. 'I hope I'm not one of the suspects.'

Hawa Singh gulped down his drink in one big swallow and asked rapid-fire, 'Do you know anyone who has been a practitioner of the ancient Indian art of Marma-Adi?'

Abhay went quiet. He poured more scotch into his glass.

'You must have heard about this form of martial art,' said Ruby.

Abhay got up, taking his glass with him. He moved away and looked up at the sky without speaking.

'So you don't want to tell us,' said Ruby.

'I have known the greatest practitioner of Marma-Adi in Benares, and known him very closely,' said Abhay finally.

'Well, we know of one, Baba Ramtirath. Is there anyone else?' asked Hawa Singh.

Abhay said with emphasis, 'I'm talking about *the* greatest.'

Hawa Singh held his breath. Ruby waited impatiently.

'He was my brother, Manvendra Singh. The cannibal locked up in the mental facility.'

CHAPTER 34

Policemen are often confronted with situations which baffle them at first. A certain crime may seem meaningless, but they have to derive some meaning out of it. They have to connect the dots, find the links, delve into its history, look for evidence, come up with a zillion theories—and arrive at the truth.

The thing is, truth is always stranger than fiction.

Hawa Singh's natural ability to interpret other people's thoughts and actions made things go faster. He was like an accomplished actor, getting under the skin of the character, feeling like him, behaving like him. A good policeman has to think like an actor to get closer to a criminal. He'll have to get inside the criminal mind.

It was 2 am. The meteorological miracle had continued and a starry blanket lay over Benares. But since there were no street lights on the long stretch of road, it was dark. And cold.

They raced towards the Sparrow Mental Health Institute, riding the Bullet. Hawa Singh drove against the wind, which was like a blow to the face, and a howling in his ears, making his eyes water.

Ruby had to shout to make herself heard. 'Manvendra is not only locked in his cell but also chained. He could not have escaped from there. Moreover, he could not have killed and returned without anyone knowing.'

Hawa Singh turned his head slightly. 'Unless' he shouted back, 'someone has been helping him there'.

True, he might have an accomplice, thought Ruby. Someone helping him or he could be working for someone else. Aloud, she said, 'If Manvendra is the killer, then your father and also the guesthouse owner, both of whom saw him dressed like a sadhu, would have recognized him by his grotesque face.'

'He could have disguised his face,' Hawa Singh argued, 'just the way he disguised himself as a sadhu. Don't forget he is a master of many arts.'

They were interrupted by the wail of a siren. Hawa Singh stopped the bike. Ahead, at the Sparrow Institute, there was chaos everywhere. Floodlights had been switched on all sides, the few guards of the institution were running here and there, looking inside rooms. Others scanned the vast lawns with torches.

Three of the guards sped out in a jeep, shouting encouragingly to each other, 'He couldn't have gone far.'

Hawa Singh and Ruby ran up the gravel path towards the building. The siren was still on. He stopped a stocky woman panting down the stairs and asked, 'What happened?'

'The cannibal has escaped,' she replied, out of breath.

Hawa Singh felt the pain of the bullet again. He tried hard to concentrate and closed his eyes. Ruby put a steadying hand on his arm. 'We need to check on Sudha,' she said.

They went to Sudha's office. The door was open. They walked in to find Sudha Krishnamurthy lying on the floor, the entire office ransacked. Books, furniture, framed pictures and shards of glass lay scattered everywhere. A cabinet had been wrenched open and files were strewn around the place.

Hawa Singh saw a deep wound on Sudha's head, which was bleeding heavily. He held her in his arms. 'Sudha, open your eyes,' he urged.

There was no response. He looked helplessly at Ruby and let Sudha's head rest back on the hard floor.

There was nothing they could do. They made for Manvendra's cell, and found the door open. There were drops of blood on the tiled white floor. Further in, Dr Binod Pradhan was sprawled on the ground, in a pool of blood. A large chunk of flesh around his throat had been torn off, as if some wild animal had attacked him. His eyes were wide open in a horrified stare. Hawa Singh noticed that Dr Pradhan was lying close to the place where Manvendra had been tied to the wall. Something had made him go up close to the cannibal. Hawa Singh looked for the iron chain. It was lying on the floor like a dead snake. The cannibal had broken his fetters.

'It looks like he escaped from here and went straight to Sudha's office,' he contrived to say, after taking a deep, shuddering breath. 'What did he want with her?'

As they walked back towards Sudha's office they saw medics bearing her out on a stretcher. A young lady doctor had examined the woman and ordered that she be rushed to the infirmary. 'She still has some life. We can save her,' she'd said. The medics ran with the stretcher down the long corridor.

The doctor seemed a bit puzzled when she saw Hawa Singh and Ruby Malik, but then recognized who they were. 'Dr Sudha spoke so much about you both. She loved your dedication and would often set you up as exemplars of hard work.'

Hawa Singh looked at the badge on her coat. Dr Shruti Srivastava. 'How did he escape?' was all that Hawa Singh could manage in return.

Shruti sighed deeply. 'It was around 12.30 am that Manvendra started screaming and shouting. He complained of severe headache and even started to beat his head against the wall. I was on night duty. I tried to give him sleep-inducing pills but he threw them away.'

Shruti went on. 'Manvendra continued to bang his head against the wall so I called Dr Binod Pradhan and Sudha. Most of the doctors live in staff quarters close by and they were here in a few minutes. Dr Binod went up to him and they seemed to have a fiery argument. I was outside and didn't hear much.'

'You must have heard something?' asked Hawa Singh.

Shruti tried hard to think and said, 'Manvendra was shouting, "I'll kill you all. I'm the Butcher."'

'What happened next?'

'I was too scared to go anywhere near Manvendra so I ran down to Sudha's office. Then I heard a scream. I knew it was Dr Pradhan, but my entire body refused to move. I was too nervous to react. Hearing the scream, a few of our night guards ran up and saw Dr Pradhan lying there. Manvendra had managed to break free from the chain. He escaped.'

Ruby tried to appear calm. 'Where did he go from there?'

Shruti looked at them with fearful eyes and said, 'He straightaway rushed inside Sudha's office. He started to look for files and ransacked the entire place.'

'Where was Sudha?' Hawa Singh interrupted.

'She had not yet come in. So he went on searching through the files. He was probably looking for his own, in order to destroy the records. I think it was another ten minutes or so before Sudha walked in on him.'

'Did he attack her straightaway?' asked Ruby.

'No, he wanted her to hand over his file. He kept threatening to kill her. Sudha was too terrified to anything. He kept smashing things on the floor. He even punched her and banged her head against the wall.'

'Did he finally get his file?' Hawa Singh asked.

'I have no idea,' Dr Shruti replied. 'Later, Manvendra closed the door and we heard him shouting at her. I couldn't hear what he was saying. Then the door opened and he came running out. The guards tried to stop him but he was uncontrollable and escaped into the darkness.'

'Where were you all this while?' asked Ruby clutching for Hawa Singh's hand.

Shruti looked down in shame. 'I was hiding behind the stairs.'

'You don't need to feel ashamed of that,' said Hawa Singh. 'You did the right thing. He would have attacked you.'

Ruby realized that the siren had stopped. The air felt still. 'Do you think Dr Sudha will be okay?' she asked the doctor.

'There were a few faint signs of life,' she replied. 'We have our infirmary and I hope the doctors there have been able to revive her. I will have to rush and check on her.'

She almost ran, her heels clacking down the corridor. Hawa Singh turned to Ruby and gently put his hand on her head. She hugged him tightly, wishing her terror away.

But only briefly. Then she pulled away, returned to her professional self, and spoke without sentiment. 'Where would he go?' she asked.

Hawa Singh didn't have to do any arithmetic to answer that one. 'He had drawn my horoscope chart on in the Jantar-Mantar, remember?'

As an afterthought, he added. 'He also drew my father's.'

Ruby looked at him wide-eyed. 'You mean he will go after your father?'

'In all probability, yes,' said Hawa Singh.

CHAPTER 35

It was 4 am. Mukti Bhawan stood like a skeleton, its bricks showing through the lime wash. A body pressed itself against a wall, and looked into the darkness with vacant eyes. The body was naked but felt no cold. The darkness covered it.

Hawa Singh and Ruby ran towards it. They saw the staring eyes. Then, the eyes blinked. They did not belong to Fauja Singh, but to another of those awaiting death at Mukti Bhawan.

Hawa Singh rushed beyond it and inside his father's room, switching on the lone bulb. The first thing he saw was the Cross.

There was the jute mat spread on the floor, on it was the tattered mattress, a dirty pillow and two thick blankets that he had newly bought for his father. The Cross had struck right through the blankets.

Ruby stood frozen to the spot while he removed the blankets with shaking hands. Fauja Singh was not there. The Cross was stabbed into a thick layer of woollens and a pillow kept under the blankets to make it look like a person sleeping there.

He looked back at Ruby. Life returned to their bodies.

'Where did he go?' asked Ruby.

'To think he was awaiting death—and narrowly missed it.'

They hurried out from there. It was 4.15 am.This was the auspicious hour when the devout woke up, had their bath in the Ganges and said their morning prayers.

Hawa Singh hastened to Dashashwamedh Ghat, Ruby following close behind. He was sure his father would be somewhere nearby. Fauja Singh would often come here and sit by the steps, looking out over the river, waiting for a death that never came.

Hawa Singh frantically searched the ghat looking for him. He was nowhere. *Is it possible that the Butcher had taken him away? Was the Cross some sort of message?*'

Ruby, too, scanned the area. She saw Naga sadhus taking a dip in the water. Water so cold that she couldn't bear to dip even her hand in it.

They ran the entire length of the ghat but failed to find the old man. Hawa Singh reflected sadly that though he'd agreed to bring his father to Benares in his last days, he had never wanted him to die. Never, ever. Memories came, unbidden, of their moments together. Holding on to his father's finger as a child, his father carrying him to school on his shoulders, their bicycle races through the green fields in the village, and their mutual fondness for Kavita.

Fauja Singh had gradually begun to love Kavita and treated her like his daughter. He had fought a lonely battle to get the village panchayat to agree to the marriage of his only son to a south Indian girl. He had learnt to laugh at her jokes, and waited impatiently for her to cook him dosas and idlis. Fauja Singh got the toilet in the house fixed with a Western-style commode, so that when the girl came home as a bride, she'd have every comfort. He had, at some cost, got marble flooring done in the rooms and bought new bedcovers.

The day he heard the news of Kavita's death, he gave up on life. It seemed that all the excitement, happiness and joy he'd ever felt had been chopped away in one stroke. Since that day he had never stepped inside the newly furbished house and lived in a small mud hut that he had built in the fields instead.

The heart disease was welcome. He didn't have the will to live.

Father and son both lived in the shadow of death. Hawa Singh threw himself in the line of fire and till now had come out unscathed. Fauja Singh decided to let Benares take his life.

Ruby had brought with her a flicker of hope but blackness overcame it. They enjoyed each other's presence in their lives, but without optimism about the future.

For now, Hawa Singh didn't want to lose his father. They had fought, argued, made each other cry, but they were a team. He would never let anyone take his father away. His eyes filled with tears at the thought of losing him.

Ruby's cry filled his ears.'There he is!'

He turned to see Ruby running down the steps and, before he could move, she had jumped into the water. He joined her. They could see Fauja Singh, with hands folded, slowly descend further and deeper into the river.

Hawa Singh yelled to him, 'Fauja, where the hell are you going?'

Fauja didn't seem to hear them, or he was too pre-occupied with his thoughts. His head disappeared underwater.

Ruby swam rapidly towards him. It was as if Mother Ganges had called out to her and taken her in Her arms, after all. It was not just a dip Ruby had taken. She had become one with the river—just like Hawa Singh.

Fauja, too, had surrendered to the Ganges. He was floating away when hands clutched at him to drag him to land. Fauja was unconscious and Ruby had to resuscitate him on the steps of the ghat. Soon, Fauja coughed up the water from his lungs, sat up and stared angrily at them.

'You won't let me even *die* in peace!' he said reproachfully.

'So you wanted to end your life like a coward, committing suicide!' Hawa Singh shouted back at him.

'I was taking jal-samadhi,' cried Fauja Singh.

Ruby held his hand and spoke soothingly. 'Look how fit and strong you are. You frightened even death away.'

Fauja softened, his teary eyes on her face. 'This CID girl saved me. When I opened my eyes under water, I saw Kavita coming towards me and holding my hand. She carried me up.'

Hawa Singh closed his eyes. The tears mixed with the water of the river on his face.

A few sadhus gathered around them curiously. 'Get away from me!' Fauja roared at them. 'I'm fine!'

Ruby helped him get up and placed his arm around her shoulders. Fauja turned to smile at Hawa Singh. 'My Kavita has come back,' he crowed.

Hawa Singh nodded and got up.

'We found a Cross in your room,' said Ruby.

'Ah, *that* Cross. Actually, I made it myself and

sharpened it to test how the Butcher uses one. I thought I might be able to help this idiot Hawa Singh, but he doesn't value my advice.'

They sat near a stall and had hot masala tea. Fauja slurped on it, beaming. 'I never enjoyed tea so much.'

Hawa Singh's mind was racing back to the Butcher. *Where could he have gone?*

At that moment Ruby and Hawa Singh looked at each other, filled with the same thought.

*

He had finally escaped his prison. He was free. He knew they were closing in on him but in his freedom he had set a trap for them. The policeman from Delhi had worried him but now he could relax. He had set them on a hunt. A hunt into a maze that he had built for them that would eventually lead them nowhere.

He liked the thought that that girl from the FBI observed him keenly. Maybe she was trained to deduce things. She definitely was smart, and he loved her clear, glowing, fair skin and her eyes. There was something about her that made him want to eat her up.

But he was in awe of that Hawa Singh. First, he survived the knife attack and then came out alive from the tunnel under the Ganga. That was definitely commendable. In fact, it was unfathomable. 'Bravo, Bravo, Hawa Singh!' he shouted to no one.

The gods seem to be favouring the policeman. Then the thought occurred to him that he, too, was divine, in a way. He belonged to the royal family of Benares. People considered the Kashi Naresh to be the incarnation of Lord Shiva, and thus, being his brother, it made him one of the pantheon of Hindu gods.

Not that this had anything to do with religion. Nor was he a fanatic. It was about Benares and its history. The historians never got it right. The ancient land of Benares was crying for blood. He was there to fulfil the need.

Throughout the ages the Vatican had imposed its rule and made a mockery of other faiths. The men of the Cross started the Crusades, targeted Muslims and killed hundreds of thousands of innocent men and women. Now they talk of Jihad, the backlash of the Holocaust and the Fundamentalists targeting *them*.

History was coming full circle.

Benares had also completed its circle and was now giving it back to them. We gave them the science of astrology, astronomy, we gave them the wisdom of the *Bhrigu-Samhita*. The stars had aligned back to defeat *them*.

CHAPTER 36

5 am.
Temperature: 1 degree Celsius.
Windy—North-westerly winds from the Himalayas.
Clear skies. No fog. Frost formation indicated.

Hawa Singh had called SSP Neeraj Thakur, and explained the situation to him. The SSP was on his way with his elite command of paunchy, samosa-munching officers. Hawa Singh sent his father away to Mukti Bhawan, asking him to change his clothes and rest.

'Don't forget I came to Benares to die, and not to be frightened by some madman. You don't worry about me. Just make sure this time that the killer doesn't get away,' said Fauja Singh.

Hawa Singh nodded.

'And don't come to me with another bullet in your head or a Cross sticking out of your chest. I want you in one piece,' called back Fauja Singh as he walked away from the ghat.

Hawa Singh turned to smile at Ruby. 'He loves me a lot.'

Ruby had a faint smile herself, as she looked at herself, drenched and shivering. Hawa Singh took out his jacket and put it on her. These were small gestures in harsh times, and swept Ruby away in a flood of emotion. Her heart was telling her that this was the man, what the world called Mr Right. You could never be more right, she dryly told her heart.

He was in his t-shirt, with water dripping from his hair, clothes and the bandages on his chest and arm. She wanted to hold him tightly and stay that way forever. She had never felt like this before.

She had her share of one-night stands, but this man was something else. She didn't want to spoil what they had by hurrying into bed. He, too, had made no demands.

Maybe he was still too deeply in love with Kavita. Maybe he would never love Ruby. Still, she could always love him.

Hawa Singh busied himself making calls. He instructed Sub-Inspector Gaya Prasad Sharma to take a team to bring the Naga sadhus to Manikarnika Ghat. He wanted to address and question both the Nagas and the Aghoris together on the famous cremation ghat.

'The Butcher had a deep connection with the Aghoris as he had lived with them here in the cremation grounds. It's possible that he might return there, as it could seem to him a good place to hide,' said Hawa Singh.

Ruby nodded saying, 'The very smell of human flesh might also draw him there. We need to get there fast.'

Hawa Singh kick-started the motorcycle. 'I feel I could be the next target.'

Ruby climbed on the pillion seat. 'I will be right by you. Let him come. It will be easy to take him down if we're together.'

He looked back at her and they both grinned.

Ruby, still wearing his jacket, wrapped her arms around him, hugging him tighter when she felt him shivering in the wind. He felt her warmth seeping into him as he sped through the narrow alleys of the town, now empty.

A few street dogs tried to give chase, but gave up soon enough, disheartened. They couldn't keep up with the Ghost. One moment he was there and then he was gone.

The sound of wailing came louder and louder as they approached the Manikarnika Ghat. Smoke, a dull grey, rose from the pyres. There were more than twenty burning pyres even at that time of day.

Gaya Prasad Sharma was already there when they arrived. He saluted Hawa Singh and Ruby, and said, 'Sir, I have brought the Naga sadhus.'

Hawa Singh saw Baba Ramtirath and his eleven disciples waiting for them. The blue eyes snapped as Ramtirath told him, 'We are trying our best to co-operate with you, but don't mistake co-operation for weakness.'

Hawa Singh walked towards Baba Ramtirath saying, 'I won't. I want you to know we now know who the Butcher is. It's just that he escaped us.'

Hawa Singh shouted to Gaya Prasad, 'Sharma, search the entire ghat and the cremation ground inch-by-inch. And bring out all the Aghoris and Doms. He could be hiding here among them.'

Gaya Prasad and team started rounding up all the Aghori tantriks, sadhus and Doms, including the Aghori leader Neelambar Nath, who was deep in some sort of pooja.

Dom Raja Sanjeet Choudhary, dressed in black, was supervising the cremations. Gaya Prasad recognized him and asked him to move out of the cremation grounds along with all the other Doms.

'We cannot leave the cremation halfway like this,' Sanjeet protested.

Gaya strode up to him, grabbed him by his neck and dragged him away. 'Next time I won't talk,' he growled. 'I'll burn you all in these pyres.'

Hawa Singh and Ruby moved cautiously through the crowd of Aghoris, Naga sadhus and Doms, now together on the ghat. The Nagas and the Aghoris, similarly ash-smeared, stood apart from each other. The Doms stood out from the crowd as they were the only ones clothed.

'Sir,' Gaya said to Hawa Singh,' we have searched the entire place. It doesn't look like he's here.'

It was 5.45 am. The sky was lightening. The boats were still anchored. The river appeared undisturbed, but reminded Hawa Singh of a crouching monster, waiting with a gaping mouth to swallow everything.

On the opposite bank there was total darkness. Above the hill there rose the ominous fort of Ramnagar. Hawa Singh suddenly swung around to Ruby. 'He must have gone to the Fort,' he said.

Just then, the SSP, carrying a clay cup of masala tea, walked up with his troop. 'Did you find him or not?' he asked, without preamble.

Hawa Singh was already on his way. 'He is not here,' he called back over his shoulder. 'We are going to the Fort. He could be hiding there.'

The SSP thought for a moment and said, 'We'll have to disturb the king for that—but I suppose that has to be done. Let's go there together.'

The SSP and his men got back into their jeep. Hawa Singh started his motorcycle and was about to ride off when a sight caught his eye. A bright light of yellow, orange and crimson cut through the grey sky.

A large Cross spread against the wall of Ramnagar Fort was burning bright, its flames leaping high.

To the many Aghoris, Naga sadhus, pandits, boatmen and other devotees, it looked like a sign from the Kashi Naresh in defiance of Christianity. It seemed that Maharaja Abhay Narayan Singh had burnt the Cross to show the supremacy of Hindus. It was his message to all of Benares that the king was with them, in their common religion, and against all others.

They didn't see the crows coming out to hover so unusually early in the day. They couldn't distinguish the smell from that which rose from the burning pyres nearby.

Only a Dom would recognize that smell. It was the stench of burning human flesh that came from the other side of the Ganges, from the burning Cross on the wall of Ramnagar fort.

It was Dom Raja Sanjeet Choudhary who hesitatingly drew Hawa Singh's attention to it. 'There's a body on that flaming Cross,' he whispered to him hoarsely.

The Butcher had struck again.

Hawa Singh shouted to the policemen, 'Everyone at the fort!'

*

6.30 am, Ramnagar Fort

The cross was hanging from a heavy iron chain and by the time the police team pulled it up, it was more than halfway burnt. The wood had turned black and the police had to pour water to douse the flames.

Hawa Singh was one of the few policemen who could withstand such a horrific sight. Even Ruby turned her face away and fought against nausea.

A body was nailed to the Cross that had charred beyond recognition. The flesh had melted and at some places clung to the wood. The skin, muscles and tissues were gone. Only some bones remained.

The SSP vomited, emptying his guts of all the samosas and kachoris he had wolfed down earlier that morning. He couldn't bring himself to go near the Cross.

It became difficult to stand there without covering one's nose. But Hawa Singh had blocked all his senses, relying only on his mind's eye. He pulled on latex gloves and bent close to the body. He could distinguish the skull, but there was no trace of skin and tissue where there should have been a face. A few lumps of skin had coagulated at the throat.

None of the policemen dared approach. Ruby stood alone to one side, watching Hawa Singh at work. She wondered how he could bear the sight and smell.

Hawa Singh continued with his work. He could see a few strands of cloth hanging on the skin near the chest. There was a gaping hole in the centre. 'The heart has been removed,' he announced. The SSP kicked at the wall filled with rage.

Hawa Singh bent even closer to the body and sniffed. 'It's hospital spirit,' he called out. The SSP only nodded, holding a handkerchief to his nose.

Hawa Singh signalled Ruby to come closer. She tied a hanky around her face and hesitatingly went to him. 'You need to block your thoughts,' he reprimanded her. 'It's just a body. So take a deep breath and calm down. I need your help.'

Ruby slowly inhaled and the stench from the burnt corpse filled her lungs. She coughed wildly.

'Focus! Focus on the smell, like its evidence. There are traces of hospital spirit in it, smell that.'

Ruby shut her eyes tightly. This time, Hawa Singh yelled at her. 'There's hardly anything left here. You'll have to look.'

She slowly opened her eyes. She saw Hawa Singh carefully remove a fine layer of burnt tissue that had mixed with the cloth fibres.

He lifted the remnants of a hand and showed it to Ruby, 'What do you see here?'

The skin had burnt off but she could clearly see that one of the fingers was missing.

She wanted to say it out loud but Hawa Singh stopped her midway. 'We need to turn the body. For that, we'll have to remove the nails.' He called for a hammer.

Gaya Prasad Sharma came running with one. He and Sharma took out the long nails with the hooked end. The body was finally free.

Hawa Singh signalled once again to Ruby. They were ready. Slowly and very carefully they started to turn over the half-burnt skeleton.

'Be very careful, the bones have become brittle and the entire body could crumble into powder,' cautioned Hawa Singh.

They managed to turn over the body. A part of the back was still covered by cloth. Hawa Singh skilfully peeled the cloth away. There was skin underneath. He could see the skin was covered with scabs. He got up and faced the cowering policemen standing at a distance.

'What?' demanded the SSP. 'Who?'

Hawa Singh exhaled and spoke softly, 'Kashi Naresh Maharaja Abhay Narayan Singh is no more.'

CHAPTER 37

They mounted vigil on Ramnagar Fort and the entire staff was put under house arrest. The museum was closed and the king's personal guards kept an eye out for trespassers in the Fort. They all had a photograph of Manvendra and were on the lookout for that distorted face.

Hawa Singh had his jacket back on, and smelt the trace of perfume Ruby had left in it. Ruby herself was dressed in black slacks and a sweater, her curves defying the sombreness of her outfit. The policemen on guard at the palace couldn't take their eyes off her.

They walked into the Darbar, the public hall in which the king met commoners. Its grandeur was awesome, with intricate pillars supporting the high ceiling, the large paintings hanging on the walls, the rows of exquisitely carved wooden chairs and, at a raised level, the majestic throne of silver.

It was said that the original throne was made of gold. The British invaders stole it and replaced it with a cheaper replica in silver. There was an elaborately embroidered hand-pulled fan cloth poised over the throne that used to be pulled by one of the king's most trusted servants. There was another throne close by, to the left, meant for the queen, and another on the right for the crown prince.

The Durbar was where Maharaja Vibuti Narayan signed the Instrument of Accession to India on 15 August, 1947. On that day, Benares merged with the new Indian state of Uttar Pradesh. With that, Maharaja Vibhuti Narayan Singh's short reign officially came to an end, although he would maintain his title for many more years.

Hawa Singh and Ruby found nothing of consequence in the Durbar. Walking through a corridor hung with portraits of past kings, they reached the door of Saraswati Bhawan.

Something made him want to go inside again. He knew that this was the vault that contained so many mysteries. Abhay himself had shown Ruby and him around, pointing out his vast collection of antiques and ancient manuscripts.

His eyes roamed, once more, over the many guns, royal carriages, the four-barrelled pistol, the mutilated coins, paintings and manuscripts sealed inside moisture-proof glass shelves. Ruby scrutinized the miniature paintings on the walls and the many handprints in yellow dye.

The handprints belonged to members of the royal family starting from the first king of Benares. She realized that the yellow colour came from turmeric paste, worn on auspicious occasions. The name of the owner was written below each handprint. She could see the mark left by Maharaja Balwant Singh's enormous hand, and those of other kings whose names she couldn't pronounce.

Hawa Singh peered at the glass shelves. He saw the original hand-written manuscript of Tulsidas's *Ramayana*, a manuscript of the *Manu-Smriti*, the original *Hanuman Chalisa*, the quill used by Tulsidas, a few leaflets believed to belong to the original Vedas, and other texts in unknown languages yet to be deciphered. It was a treasure house.

On one wall, Ruby was mystified to see a rusted iron knob in between some paintings. She looked at it curiously, put her hand around it, and turned it.

There was a slow scraping sound. The wall parted, giving way to a smaller vault inside. 'Abhay never showed us this!' Ruby told Hawa Singh when she called him over to look.

It was an ultra-modern vault, with a numbered lock and of solid, impregnable steel. They tried to unlock it with numerous permutations and combinations. Nothing worked, not even after they'd been working on it for four hours.

'What the hell could possibly be inside?' Ruby asked, after they'd exhausted themselves.

'It has to be something very precious. We'll just have to open it,' said Hawa Singh.

'The steel is tough. We won't be able to even drill through it. What we need is a master safecracker,' said Ruby.

'Abhay's obsessions lay in astronomy and astrology. It has to be something related to that,' hazarded Hawa Singh.

Ruby shrugged. 'Maybe the code is his date of birth.'

Hawa Singh smiled and casually set the numbers, 211058, not really expecting any results. But they heard the faint sound of gears inside the lock coming into position.

He had once arrested a master thief in Karol Bagh, from whom he'd picked up a few tricks of his trade. Hawa Singh had learnt from him the basic techniques of opening locks. Hearing the sound of the gears inside, Hawa Singh knew that he had got the first six digits right.

'What would the rest be?' Hawa Singh tried to think.

'Astrology and astronomy go together,' said Ruby.

Hawa Singh looked at her, not understanding her meaning.

'To make a horoscope chart one requires the date of birth *and the time*,' said Ruby.

'I have no idea about the time of his birth,' said Hawa, nonplussed.

Ruby put her hands on her hips and thought hard. Then she looked around. 'The horoscopes might also be here.' She started looking around the larger hall. 'They have preserved the handprints, portraits and even clothes of all the kings. Their horoscopes should also be a part of the royal collection.'

They looked around desperately.

In one of the glass shelves she found some texts written in Sanskrit and called Hawa Singh over. 'Look here.'

He hurried up to her and saw, with rising excitement, the many horoscopes of the royal family rolled up in bundles. He picked up a gun in the hall and, using its butt, broke the glass case open. He opened one bundle after another, and finally, there was one with 'Abhay Narayan Singh' written on it.

He opened it to find a rolled-up chart that went down to his feet. He looked feverishly for the time of birth. It was 10 am and the day was Sunday.

Hawa Singh ran back to the vault and entered the number 211010. The gears moved inside again. There was a click. Then it all stopped.

Hawa Singh gave Ruby a disappointed look. 'Nothing.'

Ruby grabbed the handle on the vault and pulled at it angrily. The vault opened without a sound. They had hit the jackpot.

They felt like children who had won at a game, and hugged each other in triumph. Inside the vault was another glass case, also moisture-proof. And inside that was what looked like an ancient manuscript. The writing here, too, was in Sanskrit.

There was one word he read clearly—*'Bhrigu'.*

CHAPTER 38

It was 7.30 pm, dark again, and windy. A light rain fell. One of the news channels had said that it was zero-degree Celsius in Benares that night. The weather forecast had warned of heavy rain and intense cold. They had advised people not to venture out as there was even the possibility of a hailstorm.

It was a full-moon night, and the Ganges roared, its waves rising high, but dark clouds prevented the moonlight from penetrating downwards.

They were sitting in the library of Benares Hindu University. Around them Shri Vishnu Shastri, Baba Ramtirath, the SSP, ACP Shishir Jha and Sub-Inspector Gaya Prasad Sharma. The library doors were locked from outside so that no curious student or teacher might come in accidentally. All the lights were switched off within. All, that is, except a table lamp, which illumined the cylindrical glass case near it. Everyone stared at the manuscript sealed inside.

'There is a legend in Benares,' said Shri Vishnu Shastri, looking up, 'that said that the original manuscript of the *Bhrigu-Samhita* lay with their kings, passed from one to the other. It said that the kings protected it with their own lives, and never revealed their secret to even the closest members of their families.'

'Why didn't you tell us this before?' asked Hawa Singh.

'Because, like I said, it's a legend,' said Vishnu Shastri. 'So many stories keep floating around in Benares about the royal family. You don't know which is true and which is not.'

The SSP cleared his throat to make his presence felt. 'Let's not wait any more.'

Hawa Singh picked up the glass cylinder and tapped it against the edge of the table. It was a hard wooden table, but it didn't seem to have any effect on the glass case. He hit it harder but the glass still didn't crack.

Hawa Singh examined it with care. 'This looks like tough glass. It could be bulletproof.'

'There has to be a way to open it,' said Ruby, coming forward. If they took such great care in preserving it, they would have to have access to it.'

Baba Ramtirath bent closer. Deep blue eyes squinted at the glass case, the centre of such attention. His fingers gently drummed over the glass, turning it round and round. He had tried to make himself presentable for the occasion, wearing beads of Rudraksha and long garlands of marigold flowers that hid his loins. By then Ruby had got used to seeing stark naked men. She briefly wondered whether it would be difficult to adapt back to her life in the US.

She had grown to love the morning sounds of temple bells, chanting, the sound of waves, the boats on the river, the colourful streets, the sadhus, the smoke from their chillums, the children flying kites from rooftops and the man she had met here, Hawa Singh.

Baba Ramtirath looked up. 'The glass case itself is a vault. It works on the mechanism of an ancient lock where the pieces of the same metal were conjoined and rotated.'

'So does it have a key?' asked the SSP.

Baba Ramtirath smiled. 'They don't have keys to them.'

Hawa Singh echoed Ruby. 'If it's a lock, then it has to unlock. Every lock is made for that purpose,' he said with irritation.

'I have not encountered such a vault in the last thirty years but, still, I'll try my best,' said Baba Ramtirath. He tried sliding the bottom and the top, but that didn't work.

'Sir, we can try using a heavy hammer,' suggested Gaya Prasad.

'We cannot take a risk with the manuscript,' warned Vishnu Shastri. 'It could turn to powder on exposure, and then we'd have nothing.'

'In ancient days,' said Baba Ramtirath, 'they used to fill such locked chambers with a chemical that came ablaze and destroyed the entire contents if anyone broke through.'

'Are you saying this glass case could also contain something like that?' asked the SSP.

'I don't know. We need to be careful,' Baba Ramtirath smiled his eternal smile.

'Can't we cut through the glass?' asked ACP Shishir Jha.

'It's *bulletproof*, Jha!' shouted the SSP.

Baba Ramtirath was concentrating on the glass case. There seemed to him to be another glass cylinder inside, that slid from both side to side, finally settling in the centre.

There was sudden excitement on everyone's face.

Baba Ramtirath saw that the manuscript had moved right into the centre in the smaller cylinder. There was no way out.

It was like a tortoise hiding under its shell, sensing danger.

The excitement died down.

Frustrated, Hawa Singh raised his fist hand high up in the air and brought it down hard on the middle of the cylinder. Nothing happened even then.

Everyone—but Ruby—gave him a look of disdain. Hawa Singh removed his hand from the case and made another fist.

There was a soft hiss. A hairline crack appeared on the glass case. They gathered eagerly around.

Another big punch. The glass case broke open.

There was a time when Hawa Singh had punched a hole through the bulletproof glass of a politician's Ambassador car as he tried to molest a female reporter sitting inside with him. His sheer determination, as always, won the day.

A smoky gas with a pungent smell coming through the crack in the glass seemed to erupt inside the case, and then, suddenly the manuscript caught fire. Everyone gasped.

Hawa Singh plunged his hand in and rescued the manuscript. The sides had charred and blackened, but it was whole.

They had the manuscript—the original manuscript of the *Bhrigu-Samhita*!

It was a parchment made of fine leather. Leaves and beaten bark were usually used for writing on during Vedic times. It appeared Bhrigu wanted material that was hardier. The sage's farsightedness served them well.

If the scroll had been of dried leaf or bark, it would have been completely destroyed in the flames.

Vishnu Shastri lifted it with both hands, and opened it delicately. Fully unrolled, it was more than ten metres long.

They couldn't make head or tail of it.

It was Baba Ramtirath and Vishnu Shastri who looked like kids who'd found a treasure trove.

Hawa Singh could see it contained many horoscope charts, drawings of the Sun, planets and some calculations. One part, the pandit told them, had descriptions in Sanskrit of the effect of the planets, Sun and Moon on Earth.

'As I told you,' Vishnu Shastri said, with obvious glee, 'the *Bhrigu-Samhita* was written in pre-Vedic times, and there was no record of its date. Now we have one!'

The others saw Baba Ramtirath and Vishnu Shastri looking with awe at a particular chart, their eyes filled with tears.

'What happened?'snapped the SSP.

Baba Ramtirath turned to them. 'Maharishi Bhrigu made a horoscope chart of Lord Krishna here in Kaashi. That means Bhrigu compiled it during the time of Krishna. That makes it not less than 9,000 years old!'

'That also makes Benares the oldest inhabited city in the world!' Vishnu Shastri joined in excitedly. 'The Vatican thought Jerusalem to be the oldest.'

Baba Ramtirath read out from the manuscript. 'Maharishi Bhrigu wrote that Krishna was the Special One and that he was Rama in his earlier life, and would come back in many avatars—as Buddha, Jesus, Mohammed. So there is no difference between any of them. They are all One.'

Ruby knew that this discovery would shake the very foundations of the Vatican.

Vishnu Shastri pointed to a crude drawing of the solar system with the Sun at its centre. 'See, Bhrigu knew 9,000 years ago that the Sun was the centre and not our Earth, while it was not till the sixteenth century that Galileo and Copernicus came up with the truth.'

Baba Ramtirath pointed out some additional parchment joined to the manuscript. It looked to be more recent than the *Bhrigu-Samhita*. The colour had not yet faded. He looked closely at the handwritten accounts. 'These were written by the followers of Bhrigu during the time of Christ, a few thousand years after Bhrigu wrote his manuscript. It seems the royal family of Benares had preserved all of this. It says that Christ had sent his disciple Thomas to teach his form of spirituality in India, and that he came to Kaashi, that is, Benares. Thomas spoke of many of Christ's teachings that don't exist in the Bible. Principles such as karma and re-incarnation seem to have been reaffirmed by Christ.'

Vishnu Shastri said, 'The Bible was not written by Jesus Christ. It was written by his disciples and other saints. Many of Christ's teachings were originally Eastern in nature, and were edited out. Imagine the implications that this discovery holds for Western Christianity and its churches?'

'Okay, so we have laid hands on this miraculous document, one that will shake the entire Western world. But what,' said Ruby, getting down to brass tactics, 'does all this have to do with the murders?'

Hawa Singh was trying to put the pieces of the puzzle together. 'All three victims were connected to the

Vatican,' he said. 'Either they were sent by the Vatican to look for this manuscript or they came independently in search of it, having heard of it in Rome.'

'You mean they didn't want the truth to come out—that Benares is the oldest inhabited city in the world, and about the original teachings of Christ?' asked Ruby.

'So why kill them?' said Baba Ramtirath.

'Yes, finding the *Bhrigu-Samhita* would have glorified Hindus and Benares. Maybe the Butcher didn't want that,' said Hawa Singh.

'Unless the killer is a fanatic Christian and didn't want the findings to shake faith in the richest religious centre in the world,' said Ruby.

'Exactly. Maybe we were wrong all the time. The killer is not a Hindu but a Christian, and the Cross is a statement of supremacy,' said Vishnu Shastri.

'We all know that Manvendra is a Hindu and belongs to the royal and supposedly divine family of Benares,' said the SSP.

'He might have considered it his royal duty, as part of the family, to protect the *Bhrigu-Samhita*.'

'Then why did he go and kill the king of Benares, his own brother?' asked Ruby, almost shrilly. They all looked out of their depth.

Hawa Singh took a deep, shuddering breath. 'Look, we've identified the killer. Once we catch him, everything will come to light. The focus right now should be on looking for him.'

'What should we do with the manuscript?' the SSP wanted to know.

'It's a great opportunity for a press conference,' said Hawa Singh, grinning inwardly. 'You can show this to all the reporters and tomorrow morning the papers will be filled with the news. Maybe that will even help in getting the Butcher out of his hide-out.'

'It'll definitely take some heat away from the Butcher case,' said ACP Shishir Jha.

It was party time, again, for the hounds.

*

By the time the SSP and other police officers finished briefing the media on the astonishing new discovery, it was 11.30 pm. The predicted hailstorm came and lashed the city of Benares. Taking the severe weather into consideration, the SSP arranged for police jeeps to drop the reporters back at their respective offices. It was another matter that he wanted the news splashed in every paper the next day. Preferably featuring him in a prominent role.

Hawa Singh had borrowed Gaya Prasad's police jeep to drop Ruby to Nadesar Palace. The storm continued throughout, hailstones clattering furiously on the jeep all the way.

Both Ruby and Hawa Singh were too tired—body and mind—to thrash through the details of the case any further. All they desperately needed was to sleep.

They ran from the jeep to the warmth and dryness of the heated lobby. It was like a different world. Hawa Singh escorted Ruby to her room. He wanted to leave, but the lure of a glass of scotch pulled him inside. He waited as Ruby went to mix him a drink.

She looked at him over her shoulder. 'Why don't you have a shower? It's lovely and warm. It'll soothe you.'

Hawa Singh felt uneasy about having a shower in her hotel room. But she pulled him up from where he was sitting and playfully pulled off his jacket. 'Now, you've begun to smell,' she teased him.

He went inside the bathroom, where there was a big shining bathtub. He worried that he might soil it. He looked at the faucets, the shower above his head, the gleaming knobs and the commode that gleamed like a throne.

He removed his clothes and hesitantly turned on the shower. A spray of warm water hit his body with a hiss. It was indeed soothing. He held his face up to the cascading water and smiled broadly. This was as good as a treat.

He felt the door open a crack, and held his breath, waiting. Ruby had also shed her clothes. Now she joined him under the shower, their eyes never leaving each other's. She looked at the wound on his chest and kissed it.

In a flash they melted into each other's arms, kissing passionately, their legs entwined. They could not recall when they came out of the bathroom and collapsed together on the bed.

It was frenzied love-making, although Hawa Singh remembered to be gentle. Later, sated with love, they lay breathlessly side by side, staring at the ceiling.

It was Ruby who turned to smile at him. 'I think I've fallen in love with you,' she said simply.

Hawa Singh restrained himself. 'I'll always be there for you,' he said, meaning it, but not wanting to give way to his emotions just then.

Ruby didn't know what he meant. She had wanted something more. But she didn't want to spoil the moment, and lay quietly in his arms.

*

He slipped into the room like air slipping through a crack in the door. He saw them lying wrapped in each other's arms amidst the tangled sheets. A smile appeared on his face. He sat himself down on the sofa and contentedly took out the Colt.

He looked at the peaceful, sleeping face of the policeman they called Hawa Singh. He pointed the Colt at his head thinking, 'This is the irony of life. You get killed by the very pistol you kept for your own safety.'

He looked at Ruby's long, toned legs. She was indeed beautiful. He saw her snuggled close to Hawa Singh, smiling in her dreams.

He lowered the Colt thoughtfully. He would love to engage Ruby in sex, but would also love to give her a special and spectacular death.

He was no pervert. He was merely working towards a purpose. Anyone coming between him and his quest was his enemy.

He laughed to himself, silently, 'We'll have a great time, Hawa Singh. I won't let you die too easily.'

He knew that they had shown the original manuscript of the *Bhrigu-Samhita* to the press. He smiled at the stupidity of those policemen. They were merely doing his job for him, walking obediently into the web he'd spun for them.

He wanted to wake up Hawa Singh and laugh in his face. But he controlled himself. He was no ordinary criminal, no senseless serial-killer. He wanted to cut each and every branch off, before uprooting the tree entirely.

For him the number eleven would not be enough. He had a long way to go, many obstacles to clear on the way.

He kept looking at the sleeping couple. They'd found love at the time of death.

Then he got up and slipped out the way he came in. At that very moment Hawa Singh got up with a start. He could sense that someone had been in the room.

A shiver ran down his body. *Did the Butcher come in here?*

Hawa Singh saw the half-open window, rushed to it and looked out. There was only darkness to be seen. He closed the window and turned back to Ruby. She was in deep sleep.

Hawa Singh had never slept so well since he had lost Kavita. But sleeping had cost him the Butcher.

CHAPTER 39

Hawa Singh had fallen asleep again, despite himself, and it was the loud ringing of the phone that woke both him and Ruby. It was Sub-Inspector Gaya Prasad. The Butcher had scored yet another time.

The news jolted them out of their dreamy state. They were out of bed and dressed in three minutes flat. Hawa Singh checked his watch. It was 5 am. Another grisly dawn awaited them.

Dawn appeared to be the Butcher's preferred time for doling out death. They reached Manikarnika Ghat and saw two police jeeps standing there. Gaya Prasad, along with five other policemen, was busy moving away the early morning devotees who had crowded around the ghat. The fire from the pyres was going as strong as ever.

'I'm sorry to have woken you up so early,' said Gaya Prasad. 'We found another body and it looks like the work of the Butcher.' He led them ahead. They walked past the Vishnu temple that was believed to be sinking slowly into the sand at an angle. They drew close to the sacred well called the Manikarnika Kund, said to have been dug by Lord Vishnu at the time of creation. It is believed that Lord Shiva had dropped his earrings in this well during his transcendental dance. Hence the name 'Manikarnika', meaning 'jewelled earring'.

The Manikarnika Ghat brings death and release face-to-face with the creation of the universe. While the power of life was generated at the *charanpaduka* of Vishnu, the actual cremation of bodies takes place at Jalsayin Ghat, the whole of which is called the Manikarnika Ghat. Jalsayin, or 'the sleeper of the water' reflects the beauty of Vishnu asleep on Shesha Naga, during the cosmic deluge consuming the ashes of the cosmos, symbolizing the endless cycle of time, the flame of which burns continuously at the Manikarnika Ghat. Shesha also means remainder; the ashes that remain to be washed away by the Ganges, and lose themselves into the cosmic ocean. In Hindu mythology, Vishnu is the seed of life, a lotus from whose navel grows Brahma, who creates the world.

Every Hindu in Benares aspires to be cremated at Manikarnika. It is believed that cremation here is a guarantee of liberation, courtesy a boon given by Lord Shiva. Nevertheless, it's a very costly affair and not everyone can afford it. The cheaper option for liberation was the Harishchandra Ghat, and most ended there.

They reached close to the perimeter marked by a rope. Hawa Singh could see a group of Doms watching them approach. Inside the perimeter was a large round slab called Charana Paduka, placed on high ground. In the middle of it stood a stone pedestal in the shape of a lotus, the top of which was inlaid with marble. The two footprints of Lord Vishnu marked the centre of the marble.

According to legend it is believed that Lord Vishnu had chosen this sacred spot for the performing of ascetic rites and the worship of Lord Shiva. Vishnu apparently stood in meditation there for about 500,000 years to please Shiva, leaving his footprints on the stone.

According to this legend, Benares would be more than 500,000 years old, but then those were just myths and legends.

Right on top of the Charan Paduka sat a human figure in a meditative pose with his hands folded. It was headless.

The torso was drenched in its own blood. The marble stone nearby was also awash in red. A fountain of it must have spurted after the beheading.

Hawa Singh ducked under the rope, followed by Ruby. They were careful not to slip on the blood when they reached the body.

Hawa Singh bent down and picked up the stub of a cigarette. It was from a joint of marijuana. So it *was* the Butcher who had done it. He had created another work of art for them to wonder at. Ruby took the stub from Hawa Singh and placed it in her evidence pouch.

The body was not that of a white foreigner. It was a male of medium height, average build, lean and brown-skinned. There were no marks of torture or a struggle on the body. There were a few scars on the shoulder blades, neck and back that looked like scars from childhood injuries. But there was the telltale cavity in the chest area, from which the heart had been removed. There was no Cross on the scene.

Although the victim was not a foreigner this time, nor had the body been pierced with a Cross, the absence of the heart seemed to echo the Butcher's modus operandi.

But the absence of the head posed a problem. It would be difficult to identify the victim. Gaya Prasad called to them, 'Sir, we also need to check inside the temple.'

Right before them was the small Adi Kesava temple that housed the Charan Paduka. Hawa Singh and Ruby proceeded to its inner sanctorum, Gaya having secured the place with policemen. In what seemed to have become a grim repetition of police procedures, no one was allowed to enter Manikarnika Ghat.

Hawa Singh removed his shoes before he entered the temple. Ruby followed suit. There was a large idol of Lord Krishna inside. The statue bore a benign face, its lips stretched in welcome, its merry eyes all-knowing.

At the idols' feet was a large brass plate with slightly curved sides, as in a thali, brimming with blood. In the centre of the tray was a severed human head.

Its head faced the idol, as if in supplication. Shoulder-length hair fell to the scarlet pool in which it stood, its ends soaked. Ruby almost collapsed to her knees, but Hawa Singh caught her in time, and firmly held her up till she calmed down. She fought to regain her equilibrium, ashamed that she'd acted like a non-professional instead of a seasoned FBI agent.

They began a thorough examination of the precincts. The first thing Ruby encountered was a long sword with a bloodied blade, the probable instrument of murder. It was unusually shaped, rather like an elongated Cross.

The floor bore bloodied footprints, too, and Hawa Singh summoned Gaya and the forensics to take copies.

'Who discovered the body, Sharma?' Hawa Singh asked.

'Sir, the control room received an anonymous call. I was patrolling so I was relayed the information, and got here at 4.25 am. Later, a few Doms collected here, but I cleared the ghat of them, and all other devotees and visitors.'

The forensics were about to wrap the head and remove it from the thali, when Hawa Singh stopped them with a gesture. He hadn't looked at it sufficiently closely. One of the forensic experts nudged the large brass plate towards them, to directly face Hawa Singh and Ruby. They well knew that person. They had met him and had spoken to him. They had heard many stories about him.

It was the head of the very man they were chasing. The Butcher, Manvendra Singh.

The cannibal had been sacrificed at the altar of God.

*

The newspapers were filled with front page articles about the finding of the ancient manuscript of the *Bhrigu-Samhita*, the reports dwelling extensively on Maharishi Bhrigu's drawings of the solar system, the horoscope chart of Krishna, and the consequent establishment of Benares' unrivalled antiquity the world over. Some of the reporters had drawn their own conclusions: the Vatican never wanted this to come out and had sent its own assassins to kill the Kashi Naresh and steal the manuscript from his keeping. They didn't care to go into why the Vatican's hired assassins got killed mysteriously themselves.

There were reports that spoke about Christ's teachings related to karma and rebirth, deemed unacceptable by the Church. One Hindu reporter went on to write that Christianity in fact emerged from Hinduism, and that Hinduism was the mother of all religions.

The people of Benares rejoiced while the TV channels went wild, broadcasting debates between representatives of the Christian community nationwide and Hindu scholars.

There was no official word from the Vatican. The historians argued on the authenticity of the original *Bhrigu-Samhita*. Hindu evangelists proudly asserted that Maharishi Bhrigu came up with the drawings of the solar system much before the West knew of its existence. Suddenly, the world was big on Hinduism.

SSP Neeraj Thakur may have garnered all the media spaces he had desired, but he wasn't exactly overjoyed. In his office, there were no exultations. 'I told you from the start that you were chasing the wrong man,' he shouted, his face purple.

Hawa Singh looked around at the other police officers in the room, who weren't daring to speak. He too, had nothing to say, but he forced himself to speak coherently. 'All the evidence pointed at Manvendra Singh,' he managed through taut lips and a dry mouth. 'The method of killing, the fingerprints, the traces of marijuana, the history of mental deterioration and the turning to cannibalism. Everything fitted so perfectly.'

'You have *nothing* to work on,' retorted the SSP. 'The one and only suspect you were chasing is slaughtered himself. We have reached a dead end.'

'Sir,' ventured ACP Shishir Jha, 'maybe you were right—that the killer could be a Christian. He used a Cross to kill on sacred Hindu sites.'

The SSP nodded, pleased. 'Yes, we need to check on all the Christians in Benares. They are a small population here and it won't be difficult to round them up. Maybe we'll come up with something—for a change.'

'It is unlikely a Christian would have drawn horoscope charts, or would have knowledge of Vedic astrology,' argued Hawa Singh.

'Then we have nothing to work on,' the SSP interrupted rudely. 'I'm going to lose my job, do you understand? The Chief Minister is right on my back. I'll have to report this new murder to him.'

'Both Kashi Naresh Maharaja Abhay Narayan Singh and his brother have been brutally murdered,' observed ACP Shishir Jha. 'The killer seems to be targeting the royal family, in addition to white Christians.'

'Why did he take away the hearts from the victims' bodies?' Sub-Inspector Gaya Prasad Sharma uttered the question on everyone's mind.

Hawa Singh had an answer. 'The hearts are his trophies,' he said plainly. 'You remember the story of the ancient dacoit-turned-Buddhist monk Angulimaal, who used to collect the fingers of his victims? There have been many other killers who collected body parts as souvenirs. We saw that in the collection of Suryadev Singh and his father B.P. Singh, too.'

'We seem to know everything that the killer has done, but not who he is. We are still nowhere close to finding him,' said the SSP, glumly.

What have we missed? Hawa Singh tried desperately to sort through the facts at hand. *Surely, those matching fingerprints should have been by themselves conclusive?*

There was something hidden in those fingerprints. Then, he remembered the handprint on the wall.

Hawa Singh rushed out, calling back to Ruby, 'I've got it. Come with me.'

*

They were inside Saraswati Bhawan at Ramnagar Fort.

'Last time we were here I saw you looking at the preserved handprints of the royal family. That should also have the handprint of Manvendra Singh,' said Hawa Singh.

Ruby hurried to the wall behind the shelves of artefacts. 'Here they are, Singh.'

They looked at the handprints and the names under them. They traced them to those of Maharaja Vibhuti Narayan Singh, and then as they moved further along the wall, to the handprints of Abhay Narayan Singh and his brother, Manvendra Singh.

The shape of the latter's suggested that the owner had been an artistic person, with long, slender fingers. It was close to the thumb area that they got the clearest image.

'You mean to say that someone faked his prints on the knife, axe and in the file?' asked Ruby agitatedly.

Hawa Singh was calm. 'Well, it seems like it now. If I am wrong, it will all have truly come to nothing.'

Ruby took the print from the wall on a transparent tape that she pasted over it and carefully removed. She then compared it in detail with the prints taken from the knife, the axe and the file at Sparrow Mental Institute.

'They don't match at all!' she cried.

'I knew it,' Hawa Singh said through gritted teeth, his colour heightening.

'What does it mean?' asked Ruby.

'That the person locked up at Sparrow's mental institute was not Manvendra Singh. His face was deliberately cut up so no one would recognize him. He was kept on drugs and maybe even mentally brainwashed into believing that he was Manvendra Singh, brother to the king of Benares. Slowly, over time, he may have even been taught to believe he was the Butcher.'

'So someone locked up that person, with his fingerprints recorded in the file, under the identity of Manvendra Singh,' Ruby sounded almost incredulous. 'Then where is the real one?'

'Manvendra was the one who'd gain most by faking his own identity. It's known all over Benares that Manvendra lost his mental balance and was admitted to the Sparrow Mental Institute. It seems he somehow contrived to lock up another person in his place. While he roamed around and killed freely,' said Hawa Singh.

'Does that mean Manvendra is in fact the Butcher?'

'Manvendra Singh is also one of the greatest exponents of Vedic astrology as well as of Marma-Adi,' said Hawa Singh slowly. 'The drawing of horoscope charts suggests knowledge of the first. The killings, the wrenching out hearts and beheadings without a single sign of struggle are clear indication that someone used Marma-Adi to paralyze the victims.'

'He is part of the royal family,' Ruby countered. 'The people of Benares know him and recognize him by face. So he couldn't just walk around the city freely.'

'Well, we know by now that he used to resort to various disguises. He could be anywhere. Maybe that's why he killed in darkness and anonymity,' said Hawa Singh.

'However will we find him?' asked Ruby.

Hawa Singh looked at the handprint on the wall and said, 'Just as a criminal is drawn back to the scene of the crime, that maniac will also return to his home.'

CHAPTER 40

The gravel crunched under their feet as they hurried to the Institute. Inside all was quiet, despite the previous night's fiasco. They moved up the stairs and gently knocked at the door of Dr Sudha Krishnamurthy, CMO, Sparrow Mental Institute. There was no reply.

Hawa Singh pushed open the door of the office. There was no one inside. The place had been tidied up, although there were still a few glass pieces lying in a corner. The files had been stacked neatly back in place. The framed picture of Sudha's family had a cracked glass. One of the edges of the table had traces of blood.

They had not received any information about Sudha's condition. They didn't even know whether she had survived or not. However, they were there because Hawa Singh was sure that was the place to look for the missing link he so desperately wanted.

As they stood there blankly, Dr Shruti Srivastava walked in. Seeing them, she looked at first amazed, then quickly regained her composure to ask, 'How is it that you are here?'

'We're sorry to bother you, but we need to meet Dr Sudha,' said Hawa Singh. 'I hope she is well?'

Dr Shruti gave a slight nod. 'Yes, she somehow survived. She is in her quarters. I'll take you there.'

They followed her through the long-winding corridors and across the lawns towards the staff quarters. At the residence of the CMO, Dr Shruti asked them to wait while she went in to see if Dr Sudha would like to meet them. Ten minutes later, she returned and invited them in.

They went in to see a pale and weakened Sudha up on a couch, a quilt wrapped around her. There was an improvised table across her lap, on which she was busy signing documents.

'It's so good to see you back at work,' said Ruby, cheerfully.

Sudha smiled back. 'Good to see you too. I have to sign these salary cheques and daily reports of patients. I'm not allowed to die.'

They all smiled. Dr Shruti asked to leave, telling them, 'I have to administer medicines to all the patients. I can't keep them waiting—or Dr Sudha won't sign my cheque!'

'You'd better not keep them waiting,' said Sudha sternly. Shruti almost ran out.

Hawa Singh sat down on a proffered chair and rested his back against it. 'There's one thing I want to understand,' he said, getting straight to the point. 'Why did Manvendra attack you?'

'It seems he held me responsible for his condition,' said a serenely smiling Sudha. 'He was locked up and chained. In a sense, the institute had become a prison for him and he desperately wanted to escape. Finally, he succeeded.'

Hawa Singh let the answer sink in. It was still short of what he wanted.

Ruby quickly picked up the slack. 'When was he admitted to the institute?' she asked.

'It was almost two-and-a-half years ago.'

'That was the time you had just joined the Sparrow Research Institute,' said Ruby.

'Yes, around that time.'

Ruby chewed on her lower lip, then asked, 'When exactly was his face disfigured?'

Sudha paused to recollect. 'I think it was within the first month itself.'

Hawa Singh took it from there. 'Did Dr Binod Pradhan attend to Manvendra right from the start?'

'Dr Pradhan was an expert on schizophrenia and had done research on cannibalism. He was the perfect man for the job.'

Hawa Singh and Ruby were in perfect sync as one took over from other smoothly.

'Dr Pradhan told us that he gave marijuana to Manvendra Singh to calm his nerves. Is that a usual practice?' asked Ruby.

Dr Sudha looked stunned. 'I was never informed about it!'

'Did you ever meet a local tourist guide called Kanhaiya?' persisted Hawa Singh. 'He supplied people with marijuana and opium.'

'Are you suggesting that I'm a drug addict?' shouted Dr Sudha.

'I never said that,' said Hawa Singh calmly.

Ruby took out her phone and showed Sudha a picture of Kanhaiya on it. 'This is Kanhaiya. Did you ever see him around this place?'

Dr Sudha looked at the picture carefully. 'Yes, I think I saw him once with Dr Pradhan. There seemed no reason to suspect him of anything.'

'Okay, that clears up one thing. This Kanhaiya did come here to supply marijuana to Dr Pradhan,' said Hawa Singh.

'Are you charging me with smuggling drugs?' Sudha flared up again.

'Not at all,' said Hawa Singh.

They had deliberately hidden the information about the murder of the man who supposedly went by the name of Manvendra Singh.

There was a sudden draught of wind through the open window. The pile of cheques on the table flew about and Sudha hurriedly picked up a heavy paperweight to keep them in place. Some escaped to the floor, and Hawa Singh swiftly picked them, pinning them under a book.

In that sudden movement, Hawa Singh noticed Dr Sudha's feet barely visible below the quilt. A toe on one foot was missing.

Sudha caught him looking at it and said, 'I was a child in a small village in Tamil Nadu, when, while playing one day, I accidentally burnt my toe. The nearest hospital was more than 100 kilometres away, and hardly any public transport available. So by the time we reached the hospital, my toe was beyond repair and the doctor had to amputate it. That was the time I decided to become a doctor, to cure others. Destiny had slightly different plans for me, so I landed up a psychotherapist.'

'You are still a doctor, treating the mentally ill,' said Ruby, appeasingly.

Dr Sudha nodded. 'I try my best, but the likes of Manvendra make me feel like a failure.'

'Where would he go?' asked Hawa Singh, returning to matters at hand.

'I really have no idea. He was not close to his brother, the Kashi Naresh. He loved to spend time with Aghoris, tantriks or reading up texts on Vedic astrology and occult sciences.'

'Could he be biding his time, planning other killings?' asked Ruby.

Ruby noticed that this sudden question had jolted Sudha. Her eyebrow twitched and there was a slight movement under the skin on her cheek, indicating hidden fury. Then it all subsided, and she was back in control.

'I have no idea what he is up to,' she said impassively.

'Did you interact with him often?' asked Hawa Singh.

Ruby fired another question almost immediately after. 'You must have had therapy sessions with him. What did you notice in him?'

For a moment Sudha sat quietly collecting her thoughts, and then said, 'There are very few cases when a doctor gives up. This was one such case. With my sessions I realized Manvendra would never heal. He reacted like a man-eater who had tasted blood. One would have to kill him to stop him. No amount of medication would help. He started attacking the staff, cut his face and became more and more violent. Finally, we had to chain him and maybe that's one reason Dr Pradhan resorted to using marijuana or opium on him—even if it was illegal.'

'You think Abhay Narayan Singh will ever accept him back in the family?' asked Hawa Singh.

'I don't think so.'

'One of the things we noticed was that he had disturbed all the files in your office. What could he have been looking for?' asked Ruby.

'I think he was looking for his own file. He wanted to destroy all his records and then disappear. He didn't want to be known as a lunatic and preferred to be remembered as a part of the royal family.'

Hawa Singh looked directly at Sudha. 'Do you think Manvendra could be the Butcher, the serial-killer we are looking for?'

Sudha didn't show any reaction and there was nothing for Ruby to read.

'I can't even imagine such a thing.'

'Why?' asked Ruby.

'Like I said, he was chained and locked shut. It would be impossible for him to go out kill someone and then sneak back in.'

'Is it possible that Dr Pradhan was helping him?' asked Hawa Singh.

This time Sudha looked truly shocked. 'Dr Pradhan was trying to help him, turn the cannibal into a human being. He would never do that,' replied Dr Sudha.

'Would it be possible for Manvendra Singh to go out and kill the king?' asked Ruby.

'Is this some sort of interrogation?' Dr Sudha was visibly annoyed. 'What kind of questions are you asking? I can't start to assume things. He is mentally ill and is capable of doing anything. He might do nothing, or he might just kill himself. There could be umpteen choices.'

They sat there for a while quietly.

Finally, Sudha broke the silence. 'Any more questions? I have a lot of pending work to finish.'

Hawa Singh and Ruby looked at each other. 'No, none.' They got up to leave. 'Thank you for your time, Doctor,' said Ruby.

Sudha kept sitting there, her smile returning.

*

At the forensic lab, Hawa Singh handed Ruby the paperweight that he had pocketed from Sudha's room. 'I saw her clearly holding it at the top. It'll have her prints.' Ruby started taking the prints from the paperweight with her handy fingerprint kit. While Hawa Singh checked on the footprint they had taken from the inner sanctorum of Adi Keshwa temple, where they'd found the Butchered head.

The forensic man showed him the print they had taken. It was of the right foot. Obviously, the man had removed his shoes before entering the temple.

Hawa Singh noticed that the outline of one toe was missing.

Almost instantly, Ruby shouted, 'The prints match with that of the handprint we took from Saraswati Bhawan.'

Hawa Singh looked at her, stone-faced. 'Sudha Krishnamurthy is Manvendra Singh, the Butcher of Benares.'

CHAPTER 41

The police team inched closer and closer. It comprised SSP Neeraj Thakur, ACP Shishir Jha, Sub-Inspector Gaya Prasad Sharma and twenty other armed men—along with, of course, Hawa Singh and Ruby. The SSP signalled to his men to surround the building. The policemen slowly spread out with their rifles pointed far out in front of them, on full security alert.

Hawa Singh had warned them, 'The killer is dangerous and will not think twice before killing you.'

Hawa Singh and Ruby checked Sudha's office and her quarters but she was not there. Meanwhile, the entire staff of the Institute was asked to move out of the building. Hawa Singh looked in on the rooms of the patients. The patients looked scared and nervous. It seemed as if the mentally ill could sense and smell the danger. They were all quiet. A few huddled in the corners of the rooms. Only three reacted violently and started crying. Hawa Singh had to call Dr Shruti to calm them down.

Ruby and Gaya Prasad checked the offices on the ground floor.

ACP Shishir Jha and armed policemen were securing the exterior, scanning the vast environs of huge lawns and dense foliage.

The SSP stood outside, looking at his watch. It was 5.30 pm. They had managed to locate the Butcher's den. If only he could pounce on the Butcher himself, put him in handcuffs and parade him through the streets of Benares!

It took the police personnel inside almost twenty minutes to go through each room and office—and come up with nothing. The members of the staff standing outside looking dumbstruck. They had not been told why they'd been asked to leave the building. Nor had they been informed of the true identity of their CMO, the revered Dr Sudha Krishnamurthy.

Hawa Singh came downstairs to rejoin the rest of the team. Only Ruby was missing. A danger signal lit up instantly inside his head. He ran through the circular corridor, calling out her name. As he rounded a corner he saw her, and stopped dead in his tracks.

Ruby looked horror-stricken. He saw the nose of a Colt pointing directly at him. Then he saw Sudha emerging from behind Ruby. Her face wore the maniacal ictus of a grin. 'So you finally tracked me down,' cackled the figure. 'But it's of no use. You cannot stop me.'

'You have nowhere to run,' warned Hawa Singh. 'The entire place is surrounded.'

The Butcher laughed. With one hand he removed the long-haired wig, casting it contemptuously aside, and then peeled off the thin layer of latex he wore on his face.

Hawa Singh saw a lean man, about forty years old, with boyish features. Manvendra Singh.

'So this is the real face of the Butcher?'

'I'm not a Butcher!' shouted Manvendra Singh.

The timbre suddenly changed but there was still something boyish about it. Hawa Singh recalled the soft husky delivery, the repeated coughing and sips of tea. They were all attempts to hide the real voice.

'You killed your own brother,' said Hawa Singh.

Manvendra looked at him with the Colt still pointing at Ruby's head. Hawa Singh knew that the slightest move of his finger on the trigger could prove fatal.

'Abhay Narayan Singh was not my brother. He was a distant cousin whom my father Vibhuti Narayan Singh adopted and gave the title of the Kashi Naresh. I was supposed to be the king but my father didn't approve of my ways—my life with the Aghoris, my interest in the occult my turning into a cannibal. Imagine! He told me I was not fit to be the Kashi Naresh! I couldn't take it and finally got a chance to kill that adopted son,' cried Manvendra Singh.

'Who was the man locked up here in the Institute?' Hawa Singh asked warily, his eyes still on Ruby and the Colt.

Manvendra laughed delightedly. 'He was Sushant Singh, Abhay's brother. Abhay took away my title and I took away his brother. He got me locked up in this place but God had his own plans for me. I got to know of a new CMO at Sparrow, Sudha Krishnamurthy, coming to take charge here. So before she could reach the Institute, I killed her and her husband. And I took her place—while Sushant took mine. I myself had cut up Sushant's face so that no one would distinguish him from me. He had a similar body structure and no one bothered to ask questions of a cannibal.'

Ruby gathered herself together and shouted, 'Hawa, don't let him go. I don't care if he kills me.'

Manvendra tittered. 'Don't worry, girl, I'm going to kill you *both*.'

'I'm sure we can work things out,' said Hawa Singh placatingly.

'*You* are going to sort out *my* life? I tried that with bringing about the escape of Sushant Singh, and then was forced to kill him too.'

'Why did you kill him?'

'In his death was my freedom. I broke his chain and urged him to escape, and in that bid, the cannibal inside him surfaced. I had turned him into an animal. He could bite into human flesh and tear it off with his teeth like he did to Dr Pradhan.'

'I, too, would have been forgotten after Sushant's death but you had to botch everything up,' Manvendra Singh told him in a high accusing tone.

Hawa Singh tried to keep him talking and threw another question at him. 'Why did Sushant attack you in the office? What was he looking for?"

Manvendra gave a maniacal laugh, saying, 'He wanted his file to prove his true identity. But even in the files he had become Manvendra Singh.'

'You are the one who killed Tailanga Swami. It could have caused riots in Benares!' Ruby shouted, trying to hide her fear.

'Tailanga was my guru but with his own weaknesses. He had helped me dispose of the bodies of Sudha Krishnamurthy and her husband. In return, he wanted the position of the senior mahant in Benares. Till date, no Aghori has held that post and never will. I wanted him to wait but he started to blackmail me and threatened to reveal my identity to the Kashi Naresh and the police. So I had to kill him,' Manvendra said.

There was a sound of heavy footsteps running towards them. Manvendra looked startled.

'I told you the police have surrounded the place. Let her go, and surrender yourself,' commanded Hawa Singh.

Manvendra tittered. 'You want the future Kashi Naresh to surrender? That will never happen!'

The footsteps were coming closer and closer.

'What about Kanhaiya? Did you kill him too?' Hawa Singh asked.

'Kanhaiya,' Manvendra uttered the name in a sing-song voice, keeping his ears open to the sound of approaching feet. 'He was a drug-dealer and supplied me with marijuana and opium. Once he saw me changing into the kind of person I am today, that was the end for him.'

They heard the SSP rapping out orders to police personnel.

'You can't run and you can't hide,' Hawa Singh warned.

'You are not in a position to say that. My work is not yet over,' said Manvendra with a leer. 'First, I'll kill her, and then I'll kill you. All of Benares will get to watch the spectacle at the evening aarti.'

Manvendra pointed the revolver at Hawa Singh and began to withdraw, dragging Ruby with him. He turned into a bend in the corridor and disappeared from view. By the time the SSP and his men arrived at the scene, the Butcher was long gone.

They heard a police jeep starting outside and then speeding away.

'Where's the evening aarti to take place?' shouted Hawa Singh.

'Dashashwamedh Ghat,' answered Neeraj Thakur.

CHAPTER 42

7 pm, Dashashwamedh Ghat, Benares

The loud blowing of conch shells broke through the greyness of the sky. The ghat was crowded to capacity by locals, devotees and Indian and foreign tourists.

The aarti started with a group of pandits, all draped in saffron robes, waving incense sticks in elaborate patterns around the hallowed epicentre of devotion. The ritual was termed *Agni Pooja*, worship of Fire, wherein a dedication is made to Lord Shiva, the Ganges, Surya (Sun), Agni (Fire itself), and the entire universe.

The heady scent of sandalwood thickly permeated the air. The pandits lit large brass lamps with many wicks, lighting up the entire ghat. The pandits began the proceedings in a well-orchestrated manner, synchronizing their movement with lamps in hand, to the rhythmic chants of hymns and the beat of cymbals.

The lamps were mirrored in the waters of the Ganges. Thousands of earthen lit diyas were placed in leaf bowls and floated downriver, causing the water to reflect the starry sky. Then came a shower of petals as if the heavens themselves showered blessings on Benares. Thousands came to witness the magic.

Hawa Singh ran through the crowded streets to the ghat. His mind was racing in pace with his legs. *What were the unfathomable depths of evil to which Manvendra would sink?* He had spoken to the man at length, on more than one occasion, face to face, discussed the intricacies of mania, even sought his god-damned advice... and failed to see him for what he really was.

The Butcher had managed to keep up the act in front of even a trained FBI interrogator such as Ruby. Her mastery over kinesics and the behavioural sciences was defeated in the face of the occult, into which Manvendra Singh had delved so deeply with tantriks, sadhus and *behrupiyas*—those experts so good at disguise that even royalty had employed them as spies down the ages—whose company he preferred.

He had not only dressed as a woman, but also completely altered his body language and his voice. He had burnt the bodies of Sudha and her husband anonymously in the cremation grounds with the help of Tailanga Swami so that no one would ever get to learn of their existence in a town so far away from their home.

He had then assumed his female persona, and presented himself at Sparrow's Research and Analysis Wing for the Mentally Ill as their new head. He had placed Sushant in his cell by force and went on to replace all his fingerprints with those of Sushant in the file. Thus began the good times of the Butcher of Benares. But, who knew then, that a totally unforeseen incident would occur when a pesky police duo would lay their hands on the handprints of the royal family inside Saraswati Bhawan?

The aarti continued, and some tourists commandeered a few boats in the river, wanting a ringside view. The chanting and beat of drums rose to a crescendo.

A boat came cutting through the thousands of lamps and flowers floating in the Ganges. Inside the boat, Manvendra stood with the Colt in one hand, the other holding Ruby to him. He was still wearing the saree and a large round bindi on his forehead, an incongruous sight. As he came closer to the ghat, he raised the revolver and fired in the air. The shot rang through the air, cutting across the music and chanting. At once, there was complete silence. Everyone looked in the direction of the boat and its weird occupants.

'I am Manvendra Singh!' shouted the Butcher, 'heir to the royal family. Your Abhay Narayan Singh was only an adopted son who snatched my title from me. From now on, *I'm* your king!'

There was no reaction from the stunned and frightened crush of spectators.

Hawa Singh who hadn't been able to find an easy passage by land through the crowds to the ghat, did the next best thing and clambered aboard a boat. This drew up now opposite the one on which Manvendra stood, posturing. 'Stop this madness!' Hawa Singh bellowed across the water.

'Oh, Hawa Singh!' Manvendra greeted him as if he was glad to see him. 'Good to see you here. Now I can kill you both.'

'You have already killed many innocent people!' Hawa Singh shouted back. 'You are a butcher!'

Manvendra's eyes bulged as he cried out, 'I'm not a butcher!' He looked around at the thousands of people watching him agape. 'Yes, I killed all those foreigners. But the real Butcher is a man who killed more than five thousand people in Benares. They were innocent men, women and children.'

'Who the hell are you talking about?' asked an exasperated Hawa Singh.

'I am talking about Brigadier-General James George Smith Neill of the British East India Company,' said Manvendra, talking at the top of his voice. 'When all of northern India was aflame with the revolt of 1857, Neill arrived in Benares. He disbanded the local native regiment, lined up the sepoys, and shot them one by one. After that an entire regiment of Sikhs stationed here was also shot dead. General Neill then embarked upon a campaign of terror, hanging every able-bodied man he could lay his hands on.'

Ruby, deathly calm, said, 'What does that have to do with these foreigners?'

Manvendra replied as if it was all perfectly logical. 'Brigadier-General Neill was an orthodox Christian who served the Vatican. He was given the task of converting Indians to Christianity. And he went about the task seriously. Anyone who refused to adopt Christianity was shot dead, hanged or brutally killed in public. Many of the bodies were stabbed with the Holy Cross and left in the open as a message to others. I'm proud to say that Benares refused to convert en masse. Remember, we are the descendants of Lord Shiva and we'll never desert Him. I took their Cross and gave it back to those Christians in their own kind.'

'But they had nothing to do with what happened more than a century ago!' protested Ruby.

'They did. They were connected to the source,' said Manvendra Singh, shortly.

Then, he appeared to rethink. *These stupid spectators of my much-awaited outing deserve an explanation. I'll give it to them. I want the show to go on... for a little longer.* He raised his voice again. 'Neill came from a family in Scotland,' he called over the wind. 'He started a tradition among his kinsfolk which entailed lifelong service to the Vatican by each and every member of the extended family. Over the years, the family scattered but they never broke the tradition. I did some extensive global research and got in touch with the more powerful and dedicated of them. I told them that the secrets of the ground-breaking *Bhrigu-Samhita*, lay hidden in Benares. Being loyal to the Vatican, they resolved never to let those secrets come out. And thanks to you, Hawa Singh, the world will now know them.'

He wasn't finished, not yet. 'The Vatican wanted to shut us up. Its servile followers wanted to destroy us. I had to do something to counter them. It was pure revenge, too, on the family of Brigadier-General Neill. After Benares, Neill went to Kanpur and forced thousands of Brahmins to convert to Christianity and inflicted the death penalty on all those who refused. He compelled the Brahmins to collect the bloodied clothes of the victims, and wash the blood from the ground on which their lifeless bodies fell to bullets. That act itself resulted in a loss of caste for Brahmins. Their options after that were two—convert to Christianity or live on as untouchable Hindus. That original form of punishment is said to have been Brigadier-General Neill's own invention, and brought him great credit.' He paused to spit violently against the sides of the boat, with revulsion and hate.

Hawa Singh was keeping an eye on his every move. The knowledge that the Colt was aimed at Ruby's head caused him to reconsider every option of his own.

Manvendra continued, clearly enjoying the awed attention he was getting for the first time in his life. 'From Kanpur, Neill marched his army to Lucknow, where he was finally killed. But look at us, you shameless people! Do you know that a memorial was actually erected in Lucknow in the name of Neill and his troops?'

Manvendra ranted on. 'The memorial is inscribed with the words, "Sacred to the memory of Brigadier-General J.G.S. Neill, ADC to the Queen, Col J.L. Stephenson, Major S.G.C. Renaud, Lieut N.H. Arnold, Lieut A.A. Richardson, Lieut J.A. Chisholm, Lieut F. Dobbs, the non-commissioned officers, drummers and rank and file of the First Madras Fusiliers who fell during the suppression of the rebellion in Bengal 1857–58". We were doubly humiliated when an island in the Andamans was named after him, as a mark of honour. And you people flock to it today as happy tourists!

'Do you even know that during the 1857 Revolt, the British pursued a murderous decade-long campaign to wipe out millions of people who dared to rise against them? There was an untold holocaust in which more than 10 million people were killed over a decade following 1857!' Manvendra shouted over the wind.

'From the British point of view, it was a *necessary* holocaust,' he said bitterly. 'They thought the only way to avenge the mutiny and subjugate the people with terror forever was to destroy entire populations in towns and villages. It was simple and brutal. Indians who stood in their way were killed. But its scale has been kept a secret. It was bigger than the holocaust the Jews in

Europe underwent, but in India, an entire chapter has been erased from our history. What, after all, were 10 million deaths? They were just a statistic. What did it matter to our governments and politicians?'

Ruby weighed her options. Should she make a dash for it while the lunatic went on with his polemics? But no, he held her too fast.

'Now, you tell me, am I wrong in killing those who belonged to Neill's family?' he snarled. 'Haven't many of our ancestors been mercilessly killed or humiliated by Neill? Don't I have the right to kill his bloodline and end the lineage? Don't *you* want to?'

There was total silence. His unwilling audience was too numb to react.

It took Hawa Singh to speak up. 'No, you don't have the right to kill them!' he hollered.

Manvendra indicated with his eyes the pistol he was touching Ruby with. 'I'm not yet done. There are still more of that family living around the world. One by one, each of them will have to die.'

The SSP had stationed the entire police force all around the ghat but they were in no position to negotiate with Manvendra.

A man came at a stumbling run through the crush at the ghat. Fauja Singh. He called to his son in a shaking voice, 'You are not going to let another Kavita die.' Hawa Singh looked towards him and gently nodded in acquiesence.

Manvendra's ravings took on a note of finality. 'I'll have to sacrifice you, Hawa Singh, to my goddess. *Hé* Ganga Maiyya, please accept his blood.' He took aim and fired. The shot rang out loud and clear, piercing the air.

The bullet hit Hawa Singh. He reeled, fell overboard and sank in the water.

Fauja Singh collapsed on his knees. He hadn't come to Benares to see his son die. It was he who was supposed to go first. Tears ran from his closed eyes.

'Hawa,' sobbed Ruby, in Manvendra's stranglehold, 'Hawa'.

She attempted to struggle but Manvendra squeezed her throat with his free hand. 'I won't kill you,' he purred into her ear, 'but any one of these thousands standing there. You better stay still—for their sake.'

The SSP ran ahead with his team, all pointing their guns at Manvendra. 'Are you really in a position to point guns at me, SSP?' Manvendra demanded of him. 'Ask your men to drop their weapons. *Right now*!'

The SSP signalled his men to lower their guns. They all obeyed.

Manvendra returned his attention to Ruby who was standing paralysed, all the fight having gone out of her. 'It's time for you—FBI half-breed!—to die,' he said, almost lovingly. He closed his eyes. His finger curled over the trigger and tautened.

Somewhere from below them, a cry rang out, 'Jai Ganga Maiyya!'

The waters seem to part with the cry and Hawa Singh emerged, like the Ghost he was. He got a grip on the boat and tipped it with his strong arms. Both Manvendra and Ruby fell into the water.

Hawa Singh looked around with murderous eyes, his face streaming. Ruby resurfaced at a distance from him and he was relieved to see the SSP and Sub-inspector Gaya Prasad Sharma hastening to her rescue.

Manvendra emerged too, right behind him, and Hawa Singh spun around to make a grab at him. They grappled together in the water.

Fauja Singh had risen to his feet by now, his eyes now hopeful, even excited. He ran to Ruby and hugged her with moist eyes. 'My boy would never let any harm come to you,' he wept with joy.

Ruby's eyes, too were, wet, as they both turned to look at the Ganges.

The water suddenly turned choppy. The only light came from the lamps bobbing in the water. Hawa Singh remembered Manvendra's knowledge of Marma-Adi and realized the best thing was to keep him away from his body. Manvendra did strike him once, close to the heart, but the blow was weakened by the pull of the water, and didn't do the job Manvendra had intended—to paralyze his heart.

Fauja Singh, in a thin reedy voice, began to sing Lord Shiva's aarti. One by one, the pandits, the devotees and then the thousands of onlookers joined in, until there was one unified chorus. Their hymn, accompanied by drumbeats, rose to the heavens.

As the two strong men fought, the turbulent water brought them close to the ghat. Manvendra had begun to claw at Hawa Singh, tearing at his arm where he was shot. Hawa Singh punched his head, sending him deep into the water. For a second, Manvendra stayed submerged, but was up again, clambering up the side of the ghat, this time brandishing the Colt. He pointed it at Hawa Singh, who stood on a step right above him.

Manvendra put his finger on the trigger, smiling his old maniacal smile, aiming point blank. Hawa Singh could see the cannibal's canines shining through his grinning mouth. He turned his concentration to Manvendra's finger. He knew that the trigger was filed and wouldn't require much pressure to release the bullet. He could see the dark tunnel down the muzzle of the revolver.

In that fraction of a second, Hawa Singh seized Manvander's shooting arm, twisted it painfully, snatched the Colt from the now loosened fingers—and shot him through the head. The bullet ripped through the skull, scattering brain matter right up several steps of the ghat. Manvendra returned to the water from whence he had come.

Hawa Singh cupped his hands and, scooping up some water in them, offered it back to the holy river. The chanting grew louder and louder as Ruby and Fauja Singh hurried up to him, and they all met in a thankful embrace.

Benares reverberated with cries of 'Ganga Maiyya ki Jai!'

EPILOGUE

The media had milled outside the SSP's office. They had all wanted to interview Hawa Singh face-to-face. It had to be a big story.

Hawa Singh had not been interested in meeting the reporters and it was only after much persuasion from the SSP and Ruby that he had come out to face the newshounds. There were television cameras, flash-bulbs that blinded him and questions fired at him from all directions.

Hawa Singh had only one answer for them. 'I'm a policeman. I just did my job.' And he had walked away.

The one-line answer had been telecast repeatedly on news channels across the country, causing many to wish their hometowns and cities were similarly policed.

The next morning, Fauja Singh had packed up his stuff, all ready to go home. Hawa Singh saw him putting his things together and asked, 'Have you cancelled your death leave?'

'I'm stronger than you and my heart feels better than ever. Let's get out of here,' the old man had responded energetically.

Hawa Singh and Ruby had celebrated with the SSP, ACP Shishir Jha, Sub-Inspector Gaya Prasad Sharma and other personnel who had been their colleagues for a while. The SSP ordered hot kachoris, samosas and jalebis for everyone.

Ruby was flying back to the US. The flight was from Indira Gandhi International Airport, New Delhi, two days later.

Hawa Singh had used the small break to take her to his village. He showed off the lush green fields, their prized tube-well, his father's little hut in their field, and the tractor, on which he took her for a ride.

Fauja Singh was a happy man again. It felt like a family reunion. It was like Kavita had come back in their lives. His tears didn't stop.

Meanwhile, Neeraj Thakur, the SSP, Benares, had made an announcement in the press that Kashi Naresh Maharaja Abhay Narayan Singh suffered a major heart attack hearing about the exploits of his brother Manvendra Singh. His body was cremated inside the walls of Ramnagar Fort with full state honours.

The time had come for Ruby to leave. Early in the morning father and son had gone to the airport to see her off. She had felt something tugging her behind. She hadn't wanted to part from Hawa Singh. They'd looked deep into each other's eyes, and held each other fast.

Fauja had quietly stepped away.

'You just have to call me, and I'll be there,' promised Hawa Singh, as Ruby wiped her tears.

There would come a time when she would call him.

The flight had taken off at 4.15 am. Hawa Singh and Fauja Singh had watched from outside the airport the massive plane spearing the sky.

'How do such heavy machines fly in the air?' asked Fauja Singh.

'You don't need to break your head with such questions. They fly because they are supposed to fly, just like I fight crime because I am supposed to do that.'

Fauja Singh had nodded thoughtfully and said, 'I feel like having filter coffee, like Kavita used to make.'

'If anyone heard what you said back home, they'd laugh,' Hawa Singh had teased him. They would say, "The Haryanvi Jat has become a Madrasi"!'

'Let them say what they want. The smell of coffee reminds me of Kavita.'

Hawa Singh had bought two cups of coffee from a vendor outside the airport. Fauja had smelled the coffee and remarked with a sneer, 'Kavita's was better.'

He had looked up at another plane in the sky, and said, 'Tell me, what do they drink in the US? Tea or coffee?'

Hawa Singh, sipping on his coffee, had said, 'Some day, I'll take you there. Then you can find out for yourself.'

'I'm not going to wait for you. I'm sure my CID girl will call me there soon.'

They had exchanged a look and laughed.